SALVATION PROJECT

THE SALVATION PROJECT

STEWART ROSS

BB
BLEAN
BOOKS

First published 2017 by Blean Books
Westfield, Blean, Kent CT2 9ER

www.bleanbooks.com

ISBN 978-0-957-1019-2-0

A CIP catalogue for this book is available from the
British Library.

Printed and bound by CPI Group (UK) Ltd, Croydon, CR0 4YY

For Finn MacDonald, and the future

I would like to thank the following most warmly
for their help in preparation of this book:

Ruby May, Robert Rayner, Anoushka Helm, Eleanor Ross,
James Wills and Megan Carroll of Watson, Little Ltd, Georgia
Law, Vaarunika Dharmapala, Marcus Bell, and, more than all
others, my wife Lucy, proofreader, patient editor and constant
support.

Stewart Ross, 2017

Contents

The Soterion Mission III
The Salvation Project

The things which I have seen I now can see no more.
William Wordsworth

The Story so Far

Phase 1 : The Soterion Mission

The Great Death

In May 2017, a highly contagious epidemic of Mini-Flu struck the world. By December, every single human was infected. Tragically, because the disease's symptoms were so mild – a low fever and a slight headache for no more than a couple of hours – no one took much notice.

They should have.

The flu mutated the DNA that controls how we age, accelerating the process to a single, terrifying Death Month. The change began a year after infection and is still with us. At some point during their nineteenth year, everyone grows rapidly older and dies in just 3-4 weeks.

When the mutation first kicked in, the Great Death wiped out everyone over the age of 19. Billions of them. Services folded, power failed, plagues swept the planet, rotting bodies piled in the streets. Within the year, science, literature and knowledge – thousands of years of human civilization – disintegrated. The United Nations prevented mass warfare only by supervising the destruction of all weapons.

Education collapsed as those aged 19 and over – the Long Dead – rapidly died out. With no electricity, all electronic devices became useless and books were burned for fuel. A group of heartbroken scholars, desperate to save what they could, placed the key works of literature, science and

11

philosophy in a sealed vault. They named it the 'Soterion', the ancient Greek word for salvation.

The books and discs of the Soterion included data from the unfinished 'Salvation Project', a medical programme set up to reverse the symptoms of the Mini-Flu and stop the horrific premature ageing.

A century later...

One hundred and twenty years after the Great Death, the human race was in the hands of those formerly known as teenagers. They had divided into two groups. Constants lived in self-sufficient farming communities where they struggled to maintain the half-remembered values and ways of their ancestors. Around them, barbaric tribes of Zeds, Z-tattooed and mostly male, lived by scavenging and plunder. Friction between the two groups was continual and merciless.

The illiterate Constants of the Alba community found the fabled Soterion, but could not read the instructions on how to open the steel door. A rescue mission of literate Constants from other settlements, led by Roxanne and Cyrus, battled through Zed territory and opened the vault.

Now, at last, the Constants had a chance of rebuilding the world of the Long Dead. The climax of their work would be finishing the Salvation Project and reversing the mutation in their DNA.

Phase 2 : Revenge of the Zeds

It was not to be.

Knowledge is power and power corrupts. Two intelligent, ambitious and unscrupulous women thirsted after the Soterion's knowledge-power. The Constant Sakamir schemed to betray Alba to the Zeds and seize the Soterion for herself. In her way stood Xsani, the bewitching leader of a rare tribe of female Zeds.

Xsani had masterminded a cult that worshipped the shrunken head of Timur, a charismatic former Zed chieftain. She used Giv, a Zed who had mysteriously learned to speak with Timur's voice, to persuade two tribes of male Zeds to accept her command.

In the middle of a drunken festivity, Sakamir opened the gates of Alba to admit hordes of male and female Zeds. Sakamir and all but three of Alba's inhabitants were slaughtered in an orgy of debauchery and violence, and the settlement, together with the precious Soterion, was burned to the ground.

Phase 3 : The Salvation Project

Cyrus, his pregnant copemate Miouda, and his young friend Sammy have managed to escape from the burning ruins of Alba. They have rescued a laptop containing the entire contents of the Soterion, including the Salvation Project. On this frail and ancient machine hangs the last and only hope of restoring the civilization of the Long Dead.

But the laptop's batteries are flat, there is no electricity to power it, and it is only a matter of time before Xsani and the thwarted Zeds set off in pursuit...

List of Characters

Long Dead

          Dr Rebekkah Askar, a scientist who helped set up the Soterion

Constants

The Mission   Cyrus, the leader, originally from Della Tallis

          Miouda, originally from Alba

          Sammy, originally from the Children of Gova

          Corby, Sammy's dog

The Saffids   The Leader

          Flossco

The Meshkis   Olo

          Rama

The Tiani   Vaarunika

          Nelith

          Pablo, a dog

Unknown origins Seyda, Kamal's prisoner

Deceased   Roxanne, the Mission's original leader

          Zavar, Taja and Navid, members of the original Mission

          Bahm and Jannat, Albans

          Sakamir, a traitorous Alban

          Ozlam, High Father of the Children of Gova

Yash, Emir of Alba

Leiss, Emir of Della Tallis

Zeds

Grozny (male)	Giv, the Malik
	Kamal, Giv's successor as Malik
	Pram, a Captain
	Peng, a Captain
Gurkov (male)	Ogg, the Malik
	Pingog, a Captain
	Soceptan, a Captain
	Thog, a Captain
Murax (male)	Eziz, the Malik
	Kemran, a Captain
	Lopz
Kogon (female)	Xsani, the Malika
	Jinsha, a Zektiv
	Tarangala, Xsani's successor as Malika
	Zilna, a Zektiv
	Yalisha, a Zektiv
Deceased	Timur the Terrible, former Malik of the Grozny

1
Escape from Alba

Malik Ogg opened his one eye. Then shut it again. His head! Zeds' blood it hurt! What was the matter? For some time, he lay motionless, trying to recall where he was and what had happened.

What was that smell? Burning. What was burning? And what was his left hand resting on? It was soft and squashy. He moved his fingers, trying to make it out. It had hair, hair caked with something. He felt lower down. A nose, eyes, a gaping mouth with broken teeth…

Like the countryside on a misty morning, the events of the night gradually emerged out of the haze.

He was in the Constant settlement of Alba, which the Zeds had destroyed last night. He had led his Gurkov tribe through an open gate and found the Albans behaving very oddly, quite unlike the fierce warriors he had been expecting. All around him, scarcely noticing his arrival, men and women were dancing and singing – and drinking a strange red juice.

They were in no state to fight, and Ogg and the other male Zeds had enjoyed the best time of their short, violent lives. Never had there been such slaughter, such ravishing, such destruction. Ogg himself must have killed at least ten, as well as setting fire to buildings and violating their inhabitants.

One of his men, hands dripping with the blood of the slain, had staggered up to him and said he had tasted the Albans' drink. It was good. Taking the man's advice, Ogg had dipped his head in a bucket of the stuff and taken a swig. The taste was bitter, but the effect…

He recalled picking up the bucket and trying to tip the entire contents down his throat. Some of it splashed to the ground and over his leather jerkin, but most he managed to swallow.

What happened next, he couldn't properly recollect. He vaguely remembered rushing about, feeling sick, falling over a few times, and lying down as the earth beneath him rose and tipped and fell. Then everything went black.

It was still black. He tried once again to open his eye, but it was too painful. His mouth felt as if he had eaten sand. Why? The truth gradually dawned on him. He had been poisoned! That drink the Albans had prepared – it was obviously poison. He and all his tribe had fallen into a vile Constant trap, and now they would suffer this slow, horrible death.

Ogg stopped thinking and waited for the end.

Cyrus, Miouda and Sammy had been half walking, half running all night, desperate to put as much distance as possible between themselves and the Zeds before the pursuit began. And pursuit there would be, Cyrus was sure of it. He knew too much to be allowed to get away.

It was now mid-morning and the heat started to take its toll. Miouda was barely able to put one foot in front of another. 'One step,' she muttered to herself as they struggled up the side of a dried-out riverbed. 'One more, one more...'

She looked down at her bleeding feet, then up at the slope ahead. Fifty paces to go, at least. Don't give up... Don't give up...

'Hey, Miouda, you alright back there?' It was Cyrus, already near the top.

'Yes, thanks, Cy,' she panted. 'Think I can make it.' She hoped she sounded more confident than she felt.

'Ok. It'll be easier once we're out of the ravine. We can't stop yet.'

'Sure.' He was right. Terrible images of the sack of Alba were sharp in her mind. The blood, the screams, the hideous laughter. She had seen only too clearly what male Zeds did to the women they caught.

She trusted Cyrus more than anyone she had ever met. What he had done was amazing. Leaving his own people in Della Tallis, battling through Zeds to get to Alba, opening the Soterion, learning to read, and teaching her and others – his drive, his passion, his strength and determination were extraordinary. If anyone could lead them to safety and get the laptop working, it would be him.

But a man with a mission was not the easiest partner. She knew he cared for her deeply, even 'loved' her, to use a Long Dead word that had been banned in Alba. But if it came to a choice between her and the Soterion Mission, she wasn't sure which he would choose.

Her foot caught the edge of a boulder and she fell forward, cutting her hand on a stone.

'Miouda!' called out Sammy, struggling up the slope behind her. Good old Sammy, she thought. Always keeping an eye out for his friends.

'Hang on, Cyrus!' he shouted. 'Miouda's all in. How about a rest, eh?'

Cyrus came bounding down the slope in a flurry of dust and small stones. 'Oh, I'm sorry, Miouda!' he gasped. He put his arm around her shoulder and led her back down to the bottom. 'Sammy's right. It's about time we stopped for a bit.'

To his surprise, Malik Ogg did not die. He lay on the ground for most of the morning as his thundering headache gradually faded away. As it eased, a nagging worry wormed its way into the back of his mind.

He had attacked Alba in alliance with the Zeds of the Grozny and the Kogon tribes. Fighting alongside the Grozny, though unusual, was acceptable. Like his own tribe, the Grozny were all male. Their chief, Malik Giv, might be young and eccentric, but at least he was a man.

But the Kogon... The very thought of his unholy alliance with females brought back the painful pounding in his brain. In Constant parlance, women were mere "flabtoads", inferior beings who existed only for breeding and incidental pleasure. There were moments when he couldn't believe he'd actually accepted them as allies. The shame of it!

But there had been no denying the lisping cleverness of their leader, Malika Xsani, and Ogg remained very much in awe of her. He still couldn't quite grasp how she had engineered the pact between her Kogon and the males of the Gurkov and Grozny. But she had managed it, and he had accepted her leadership. What's more, how she had organised the triple alliance and masterminded its attack on Alba had been, well, brilliant.

Ogg's brow furrowed with the effort of reasoning. How on earth had a mere flabtoad gained such power? Much of it was due to the unwavering approval and support of Timur, a previous Malik of the Grozny and one of the most powerful and feared of all Zed chieftains.

At this point, Ogg's understanding burst its limited banks. Timur was dead. But his head, smoked and spiked on a stick, mysteriously lived on. The grim totem spoke through the mouth of Giv, Xsani's closest ally. It announced that Timur was now the all-powerful Over-Malik, and Xsani was his lieutenant.

Ogg sighed. He knew that Timur the Terrible had to be obeyed. No question. And because Timur had to be obeyed, so too did his flabtoad deputy. Ogg knew that, too. And yet, and yet… He couldn't put his finger on it, but he sensed that something in this highly unusual set-up was not quite right.

Malika Xsani stood on the edge of the plateau above Alba and looked down on the handiwork of the previous night. She turned to the raven-haired woman at her side and sighed in frustration. A meticulous organiser and a leader of ruthless brilliance, she had never before known failure. And now the greatest action of her rule had gone disastrously wrong.

It had started so well. The traitor Sakamir, a Constant turned Zed, had unlocked the gates of Alba as promised. The Zeds had swarmed in, Xsani leading her Kogon warriors to the Ghasar building where the precious books of the Soterion were stored.

The slaughter that followed, she had expected. More than that, she had welcomed it because while the male Zeds of the Gurkov and Grozny tribes were busy with their orgy of rape and murder, she had planned to seize the Ghasar and capture a literate Alban who would teach her to read. The secrets of the civilization of the Long Dead would then be at her command.

Sakamir had shattered this dream. Like Xsani, she had schemed to double-cross her allies and make the Soterion her own. But Xsani struck first. Sakamir was killed, the Ghasar was set alight, and the books of the Soterion were consumed in the flames.

Angry and bewildered Zeds were now camped amid the ashes of their ambition.

Xsani had another, more personal problem. Before forming the coalition with Ogg and Giv, she had become intrigued and then obsessed by an ancient image painted on the wall of her barn-like headquarters in the Kogon settlement of Filna. She called it the Man in the Yellow Hat. Its mysterious message seemed to challenge every Zed value she had ever held.

Gazing on the smouldering ruins of Alba, she recalled her disturbing vision of the previous night. She had been staring at the blazing Soterion when a man appeared on the hill behind the fire. As he stood surrounded by her furious warriors, his head was briefly framed by the full moon.

A living embodiment of the Man in the Yellow Hat had appeared before her very eyes, and she could not bring herself to order his death. The more she thought of the incident, the more she realised she needed to find this man and talk to him. There was so much she did not understand.

An angry scuffle between a pair of hung-over Grozny caught her attention. What had got into those stupid men last night? she wondered.

When they drank that strange red juice the Albans had made, they became even more befuddled and violent than usual. They forgot what they had been told. To Xsani's fury, they had started fighting with their Kogon allies, even trying to assault them.

Seeing the situation getting out of control, Xsani had led her women to the hillside terraces overlooking the town where she now stood. Here, the Kogon and their extraordinary Malika would be safe – for the time being at least.

2
The Long Dead

Sammy shifted on to his elbow, trying to make himself comfortable on the stony floor of the ravine. When he was finally able to relax, he looked admiringly at Cyrus. The leader of the Mission was sitting with his back against a rock and Miouda's head pillowed on his thigh. He was running his fingers through her fair hair, picking out bits of leaf and untangling its twists and knots.

'You really reckon they'll come after us?' Sammy asked.

'Pretty sure. Anyway, there's no point in hanging about just to see whether they will or not.'

Miouda examined the cut on the palm of her left hand and wondered whether she should waste precious water cleaning it. 'We were seen leaving Alba,' she said.

The image was still vivid in her head. As they were fleeing the massacre, they had come face to face with the oddest procession. Three hideous Zed warriors were guarding a gaunt young man who held a spear vertically in front of him. On the point of the weapon was skewered a blackened, shrunken head.

The spear-carrier, Giv, she hadn't seen before. But the head she recognised immediately. It belonged to Timur, Giv's predecessor as Malik of the Grozny Zeds. Charismatic, merciless, and fiendishly clever, he had been killed while trying to seize the Soterion for himself. The Albans had left his body to rot in the wilderness. Not long afterwards, Sammy discovered that the head was missing.

Cyrus had quickly worked out what was going on. A Zed of unusual insight and intelligence, seeing the potential power such an icon, must have preserved it, and was using it as a symbol of power and authority. Though Cyrus didn't know their name, he now believed he knew who that person was – the short woman with thick, fair hair who had spared his life as he stood beside the burning Ghasar.

Sammy interrupted his thoughts. 'The man carrying Timur's head actually spoke how you said the real Timur did. He sort of ranted and used those odd words like "ratbrain" and "batshit".'

Miouda looked up at her copemate. 'Yes, that weird man saw us leaving, Cy. But the books have gone and no one knows we've got a laptop, so why'd he or anyone else want to come after us?'

Cyrus tapped the silver-grey machine lying on the ground beside him. 'It's not this they want. It's us.'

'Why?'

'One of them at least was told by Sakamir that we'd been studying the Soterion books and have a load of valuable information in our heads.'

'Ugh!' Sammy snorted. 'Don't like the idea of being hunted for my head.'

'Nor what they'd do to get stuff out,' added Miouda.

'It's up to us to make sure she doesn't get the chance,' said Cyrus.

Miouda sat up sharply. 'She? What makes you think there's a woman after us?'

Cyrus explained how, when the fair-headed commander of the Kogon had him at her mercy, she had allowed him to escape. 'She shouted, "Stop! Leave him!"' he explained. 'And as her women backed off, I ran for it.'

'She has good taste, at least,' smiled Miouda.

'Or she's short-sighted,' added Sammy.

'Come on,' said Cyrus. 'This is serious. Sakamir must have told that Zed woman about me, and she must then have let me go because she wants me alive. When she can't find me, she'll learn from the weird bloke carrying Timur's head that someone fitting my description was seen leaving.'

'I'm pretty certain they'll be on to us,' said Miouda. 'Might even have set out already. Oh shit! What a horrible mess! And a few days ago, everything was going so well...'

She stared up at the sky for a moment before adding, 'You know, I still can't believe we were the only ones to get out...'

She paused, struggling to control her emotions. All her friends, everyone she had grown up with, had been slaughtered. Or worse.

Cyrus laid a hand on her arm.

'It's alright, Cy,' she said quietly. 'I'm ok.' She took a deep breath. 'Have to be, don't I? We three—'

'And a half,' interrupted Cyrus, placing a hand on her stomach.

She put her hand over his. 'Yes, three-and-a-half. Anyway, everything depends on us now, doesn't it?'

Cyrus nodded. 'And on the laptop.'

'So long as it's got the Soterion stuff in it,' said Sammy. 'And we can get at it.'

He spoke with great feeling, as if he felt a sort of personal attachment to the machine. Having grown up with a strong mistrust of authority, when asked to bring the laptops from the Soterion vault into Alba, he had left one behind. The other five had burned in the fire that destroyed the library.

As they fled Alba, the Mission collected the one Sammy had hidden. They could not be sure it held the Salvation Project data and a digital version of the burned books, but if it did they might yet be able to access the knowledge left to them by the Long Dead.

But the laptop needed electricity. Unless they came across a source of power, ideally an intact solar panel, all their efforts would be in vain.

Cyrus shifted uneasily. They owed it to themselves, and to everyone who had given up their lives for the cause, to make it to safety.

Miouda felt her copemate stir and sensed his thoughts.

'Come on then,' she said, climbing to her feet and putting out a hand to help Sammy. 'No point in sitting here worrying.'

Cyrus put his arms around his friends. 'Three as one!' he said, hoping he didn't sound too melodramatic. 'And from now on, let's try not to think about the past. The future's what we're about, ok?'

Without another word, he collected the laptop and led the way up the side of the boulder-strewn ravine. The conversation had reminded him of the awesome weight of his responsibility, and a frown spread across his handsome face. In his hands he carried the only hope of restoring the lost civilization of the Old World.

Malika Xsani again scanned what was left of the Alba settlement, wondering whether any Constants had managed to get away. Not a building had survived the conflagration unscathed. Those built of stone or concrete had lost their roofs; the wooden ones had been reduced to charred stumps.

The bodies of scores of men, women and children, some horribly mutilated, lay scattered among the wreckage. The sickly stench of scorched flesh told that a number had been burned alive. Several Gurkov and Grozny were wandering aimlessly amid the debris, searching for something to eat. Apart from a few half-hearted scuffles, the whole scene was eerily quiet.

What next? thought Xsani. With the Soterion gone, she knew what she wanted to do. But it would be such a wrench, such a betrayal. First, she had to secure her own position.

She had been raised to consider all those of the opposite gender, especially Zeds, as mere "dumbmans". The scene spread out below confirmed her contempt. Turning to the woman standing close beside her, she asked in her unmistakeable lisp, 'It was exthpected, I thuppothe, Jintha. Can you thee Ogg down there?'

Jinsha shielded her eyes from the morning sun. 'Yes, my Malika.' She touched Xsani on the arm and pointed to a figure sprawled on the cobbles alongside the well. 'That's him, I think.'

Xsani leaned forward slightly and followed the line indicated by her Jinsha's finger. 'Ah yeth! He'th very thtill. Do you think he'th… dead?'

Jinsha shook her head. 'No, Malika. I saw him move his arm. And look! One of the Gurkov draws near. I think he brings water for Malik Ogg.'

Xsani was only half listening. 'Tho he'th not dead,' she muttered, more to herself than to her kumfort. 'Then perhapth it ith time he wath.'

3
In the Forest of the Night

The Mission pressed on for three days, with no more than brief stops to sleep and eat. Travelling day and night, they survived by scavenging for food and drinking from the trickles of bitter-tasting water that seeped from the rocks. Staves and the home-made knives carried by all Constants were their only weapons.

The noonday sun was their compass, a beacon drawing them forward step after weary step. Although they had little idea where they were headed, their aims were clear: put as much distance as possible between themselves and the Zeds, cross a river to throw hunting dogs off their scent, and, most important of all, locate a solar panel capable of powering up the laptop.

By the fourth day, with no sign or sound of anyone on their tail, they allowed their pace to slacken a little. Picking their way through the thorny scrub, and keeping a wary eye out for the venomous snakes that from time to time squirmed across their path, they relaxed and chatted easily.

Sammy asked Miouda how she was feeling. 'Fine right now,' she replied. 'I'm not worried about me. But I'm in my sixteenth year, Sam, and we need to end up in a community where my child can be cared for when I'm gone.'

Like all Constants, she accepted death in a matter-of-fact manner that the Long Dead would have found odd, even callous. But when all lives were short and ended at a fixed time, death was no more to be feared than birth. Excessive sorrow would have been a waste of emotional energy.

'Don't worry,' said Sammy. 'You know Cyrus. He'll take us somewhere safe, I'm sure he will. And I'm only thirteen – I'll be around for a bit to care for you and your baby.'

'Thanks, Sam I know you will.'

'Pity old Corby's not here,' Sammy added wistfully, remembering how his faithful dog had disappeared during the Alban holocaust. 'He'd have helped me look after your child.'

Miouda smiled at the image of Nurse Corby and, as the daylight began to fade, they walked on in silence towards a wooded valley where they hoped to find running water.

'You know, Miou,' said Sammy, following Cyrus down a gentle slope to where the scrub gave way to thicker, more lush vegetation, 'there were some strange things going on back there in Alba.'

'I know. I still can't get over a whole tribe of women Zeds.'

'Yeah. Bit of a contradiction, really. And that guy carrying Timur's head was creepy, too. Downright sinister, he was. Hope he's not after us.'

Whether he was or not, at that moment the Mission faced more immediate dangers. Humans were the only species affected by the Mini-Flu. During the Great Death, zookeepers had released their animals into the wild rather than leave them to die of starvation in cages. With few natural predators, and free to roam in a world no longer dominated by human beings, beasts large and small thrived.

Cyrus was first to hear the noise – a deep, throaty growl in the trees some way to their right. He stopped on the fringe of a glade and held up his hand. 'What was that?'

Sammy knew at once. 'I've heard it before,' he muttered, glancing anxiously at the shadowy trees. 'And I don't like it, neither.'

The three Constants edged closer together and Cyrus put an arm around Miouda's shoulder. He wished they were better armed; their short knives would be useless in a Zed attack.

Miouda seized Sammy's arm. 'What is it?'

'It's an animal,' he whispered. 'I saw one when I was in the Gova place. It was in the evening. First we heard a noise, then this great big cat – enormous – came looming out of the darkness.'

'Cat?' Cyrus' voice was hoarse with anxiety. He had a good idea what was coming.

'Well, not exactly a cat. I looked it up in the encyclopedia from the Soterion. It was a tiger. You could tell by the dark lines all down its body.'

'Stripes,' said Miouda, whose vocabulary had developed quicker that anyone else's in Cyrus' reading class.

'Whatever they were,' said Sammy, 'the thing was really scary. We were alright 'cos of the fence, but we saw it grab the corpse of a dead Zed and carry it off in its mouth, as easy as anything. Like a dog with a rabbit.'

Miouda shivered and edged nearer Cyrus. Her hand moved instinctively over her stomach to protect her unborn child.

'What else did you read about tigers?' asked Cyrus. 'Killers?'

'Can be. They eat anything, dead or alive.'

'And what's that roaring mean?'

'The book said it meant it was talking to other tigers.' As if to confirm this, a second roar reverberated through the trees, much louder and coming from the opposite side of the glade.

'Two of them,' muttered Cyrus. 'And one pretty close.'

Miouda took her hand from her stomach and raised it to her lips. 'Shh!' she hissed softly. 'No way can we fight them off. Just have to make sure they don't find us.'

She drew her knife and edged towards the thicket behind her. Cyrus and Sammy followed. More concerned with the tiger than looking where they were going, the inevitable happened: Sammy's foot got tangled with a thorny tendril and he tumbled noisily to the ground. In the stillness of the evening, the sound crashed around the trees like a drum roll, sending a murder of birds screeching into the purple-blue sky overhead.

Sammy was in the middle of mouthing 'sorry' when Miouda tapped him gently on the arm. Eyes wide in amazement, she was pointing at the opposite side of the clearing. There, standing half Sammy's height and with ox-like shoulders more than twice his width, stood an enormous tiger. It was unreal, a beast of dreams. Gold-green eyes set in a massive melon-round head gazed at them unblinking as it pondered how to react to these smooth, sort of monkey creatures that had dared intrude upon its territory.

Cyrus did his best to meet the beast's stare without flinching. If animals could indeed smell fear – as he had heard – he hoped the tiger could not sense the terror gripping the humans standing before it.

An experienced fighter, Cyrus tried to take stock of his enemy. Amid all that sleek power, what held his attention most vividly were the feet: from soft pads the size of a baby's chest, claws stretched down, smooth and pointed and each one as long as a dagger. In a fight with such a magnificent war machine, no human warrior would stand a chance. As if to emphasise the point, the creature opened its jaws to reveal an array of perfect teeth, sharp and deadly.

The tiger would probably have moved on if the Constants had stayed where they were. As long as they remained motionless and quiet, the animal did not regard the strange intruders as a threat. Its main concern was the other tiger nearby.

Sammy didn't know this. Tigers, he had read, rarely attacked humans. If challenged, they backed off to look for easier prey. Unfortunately, his information came from a work of fiction and was dangerously untrue. When he stood up and took a hesitant step in the tiger's direction, waving his arms, the beast snarled and crouched low, ready to spring.

Too late, Sammy saw what was happening. By the time he had started to turn, the tiger was flying towards him like a dazzling javelin of yellow and black. Miouda froze, too horrified even to scream. Cyrus dropped the laptop and, holding out his knife as if it were a sword, sprang forward to help his friend.

Had there been no intervention, the two Constants would have died, leaving Miouda to continue the Mission on her own. But someone, or something, did intervene. While the tiger was in mid-air, a bolt of brown fur thudded into its neck. The unexpected blow knocked it sideways and it fell heavily on its flank a foot or so to Sammy's left.

For a split second, Sammy stared at his saviour in disbelief. It was impossible! It must be a ghost, some sort of phantom of the forest. But no! There, his teeth firmly embedded in the folds of skin about the tiger's neck, was his faithful Corby!

No sooner had they realised who their rescuer was than Sammy and Cyrus saw what peril he was in. The tiger was up on its feet, snarling and swatting at the dog with its lethal claws. Corby's flank was already scarred with parallel lines of blood.

The fight was an unequal one. With a violent heave, the tiger sent Corby sprawling to the ground where he lay panting and bleeding from a dozen claw wounds. As the beast turned to face Sammy, Cyrus saw his opportunity and lunged forward. He aimed for the throat.

Out of the corner of its eye, the tiger saw Cyrus coming and twisted to face him. The move proved fatal. Had Cyrus struck as he intended, his knife might not have pierced the tiger's tough hide. In the event, the blade found a much softer target.

Cyrus altered his aim slightly and, more by accident than design, the point of his knife slid off the edge of the tiger's eye socket and continued through the eyeball into its brain. It died instantly, swaying slightly before crashing to the forest floor.

There it lay, motionless. From the wound in its splendid face, a trickle of blood dropped to a spreading puddle of crimson.

Sammy ran over to his beloved Corby and, shaking violently, cradled the dog in his arms while he examined his wounds. Happily, they were less serious than he had first thought. Corby had been winded and perhaps one or two ribs had been cracked, but the bleeding from the gashes on his side was already slowing. The wounds would not worry him for long, though the scars would be there for the rest of his days.

Smiling, Cyrus and Miouda knelt down beside their friend and his long-lost companion. Silly old thing, Corby! Where had he been all this time? He had had them so worried! But he'd more than made up for it, hadn't he? Saved their lives, brave, lovely friend! How could they ever thank him?

Sammy, who had been kissing Corby's ears and telling him how much he had missed him and how brave he had been to attack a tiger so much bigger than himself, asked Cyrus and Miouda to clean the dog's wounds while he held him still. When the operation was over and Corby began to return to his old, relaxed self, they left the two of them together and went over to examine the body of the tiger.

For a while they stood in silence, gazing down at the glorious wreck. Even in death, the huge beast was both terrifying and incredibly beautiful: not just an astonishing display of colours, but a near-perfect combination of sinew and muscle, power and glory.

'I wish we hadn't needed to kill it,' said Miouda, stooping down and running her hands over the still-warm body. 'It's almost what the Long Dead called a "sin". I know it was going to kill us, but I feel what we did was somehow, well, wrong. I can't help it, but I feel guilty at what we've done.'

Cyrus nodded. 'I know what you mean.'

'The Long Dead hunted them things for fun,' Sammy called over to them. 'Big Game hunting they called it. Almost wiped tigers out.'

'For fun?' echoed Cyrus. 'Strange thing to do.' He locked Sammy's remark away at the back of his mind. Later, nearing the end, he would take it out and ponder afresh its meaning.

For the moment, there was no time to stand and stare. It was already quite dark and there was another tiger in the vicinity. If it found them, they might not be so fortunate a second time.

Checking that Corby could walk without too much pain, they went to find a safe place to rest. It couldn't be for long. If Corby had managed to trail them from Alba, Zed hunting dogs would have no trouble doing the same. And, unlike Corby, they would not be coming to save Constant lives.

4
The River

Around mid-morning, Malika Xsani was alerted by a disturbance within the ruins of the town. Flanked by her beloved kumfort Jinsha and her bodyguard of eunuchs, she went to see what was going on. A small band of Zeds was winding through the wreckage. Three of the men were guarding a fourth, who was holding a long spear with a black object spiked on top of it.

When the procession drew near, other Zeds stopped what they were doing and stood with arms upraised, chanting. 'Ti-mur! Ti-mur! Ti-mur!'

The familiar sound floated up to Xsani. Over the incantations, another voice became audible, a shrill yelling. 'Bow ratbrains! Bow before the Over-Malik! Bow to the Mighty Timur, bringer of all pleasures!'

It was Giv. His voice and vocabulary were precisely those of his dead master, Timur the Terrible, onetime Malik of the Grozny Zeds. And the object on the top of his spear was nothing less than Timur's head, preserved by smoking and now used as a sacred totem for all Zeds. Its elevation into a symbol of authority had been Xsani's idea, and a hint of a smile crossed her lips when she saw how effective the cult of Timur still was.

She could rely on Giv. He owed her everything. She had allowed him to be educated by a Constant captive, and – using the power of the head – had made him Malik of the Grozny. Above all, he adored her. Yes, she could rely on Giv.

But Ogg was different. He believed in the shrunken head, of course, but as much out of fear of castration as genuine reverence. Besides, he was so coarse, so crude – a typical dumbman Malik, all muscle and no finesse.

Watching Giv's procession make its way up the steep path, Xsani saw how Ogg could be removed and Giv made Malik of both the Grozny and the Gurkov. She would then have three tribes under her direct command, making her the mightiest Zed of all. She would be idolised and feared, perhaps even more than Timur had been.

And yet, even as these dreams of majesty flitted through her thoughts, Xsani was aware of a gnawing uncertainty. She was vaguely aware that power and glory were no longer what she truly craved. She had set her heart on the knowledge contained within the Soterion, the secrets of the Long Dead. But who were they, those ancient people whose ruins lay so impressive all around?

The question was at the heart of Xsani's confusion. As far as she could tell from the faded images she had seen, the Long Dead had not been divided between Zed and Constant. What did that mean for her and the other Zeds? And what about males in the Old World? They didn't seem like the dumbmans she had encountered, certainly not like Ogg. One in particular appeared the very opposite – who was that Man in the Yellow Hat?

So many tantalising questions, and the building that had contained the answers had gone for ever, burned to ashes. But what if some of the books had been left outside the Ghasar, in the secret place where the Albans had originally found them?

Only one person could answer that question. She needed to find the man Sakamir had called Cyrus. She was sure he was the figure she had seen on the hill, the living embodiment of the Man in the Yellow Hat. He must have escaped the holocaust when she ordered her warriors not to touch him.

She hoped with all her heart that that he was still alive. He would know not only whether any of the books had been saved, but also about the ways of the Long Dead. When she found him, thought Xsani, she would get him to share his knowledge with her. And then, and then… She sighed and looked down again into the ruined town.

Maybe Giv knew where Cyrus had gone?

Jinsha's voice brought Xsani back to the present. 'Malika, Giv is coming.'

'Ah yeth! Giv. Firtht thingth firtht. The head he carrieth will be utheful to uth. I have a plan. We cannot deal with Ogg by ourthelveth. Giv cannot deal with Ogg by himthelf. But if we work with Timur…'

Following an uncomfortable night in the forest, the Mission

continued their hunt for a river. As had happened on the way to Alba many months previously, Corby's nose did the trick.

When Cyrus mentioned to Sammy how the dog could sniff out water a long way off, the young man called Corby to him. 'There's a good boy!' he said, stroking his soft, floppy ears. 'You're hot, eh? Thirsty?' The dog looked up at him and wagged his tail. 'Thought so. Right. Find drink – go on, boy! Drink!'

No sooner were the words out of Sammy's mouth than Corby was off, weaving a path through the tangled vegetation of the jungle. The Constants trailed after him as best they could, skirting around the larger trees and using their knives to hack at the undergrowth that grew thicker the further they went. Snakes were an even greater danger. Corby appeared to dodge them by instinct, but on several occasions the Mission had to stop and wait for a silver-green body to concertina slowly across their path.

By mid-morning, Corby was so far ahead they couldn't even hear him. It didn't matter. The foetid smell of the river was unmistakeable. Soon afterwards, they burst out of the bushes on to the muddy bank of a wide, slow-flowing river overhung with huge trees whose roots trailed like tentacles into the green-brown water.

'Wow!' said Sammy, going up to Corby and patting him gently on the part of his flank unscathed by the tiger's claws. 'Well done, old boy! I said drink, and you found one alright, didn't you? Enough here for an army!'

'And there's no way the Zeds'll be able to pick up our trail on the other side,' said Cyrus. 'As long as we can get over there.'

'A big if,' said Miouda, who was stooping down and filling the water bottle from the shallows beside the bank. 'You're the only one who can swim, Cy. Even if I could, I wouldn't risk it. Bound to be crocodiles.'

'Yes, sure,' agreed Cyrus. 'Wouldn't surprise me if this was the same No-Man River we crossed when Timur was after us. Broader here, though. Must be nearer the sea.'

Sammy shuddered as he recalled the yelping fate of the Zed hunting dogs that had fallen into the river from the collapsing railway bridge. No, being dragged down beneath the slimy waters by a giant crocodile was not the way he wanted his life to end.

Crossing proved easier than they had expected. Exploring the bank downstream, they entered the site of a trading settlement. The wooden houses had largely rotted away. To their disappointment, the solar panels that had once lain on the north-facing slopes of the roofs lay broken and buried beneath layers of tangled foliage. The jungle had taken over the roads, too, and the few brick-built official buildings were now little more than huge flowerpots. Only one stood relatively undamaged.

The boatyard had been built half in the river and half out, allowing newly constructed vessels to slip easily into the water. Fittings of wood and iron had disintegrated, but the concrete shell of the building was more or less intact. Cyrus peered into the open doorway and went inside.

The rusted remains of a pleasure steamer lay with its bows submerged in a blanket of weed and ooze, and its stern, rising into the air like a rusty whale, had serpents of creeper twisting through its shattered windows. Ribbed skeletons were all that was left of a pair of wooden fishing boats; the plastic hulls of the half-dozen speedboats littering the dock had cracked like eggs.

Cyrus was about to leave when Miouda pointed to a green dome at the far end of the quay. 'There's something over there, Cy. What do you think it is?'

'No idea. Whatever it was, it's had its day.'

'Can't do no harm to take a look,' said Sammy, who was picking his way between the shattered speedboats. When he reached the green mound, he gave it a kick with his sandalled foot. The dome responded with a hollow boom.

'Wait a minute!' He picked up a piece of fallen concrete and scratched away at the moss and algae to reveal the metal beneath.

It was a small, open fishing boat lying upside down. Strongly constructed of stainless steel and aluminium, it had withstood the passage of the years well, and once the Mission had scraped it clean, turned it over and lowered it on to the water, it floated as securely as it had done all those years before.

The boat had originally been powered by an outboard motor. As this was now out of the question, they had to find another way of propelling it. Sammy suggested shoving off from the bank and letting the current carry them to the other side. 'It's bound to get across in the end,' he concluded, not very convincingly.

'Yes, in the end,' said Cyrus. 'But that could be days.' He wondered about using their clothes as sails, like the ones pictured in the Soterion encyclopedia.

Miouda was sceptical. Paddles would be simpler and more reliable, she insisted, and her suggestion prevailed.

Armed with crudely shaped paddles cut from branches, they clambered gingerly aboard their little vessel and pushed off from the jetty. Miouda sat at the stern with Corby at her feet and the precious computer cradled on her lap. Cyrus and Sammy knelt on either side and did their best to guide the boat with the paddles.

At first their progress was erratic, and the two men exchanged a few sharp words before they got the hang of steering the craft forwards rather than in circles. Even then they advanced only slowly: for each metre they went across, the current carried them three downstream. But they finally made it without incident, and gave a small cheer when their boat nosed into the soft mud of the bank and stuck firm.

Sammy was about to jump ashore with Corby at his heels when Cyrus put a hand and grabbed his leg. 'Hang on Sammy! What's that?'

Blinded in one eye on the way to Alba, Sammy had not noticed something lift itself up out of the slime a couple of paces to his right. He turned to see the thing raise its head and stare in his direction.

'Crocodile!' screamed Miouda. 'Get back, Sam!'

Talking about it later, they agreed that Miouda's cry had probably saved their lives. Its urgency startled Sammy so much that he turned, tripped over Corby and tumbled down beside Miouda. The bows of the boat were already much higher than the stern, and the sudden movement pushed the gunwale behind Miouda beneath the surface. Water poured in over her seat.

Fortunately, as the stern dipped, the bows lifted clear of the muddy bank. Cyrus saw what was happening and paddled furiously, driving the boat backwards. Sammy shifted his weight forward at the same time and the flood of water over the stern stopped. The danger had passed. On the shore, the crocodile lowered its head, closed its eyes and decided to wait for a more accessible meal.

They continued downstream until they came across a sandy bank free of hazard. Here they beached the boat and went ashore. Cyrus put his arms around his two friends and looked at the distant bank.

'Stage one complete,' he said with obvious relief. 'I don't think there's much chance of the Zeds catching up with us now. At last, we can focus on stage two: finding a solar panel and seeing what's on that laptop.'

He relaxed his grip and continued in a lower, more sombre tone, 'You know, if I'm honest, there were moments when I wondered whether we'd ever get this far.'

'We'd never have guessed,' said Miouda, smiling at Sammy.

He saw the look. 'Ok, but better that way, isn't it? I've brought you on this Mission, so it's up to me to see it through.'

'Of course,' said Miouda. 'If it wasn't for you, we'd be skewered on the end of some Zed's gut-ripper back in Alba.'

'Or chewed up inside the belly of a tiger,' added Sammy.

'So don't you go doubting yourself, or us,' said Miouda, giving his hand a squeeze.

Nevertheless, for all her reassurance, she knew Cyrus did not have – could not have – her undivided loyalty. Part of it at least she owed to the child she was carrying.

She desperately hoped she would never be asked to choose between the two.

Malika Xsani needed to act fast. Her dumbman allies were growing restless. Many had sore heads and all were hungry. Giv had taken steps to bring the Grozny tribe under control, gathering them near the Soterion Gate and sending out parties to hunt for food; but the Gurkov were becoming dangerously chaotic. It was all the fault of their leader, Malik Ogg.

The hung-over Malik had dragged himself to his feet in the early afternoon and wandered about enquiring angrily after the man who had given him the Alban 'poison'. He swore to tear whoever it was limb from limb when he found him. But as he couldn't remember the fellow's face or name, the threat remained as empty as his head. This brutish, stupid behaviour reinforced Xsani in her decision to get rid of him.

By early evening, some of the Gurkov were fighting among themselves. Others stood staring lasciviously up at the Kogon women guarding the terraces. Xsani knew she had to act by nightfall, before the situation got out of control.

She had decided to use the force that had brought the tribes together in the first place: Timur's head. With the setting sun casting a rich red hue over the upper terraces, Giv ordered his Captains to assemble the Grozny on the lower platforms, facing the summit. He then managed to persuade Ogg and his Gurkov captains to do the same. All of them, he promised, would 'taste of the glory of Timur'.

Amid the debris of the previous night, one of Giv's Captains had found a drum and managed to beat out a regular, throbbing rhythm. He was now seated near the front of the plateau, just out of sight of the crowd below. When the massed ranks of male Zeds were in place, and the sunset was at its crimson richest, he began to play. At first, his audience gawped in open-mouthed surprise. Then one of them smacked his hands together, and soon both tribes were clapping their hands, slapping their thighs and thumping their chests more or less in time to the rhythm of the drum.

When the noise was loudest and the sky most glorious, Xsani stepped forward to the edge of the plateau. The drummer stopped and the din gradually subsided. She took a deep breath.

'Thedth! O Thedth! Thith ith a great time for uth! We have uthed the power of the Mighty One, the Over-Malik Timur, to thcore a great victory over the Conthtantth! Thankth be to Timur!'

'Ti-mur! Ti-mur! Ti-mur!' howled the mob.

Xsani raised her arms. 'Our Mathter ith tho pleathed with uth, he hath thent a reward, a prithe!'

Again the chant echoed over the terraces, and once more Xsani called for quiet. 'Come forward, great Thed warriorth of the Grothny and Gurkov, and retheive your prithe! Captainth, thend up one man at a time.'

After much pushing and shoving, the eager Zeds were arranged into something approaching single file and led up to the plateau. There, each man was given a cupful of bittersweet liquid scooped from a large bucket. It was wine. The Kogon had discovered an untouched barrel of the Alban liquor. Giv had explained its effects to Xsani and she had immediately resolved to use it in the Timur ceremony.

The effect of a single cup was as she had hoped – it deadened the men's already feeble reasoning, reducing them to little more than grinning slaves. At her command, the women of the Kogon did not partake of the sacrament; Jinsha had explained to them earlier in the day that the befuddling liquid was suitable only for dumbman Zeds.

It was almost dark by the time the last man had drained his cup and resumed his place on the terrace. The summit was lit by flaming torches and, as the drumming resumed, a shape appeared against the backdrop of the night sky. In the flickering orange light, the Head of Timur the Terrible seemed alive, grinning in grizzly delight. The Grozny and Gurkov were so transfixed by the sinister symbol of majesty that they failed to notice the man holding the stick on which it was skewered. Fired by alcohol, they rocked and moaned in awe.

'I am Timur,' began the familiar voice, 'the Mighty Zed who lives for ever. Ratbrains, look on me and tremble.' Whether or not they understood the meaning of 'tremble', the audience did as they were told.

'I am the Mighty One, you volepizzles! And I am terrible! Obey me – or die!'

The audience was quiet, mesmerised by the sights and sounds of the ritual.

'You destroyed Alba – that pleased me. I have rewarded you with the drink of flames. Do further great deeds and I will give you more.' A whisper of pleasure ran through the crowd.

'Silence, batshit vermin! Now, Ogg, Malik of the Gurkov, come to me!'

Ogg rose and walked unsteadily up to the plateau. Able to see Giv holding the spear, he turned to the crowd and opened his mouth to speak.

'Gag him!' screamed Giv in his Timur voice. 'Blind him, too! The piganus has betrayed me!'

Six of Xsani's bodyguard sprang forward, seized Ogg, and threw him to the ground. While one of them put out his remaining eye with a dagger, another tied a rope around his mouth. He was hauled back to his feet.

'You do not behave as Malik,' yelled the voice. 'You wander like a dumb ox! You are an insult to me, to all Zeds! Traitor! Flab-bellied, wood-brained, turnip-headed bucket of snakepiss! Take him away!'

Xsani watched as her bodyguard bundled Ogg over to the precipice on the reverse side of the plateau and threw him to his death on the rocks below. Eathier than I had antithipated, she thought. And, not for the first time, she wondered at Giv's extraordinary creativity. It was uncanny. When in full cry, he didn't just sound like Timur – he was Timur!

The voice had resumed. 'So perish all snailslime traitors! Never forget: I am that I am, the Mighty One! Grozny, Gurkov, Kogon – all Zeds are one under me. Malika Xsani knows my will. Obey her, and you obey me! Obey, vermin! Obey! Obey! Ob-ey!'

As the voice faded away, the Head withdrew into the darkness. Xsani came forward. 'Lithen! Timur hath thpoken to me and thith wath hith command: Ogg ith dead; the Grothny and the Gurkov will now be one, and Giv will be their Malik.

'Together we are thtronger. Beat again, drum man!'

As the steady throb quivered into the warm air of the night, she lifted her arms and led the chant herself.

'Ti-mur! Ti-mur! Ti-mur!'

5
The Man in the Yellow Hat

The Mission had had enough of the jungle. It was dangerous and unhealthy, and there wasn't a hope of coming across an undamaged panel in such a hostile environment. But leaving was not easy. Their quest for a river had brought them deep into the steamy undergrowth, and they had lost all sense of which way they were headed. The leafy canopy overhead was so dense that at times they even lost sight of the sky.

Sammy solved the problem by climbing the tallest tree he could find. Hundreds of feet above the forest floor, with only parrots and small, sad-faced monkeys for company, he clung to a swaying trunk and gazed about. On all sides the green sea of the forest stretched as far as his eye could see... No, not quite. In line with the midday sun – Miouda explained later that the Long Dead knew it as south – he could just make out the land rising.

'It looks like hills,' he called down. 'Miles and miles and miles away. Sort of blue-brown. There's something further away... Can't really see, but it could be mountains.'

He clambered down to the ground and explained more carefully what he had seen. Taking their bearings from the sun, the Mission set off for the distant hills. The journey was long and arduous, but after ten days the vegetation thinned out and the jungle gradually gave way to a verdant landscape dotted with exposed rock and cut through by deep gullies. Hawks wheeled in the breeze and herds of wild goats grazed on the lush grass.

Late one afternoon, they stumbled upon a small mountain settlement of strongly built houses clustered around a rushing stream of clean water. Designed to withstand the roughest weather, the roofs and windows of several houses were still intact. The stony roads were quite clear, too, giving the impression of a village frozen in time: a museum of the Long Dead.

They wandered up and down the streets, staring at the houses and wondering at their remarkable state of preservation. For some reason, perhaps because of its remote, elevated position, the village had escaped pillaging by Zeds. On the roof of a house near the edge of the village, peeping out from beneath a layer of grass, they saw the unmistakable corner of a solar panel.

Cautiously, Cyrus opened the door and went inside.

Xsani was served by four officers, or "Zektivs": her adored kumfort Jinsha, Tarangala, Zilna, and Yalisha. All four were uneasy living at close quarters with dumbmans. Despite Timur's exhortations, which they knew came from the mouth of Malik Giv, they didn't trust their allies. But when they told Xsani of their worries, her response was always the same. She was not yet ready to move. However, should they wish to go off on their own…

The Zektivs accepted the decision without question, though they found it hard to understand. With the Soterion burned to the ground, what was the point in staying? They imagined it was because their Malika enjoyed being in overall command of three tribes. Only Jinsha, who alone sensed the turmoil behind Xsani's cool exterior, understood there was a far more significant reason: she was hoping to find someone.

The Zektivs took heart from the Gurkovs' improved behaviour now Ogg was out of the way. Following a few floggings, and the spectacular public execution of a potential rival, the tribe accepted Giv as their new chieftain and joined eagerly in the hunting and scavenging parties he organised. He got others to patch up the Alban dwellings that were still usable, and had the dead bodies collected and burned. The tribes' dogs, breeding slaves and children had been left behind at the time of the attack; they were now brought into the town and housed in the blackened shells of the larger storerooms.

At the end of each day's labours, Giv assembled his men before the shrunken skull for a short ritual of Timur worship. For many of them, Giv's leadership brought greater stability and comfort than they had ever experienced.

Meanwhile, Xsani and Jinsha sought Cyrus amid the ruins. They peered into every corner and checked every body before it was burned. Nothing. Of the tall, strong-looking man with the dark brown hair and wise, grey eyes there was no sign.

In the end, the anxious Malika concluded that the person she longed to talk to had escaped.

That night, lying beside her kumfort in a tent of salvaged plastic sheeting, Xsani considered her position. Continue her search or abandon it? If she gave up, she would either have to set up the Kogon in a new base or continue with the experiment of living with Giv and his dumbman Zeds. Leading the Kogon away would mean giving up much of her power and reverting to being a Malika of a single tribe.

But would the Kogon-Grozny-Gurkov coalition last? Her immense authority rested on a smoked head and a strange, half-mad dumbman. If Giv died or turned against her, the whole enterprise would crumble...

Continuing to search for Cyrus would be even more perilous, but how else could she settle the doubt growing within her? Like a malignant disease, it threatened to undermine her very existence. It fed on Jinsha's beauty, on the wreckage of Alba, and on the Man in the Yellow Hat. Finally, she made her decision.

'Jintha?'

'Yes, my Malika?' The young woman opened her dark eyes and smiled up at her mistress. 'What can I do for you?'

'Tell me the truth, Jintha.'

'I do not understand, Malika.'

The older woman stretched out her hand and, in the pale moonlight shining through the tent walls, drew her fingers over the smooth nape of her kumfort's neck. 'Are we Thedth, Jintha? Are we all Thed, every piethe of us?'

Jinsha raised her lips to the triple Z scars burned into the

Malika's forehead and cheeks. 'We are marked as Zeds.'

'Inthide ath well ath outthide?'

'I don't know, Malika.'

'Nor do I, lovely Jintha. Nor do I.' Looking into her kumfort's eyes, she paused for a moment before announcing, as much to herself as to her companion, 'I am leaving, Jintha.'

Jinsha stared at her blankly. 'Leaving what?'

'Leaving Alba and the dumbman Grothny-Gurkov.' She hesitated. 'And leaving the Kogon as well.'

Tears brimmed in Jinsha's eyes. 'Leaving me, Malika?'

Xsani gently shook her head. 'I hope not, Jintha. Will you come with me? It will be very hard and we may not thuctheed.'

'I will go anywhere you take me, O my Malika. And do anything you command. Where are we going?'

Xsani gazed beyond the roof of the tent at the vast emptiness of the night. 'We are going to find the Man in the Yellow Hat.'

The Mission could probably not have gone on without the short interlude in the mountains. Their time in the jungle and the long climb up to the village had taken a harsh toll. Their clothes were in rags, their feet blistered, their bodies swollen and scarred with scratches and the bites of a thousand insects.

Emotionally, too, they were exhausted. The ghastly night of slaughter in Alba and the days of painful uncertainty that followed had stretched their nerves to breaking. Sammy, normally so cheerful, withdrew into himself. Miouda snapped at Cyrus on several occasions, accusing him of putting the Mission before the security of their child.

'I know what you mean,' he replied, regarding her with

serious, sorrowful eyes. 'And in a way you're right. I'm sorry, but we can't turn back, can we? The success of the Mission and the safety of our baby are one and the same now.'

She knew this made sense. But it was painful to hear.

Happily, they found the house in the mountains before anyone said or did anything they would later regret. Once safe inside, they drew the rusty bolt on the door, swept the dust off the beds and lay down. Sleep fell upon them as water to parched flowers. It soothed their aching limbs, calmed their troubled minds and restored the frayed edges of the affection that bound them together so tightly.

Having slept through to the afternoon, they were woken by the wind moaning in the eaves like a lost spirit. Rain hammered against windowpanes filthy with grime and spiders' webs. As evening fell, the storm subsided. The three friends lit a pair of candles they had unearthed beneath the staircase, and gathered around the kitchen table to plan what to do next. First, food. The contents of the cupboards could not be trusted. As soon as it was light, Cyrus would go out and try to kill one of the goats they had seen on the hillside. Miouda would look for fruit and vegetables in the long-neglected gardens.

Sammy's job was to climb on to the roof and clear the grass and muck off the solar panel. Miouda said she would trace the wires from the panel and try to make sense of how the system worked. All they had to go on were hazy memories of diagrams they had seen in the books of the Soterion back in Alba.

Everything went according to plan. Sammy cleaned the panel until it shone like new. As he worked, he intoned the prayer of the Gova settlement where he had grown up. 'Glory to Gova! Polish the panel!' he chanted, except he replaced 'Gova' with a rude word of his own and added an ironic second verse about Ozlam, the corrupt head of his former community.

Miouda found a cupboard on the landing where the electric cables entered the house. It had two supplies, one from wires that came in from outside, and one from the panel on the roof. The latter passed through a switch, currently set at "Off", and via a dusty plastic box to a larger container on the floor marked Longstore® Batteries. That, she imagined, was where the electricity was stored when there wasn't enough light to power the panel. The only way to find out whether it all still worked was to move the switch to "On".

Towards the end of the morning, as the sun was coming out, Cyrus came back carrying the legs and ribs of a goat. He had caught the creature in a meadow, skinned and butchered it on the spot – and left the bits he did not want on the grass for the birds and wild animals.

That was his first mistake.

When he had finished on the roof, Sammy took a basket and went off to help Miouda gather vegetables. They came back with baskets laden with potatoes, onions and an array of green, cabbage-like plants. Cyrus lit a fire in the living-room grate and hooked up the goat to roast over the flames. Beside it, Miouda hung an iron pot in which to boil the potatoes and cabbage.

Long before the meat was thoroughly done, they were all slicing thick brown chunks off the outside and stuffing them into their mouths. As the rich juice ran down their chins, they turned to each other and grinned. It was the first cooked food they had tasted in over a month.

After they had eaten as much as their stomachs could hold, Miouda led them upstairs to the solar panel switch.

'Shall I?' she asked, putting her fingers on the plastic handle.

'Alright,' said Cyrus. 'Go!'

Miouda pulled sharply downwards – and the handle broke off. The switch remained in the "Off" position.

'Damn!' muttered Miouda, using a Long Dead word she had picked up from Cyrus. 'I must have pulled too hard.'

Cyrus examined the handle. 'No. Not your fault. It's the same with everything the Long Dead made of plastic. In time it gets weak and breaks. But I think I can make it work.'

He drew his knife and inserted the point into the hole where the handle had projected. Jamming it on to the spindle, he levered upwards. With a snap, the switch sprang to "On".

Nothing happened. They ran around the house flicking all the light switches, but not one bulb lit up. When they gathered back by the main switch, Miouda bit her bottom lip in frustration. 'It doesn't work,' she said, trying to hide her disappointment. 'It's probably been left too long. The panel must be broken.'

'But the one in Gova worked,' said Cyrus. 'Why shouldn't this one? There must be something we're not doing right.'

'Stupid thing!' snorted Sammy. 'Getting our hopes up like that!' He thumped the box next to the switch with his fist, sending a cloud of fine dust into the air.

Whatever was in the box, or what it was for, they never knew. But Sammy's blow did the trick. Above their heads a bulb glowed, faint to begin with but rapidly brightening until it shone like a little star of hope.

Sammy did a dance of joy. Cyrus kissed Miouda and told her their dark days were over. They would leave the light shining all night.

That was his second mistake.

6
Xsani's Decision

Officers of the Kogon tribe went through a long and testing period of training. Xsani chose the candidates with great care, selecting the brightest and keeping a keen eye on their progress. Only four or five ever made it to the position of Zektiv. Of these, she singled out one as her kumfort and successor.

Jinsha had proved outstanding from the beginning. Female Constant prisoners taught her to speak clearly, to count and to reason. Zilna and Yalisha, the senior Zektivs responsible for military training, declared Jinsha to be the ablest of all their pupils. Xsani herself taught Jinsha the most important lessons: to loathe and mistrust all dumbmans, especially Zeds, and to harden her heart against feelings that might endanger the tribe.

Jinsha learned all these things and, like her mistress, built around herself a defensive shell of insensitivity. For this, and for her unstinting devotion to the Malika, she was rewarded with exemption from the indignity of breeding. As a consequence, every Kogon knew that unless she was carried off by war or disease, Jinsha would succeed Xsani as Malika of the Kogon.

It was not to be. The sack of Alba and destruction of the Soterion affected Xsani more deeply than she realised. She was forced to confront questions that had been troubling her for over a year.

'You thee, my thweet Jintha,' she explained after telling her that she planned to leave Alba and the Kogon, 'I have been thinking about everything. About how we live our liveth. The Thoterion, with it'th bookth and withdom, might have shown uth a different life.'

'The life of the Long Dead?'

'Yeth, that life.' She put her arm around Jinsha and kissed her. 'Dumbman Thedth don't do that, do they?'

Jinsha smiled and shook her head.

'But dumbman Conthtantth do…' She paused. 'All my life, ever thinthe I wath a little girl, I wath told that I mutht hate the Conthtantth. But a Conthtant opened the Thoterion. What wath he looking for? I wath told that the dumbman Thyruth wantth to return to the wayth of the Long Dead, when there were no Conthtantth and no Thedth.'

'Cyrus, the Man in the Yellow Hat, Malika?'

'Yeth. Thyruth appearth like the dumbman in that picture. The image thpoke to me, Jintha. I can't get it out of my head. I think… I think…'

Wide-eyed with expectation, Jinsha leaned forward. Such talk from any other lips would be treason, punishable by torture and death. 'Yes, my Malika?' she asked, her chest tight with anticipation. 'What do you think?'

'I think not all Thedth are the thame.'

'I know. Kogon and dumbmans—'

'More than that, my dearetht Jintha. When I thee what happened here, what the Gurkov and Grothny did – I feel more like a Conthtant than a Thed.'

Her kumfort gasped and instinctively drew back. 'But I am a Zed!'

'You have the markth on your thkin, Jintha, but not I think on your heart.'

Jinsha began to sob. 'What are you saying, Malika? I don't understand!'

Xsani stretched out her arms and held her tight. 'I am only thtarting to underthtand mythelf, dearetht Jintha. We muth find thith Thyruth – Giv will help uth – and learn what he knowth. Thingth are changing, Jintha. Thingth are changing.'

Outwardly, Xsani gave no indication of her inner turbulence or of what she was about to do. In the morning, she arranged for her tribe to be fed and for the Zektivs to organise drills for the warriors. This done, she waited for Giv to appear. He did not do so until late in the afternoon, marching up the hill with a posse of Grozny servants bearing the grim symbol of his authority.

When he was some way off, Xsani sent Jinsha down to him with a request that he leave his men and advance alone. He obeyed immediately.

'Great Malika,' he began, kneeling and gazing up at her face in adoration, 'most favoured of the Mighty Timur, Giv is here!' After learning to talk in sentences, he had developed this odd style of speech for use on occasions of great importance.

'Tho I thee, Giv,' said Xsani dryly. 'Now do thtand up. I have thomething very important to dithcuth with you.'

The newly created Malik of the Grozny and Gurkov stared in open-mouthed wonder as she explained how Timur, the Mighty Timur, had come to her in a dream the previous night. It was an experience she would never, ever forget.

Giv nodded wildly. He understood. Yes, he understood. 'And did the Great One speak?' he asked, twisting his spindly fingers.

'Yeth, Giv. But hith wordth are thecret.'

'Tell me, Giv begs you, O wondrous Malika!' His fingers were now so entwined that she feared he might never be able to undo them.

'It conthernth you…'

'Me? O… O Malika!'

Xsani's bodyguard of loyal eunuchs, anxious Giv might lose control and throw himself on her, raised their spears and took a step forward. Xsani waved them back with a gesture of irritation. 'Timur wantth uth to do thomething for him – together.'

'Together?!'

'Yeth. He wantth uth to find Thyruth.'

Giv's face looked blank. 'Thyruth? I mean – O have mercy on Giv, Malika! – Giv mean say Cyrus. Who is he?'

'Thakamir thpoke of him. He ith the Conthtant who opened the Thoterion and ith teaching the people of Alba to read. He knowth much.'

'Is he not blooddead, Malika? Slain?'

'I think not, Giv. I thaw him by the Ghathar – and I let him ethcape. Did you thee any Conthtant leaving Alba? Perhapth he wath not alone. Thakamir talked of a woman and a boy – and a dog.'

'No, Great Malika. Giv's eyes were not seeing – Wait! Yes, Giv remembers. As he entering Alba with the Master, he sees three Constants passing by…'

'And a dog?'

'Er, no Malika. Giv sees no dog.'

'It ith not important. You thaw the Conthtantth, that ith what matterth. Now, thith is what Timur orderth uth to do…'

First, Giv was to make sure that three of his tribe's best hunting dogs were moved to a safe place near the Soterion Gate. When all his men were asleep and the moon was at its highest, he was to go to the gate, bringing with him the Head of Timur and his most reliable and experienced Captain. Xsani, Jinsha and their eunuch bodyguard would meet them there.

As Xsani outlined her intentions, Giv nodded in blind obedience.

'We will leave Alba, Giv, and go to find Thyruth.'

'Good, O Malika! Zeds like hunting. Tribes will happy be. Smiling.'

Xsani paused. This was the crucial moment. If Giv questioned her, she was unsure what to do. But it was a risk she had to take. 'No, Malik Giv. No tribeth. Jutht Giv, one Captain and three dogth. The great Timur hath commanded and I, your Malika, mutht obey. Tho mutht you.'

She stared at Giv's face, reading the thoughts and emotions that flashed across it. Follow this bewitching flabtoad? Abandon his tribes when he had just been made their Malik?

But the order had come from Over-Malik Timur, the one who had given him the gift of speaking. There was no choice: Giv too would obey.

'Giv at gate will be.'

'Good. With man and dogth?'

'With Captain Pram and three dogs, O Malika.'

Xsani resisted the temptation to smile and reminded Giv that the plan was secret. No one, not even this Captain Pram, must know what was going on. Having assured him that Timur would reward his loyalty, she sent him back to his people.

Phase two of the Malika's plan was more painful to explain. At dusk, she summoned Tarangala and told her that from now on she was Malika of the Kogon. The tall Zektiv frowned.

'You are the Malika, Xsani.'

'Thoon I will not be here, Tarangala. I am going away.'

'Is our Malika in the Death Month?' Tarangala asked, her voice quavering in dismay. 'She will be dead?'

'No, I am not yet dying. I am jutht leaving Alba and the Kogon.'

'And Jinsha. Is she not new Malika?'

'Jintha cometh with me.' She lifted her blue silk gown, slipped it over her shoulders and handed it to the astonished Tarangala. 'Here, you mutht now wear thith. It ith the thymbol of the Malika. Take off your dreth and give it to me.'

Too shocked to speak, Tarangala did as she was told. When the exchange was done, Xsani gave her final orders. The new Malika was to rouse the Kogon before dawn and lead them out of Alba. Once in the woods, they were to meet up with those left behind at the time of the attack: the sick, the pregnant and the dying, as well as the dumbman breeding slaves and their guards. The whole tribe was then to leave the area as quickly as possible and find a new, secure base.

By the time Xsani had finished, Tarangala had regained her composure. Yes, she would obey the Malika…

'No, Tarangala. Remember, you are the Malika now. You give the commandth, not me. Now go – and take care of my Kogon with all your thtrength.'

As the new leader turned to go, she noticed Xsani's mouth moving in a way she had never seen before. It was almost as if she were trying not to cry.

The light in the mountain house did not shine all night. There had been insufficient hours of daylight to charge the Longstore® batteries, and after a couple of hours the bulb flickered and went out. The three Constants had fallen asleep long before this, stuffed with rich food and exhausted by the exciting developments of the day.

When the electricity had come on, they had hurried from room to room to see how many lamps and gadgets worked. For a second, as red and orange lights glimmered into life behind curtains of cobweb, the kitchen twinkled like a fantastic Milky Way. But the vision faded as quickly as it had arisen. One by one, the ancient bulbs burned out and the room was once more swathed in the uniform greyness of dust. Elsewhere in the house, just three lamps still worked. Cyrus unscrewed one of the bulbs and moved it to a socket in the kitchen ceiling.

The fuses in the electric kettle, cooker and microwave blew as soon as they were switched on, but they had better luck with the food mixer. Miouda almost jumped out of her skin when it roared into life.

The tiny batteries inside all the other sophisticated electrical gadgetry had disintegrated. None of the televisions worked, nor, to their intense disappointment, did a large desktop computer. In one of the bedrooms, however, a digital clock came on. It read 09:47 : Thursday : 19 September : 2019.

Cyrus looked at it wistfully. 'The time when they turned off the electricity, I suppose.'

Miouda took his hand. 'Yes. And I wonder who they were? Obviously they chose not to die at home.'

She was wrong. In their first search of the building, they had missed the heavy oak door at the entrance to the cellar. On the morning of their fourth day, as they were looking for spare light bulbs and a lead for the laptop, Cyrus lifted the latch and pushed open the cellar door. He found himself at the head of stone steps descending into darkness. A strange, musty smell hung in the air.

'Hey, Miouda! Sammy! Come here! I've found another room.'

He pressed the switch on the wall to his right and was surprised when a pale yellow glow flooded the room below. As soon as Miouda and Sammy joined him, he led the way down.

The air was colder and damper than in the rest of the house. At the foot of the stairs stood the rusted, barely identifiable carcass of a washing machine. Mildewed wine racks lined the wall on their left; opposite lay the corroded frame of a child's bicycle, surrounded by mouldering boxes of discarded toys. The rotten remains of garden implements hung precariously on tarnished hooks. Through the tiny fissures between the ceiling and the clammy walls, gnarled tree roots twisted like fingers. Slowly but inexorably, nature was reclaiming the kingdom the Long Dead had believed was theirs.

The couple that had lived in the Alpine house had chosen to die here, out of sight of the civilization crumbling above. Their end had not been violent, as so many had been, but dignified and carefully thought out. They had switched off the electricity and entered the cellar in the dark, shutting the thick door of their tomb behind them.

They had died sitting at a table laid for a meal. In the damp atmosphere, the wooden furniture had decayed to a soggy pulp, allowing the corpses to roll forwards on to the floor amid a sad mosaic of broken plates and tarnished cutlery.

Little now remained of the bodies. Clothes and flesh had decomposed long ago, leaving bits of shoe, crusted jewellery and a few crumbling bones. The skulls, lying some distance apart, were still recognisable beneath the multi-coloured fungus sprouting from the empty eye sockets.

Miouda stooped and picked up a piece of cracked slate that had fallen from the table when it collapsed. A simple message was scratched into the hard surface. She wiped it with her hand and read, 'God have mercy on us.'

As she spoke, the lamp gave out. Without a word, the Constants fumbled their way up the stairs to the light. It was a long time before any of them talked about what they had seen.

They spent the rest of the day bathing in the icy stream and scouring the village for books and a serviceable computer cable.

The books had all gone – used as fuel during the Great Death of 2018-19 – but they did find a variety of electronic machines. Though several of the cables were undamaged, all the plugs were too large for the socket in the SP laptop. They continued the search over the next two days, always with the same result. It was as if their laptop was a one-off, Miouda concluded.

'Do you think that's possible?' asked Cyrus, staring at the inert computer. It was evening, and the three friends were gathered around the kitchen table after supper. Corby snoozed at Sammy's feet.

'Makes sense,' Cyrus said. 'Most have names on them, like Dell and Acer. Ours just has SP.'

'If whoever set up the Soterion—' began Miouda.

'Dr Rebekkah Askar,' said Cyrus. 'Her name was on the letter we found in the vault.'

'Yes, I remember. Anyway, this Dr Askar must have hoped the machines would work when they were switched on, mustn't she? Even years and years later. Otherwise, what would've been the point in leaving them?

'Because she knew normal computers wouldn't last, ours was made better. It's bigger than the ones we've seen, isn't it?'

'And heavier,' said Cyrus.

While they were talking, Sammy had leaned forward, flipped up the top of the laptop and examined it carefully, tapping the casing. When he had finished, he rested it clear of the tabletop on two pieces of wood and started pressing the keys. He began at the top left and worked his way down, one at a time, row by row, until he reached an unmarked key at the bottom on the right. As he hit it, there was a sharp click.

'Yes!' he exclaimed, lifting the computer in the air. A small compartment had opened underneath, and from it had fallen a small metal and plastic object shaped like a tube. Sammy grabbed it and slotted it into a port on the left-hand side.

'There we are! I bet you one of the wires fits into that.'

It did.

Miouda produced the cable she had found with its transformer and plastic insulation still intact. She plugged one end into a socket on the wall, and the other into the adapter projecting from the side of the laptop. Sammy, who had moved to her side, peered eagerly at the blank, black screen.

Too anxious to remain seated, Cyrus looked over her shoulder. If the machine didn't work, all the sacrifices of the Mission would have been a tragic waste of time. He could hardly bear to think about it.

Miouda's finger hovered over the button marked "On". 'Are we ready?'

'Please work,' whispered Sammy.

'It will!' said Cyrus. 'It must!'

Miouda began to bring her finger down. 'Here goes!'

Before it reached the button, there was a loud crash. Corby woke with a start. Miouda gasped and jumped back from the table as shards of glass showered into the room and a large rock thudded on to the floor beside her.

7
Kemran's Patrol

An equally dramatic shock had struck the Zeds when they discovered that Xsani and the Kogon had disappeared overnight. The guard on the Patrol Gate was first to notice something was amiss. Waking at dawn, his first reaction was panic: sleeping on duty was punishable by a severe flogging and probably the loss of a few teeth.

He looked around. Relief. No one else was stirring. He glanced up at the terraces, hoping to snatch a glimpse of a shapely Kogon. Nothing happening up there, either... That's odd... Nothing happening? There were always guards patrolling the perimeter of the Kogon camp.

The Zed went to investigate. Who knows, he told himself as he climbed the slope, he might find a defenceless flabtoad with whom to slake his lust.

On reaching the plateau where the Kogon had camped, he stared about him in bewilderment. There were no defenceless flabtoads – in fact, there were no flabtoads at all. The ashes of a few fires, a couple of broken spears and a toilet pit were the only signs of the site's recent occupation. Moments later, he was hurtling down the hill towards the shell of a grain store that Giv had made his headquarters.

'Malik!' he panted as he approached the building. 'Malik! Flabtoads gone! Flabtoads gone! Flabtoads...'

The building was empty. What was happening? First no Kogon, now no Malik. He didn't understand it at all.

Within five minutes, the entire Grozny-Gurkov camp was in chaos.

Raised as hunters and fighters, the common Zeds who had sacked Alba had nothing but scorn for the arts of peace practised by the Long Dead and their Constant imitators. So-called 'civilization', their Maliks asserted over and over again, had failed – one only had to look around to see that. The world belonged to the fearless male, the tough male, the brutal male.

But Zed warriors were pack animals, and every pack needs a leader. When they found their Malik and the totemic Head of Timur had disappeared, they milled about in angry confusion. A number climbed the terraces to confirm with their own eyes that the flabtoads were no longer there. By late morning, they were fighting among themselves.

As with creatures in the wild, the Zeds knew instinctively who among them wielded authority. It tended to be the older and stronger men, those who had seen sixteen or seventeen winters. They were physically well-developed and some had learned from Constant prisoners how to speak and think reasonably coherently. The more promising had been singled out by their Maliks as Captains. As with the Kogon, the chiefs also picked their successors.

But Giv had left before he had time to select an heir. It was therefore up to his Captains – nine in number now Pram had gone – to select one of themselves as the new commander. Three stood out, two Gurkov and one Grozny.

The acutely myopic Pingog had once been in line to succeed Ogg. He was a tall, cunning warrior with a shark fin nose. The second possibility, Soceptan, was renowned for the quick and furious temper that cloaked a somewhat dim wit. Kamal, the Grozny candidate, had the advantage of having once been appointed by the legendary Timur to take over in his absence. His disadvantage was a missing right hand, chopped off in battle at the age of thirteen.

The fighting started when an ambitious Captain, making a bid for the leadership, called Soceptan a 'hippobum'. It ended a minute later when the challenger's head was removed with a single blow from the older man's axe.

Pingog feared this victory would make Soceptan favourite to replace Giv, so he deliberately provoked his rival into a showdown. 'You skull rattle – nuts in bucket,' he teased with a rare flash of imagination. 'Soceptan big head, little brain!'

Soceptan shivered with fury and charged, spinning his axe around his head.

Pingog, using his long, spindly legs to advantage, stepped neatly to one side and watched his foe thunder harmlessly by. 'Nutbrain!' he chanted 'Nutbrain! Nutbrain!'

It was like a Long Dead bullfight, and it ended in a similar manner. Soceptan, growing more and more angry, made three further charges. On the third, Pingog ducked beneath the whirling axe and stuck out his rusty gut-ripper.

Soceptan tripped and sprawled headlong to the ground. As he landed, his axe spun out of his grasp and slid away over the cobbles. Pingog was on him in an instant. A bone-splintering hack, a skewering thrust to the belly – and it was all over.

'Feed corpse to hunting dogs,' commanded Pingog, already giving himself Malikian airs.

Kamal had observed all this with interest. Pingog's victory made him a real threat, and one that needed to be dealt with swiftly before his status became embedded. Kamal planned his campaign carefully. While he could only fight one-handed, his enemy's myopia meant objects more than four paces away from him were just a blur. To take advantage of this disability, the wily Kamal had decided to fight at long range.

Carrying four metal-tipped Alban spears, he climbed on to the wall between the Soterion and Patrol Gates and shouted for Pingog to come and fight. 'Giv tell me I new Malik!' he lied. 'Pingog spindly stick-man coward!'

The lanky Gurkov could hardly ignore the challenge. Grasping his gut-ripper, he moved cautiously nearer the wall. Around him, Zeds stopped what they were doing and gathered to watch. There was no better sport than a fight to the death – as this would surely be.

The contest was less gorily spectacular than many had hoped. When Pingog reached the foot of the wall and was looking short-sightedly for the stairs to the top, Kamal launched the first of his spears. It struck the Gurkov on the side of his head, slicing open a long wound as it ricocheted off his skull.

Undaunted by the blood and severed right ear flapping

against his cheek, Pingog located the steps and began his ascent. Kamal raised a second spear and flung it down with all his strength.

Quite by chance, at that moment Pingog raised his gut-ripper. The spear struck its serrated metal blade and fell harmlessly to the ground.

'Now, stump-hand coward, die!' shouted the Gurkov, loping quickly up the remaining steps to the wall-head. By the time he reached the top, Kamal had retreated to a safe distance and raised his third spear.

Pingog stared about him, trying to work out which of the blurred shapes on the edge of his vision was the enemy. From the direction of one of them, something was coming towards him, something that hissed and flashed. Too late he recognised it as a third javelin.

The missile embedded itself in his stomach and brought forth an involuntary grunt of pain. Without trying to remove the shaft sticking out in front of him like a broom handle, he lurched blindly forward. He had taken no more than half-a-dozen steps before the fourth spear struck.

At close to point-blank range, Kamal could not miss. The weapon pierced deep into the Gurkov's chest, severing an artery. He crumpled to his knees, fell backwards, and rolled over the side of the wall to the cobbles below.

Seeing a number of fascinated Zeds running forward to inspect the corpse, Kamal lifted his arms in triumph. 'Kamal is Malik,' he yelled. As some Grozny probably recalled how much they had hated him during his last period of leadership, he added in an unusual flash of inspiration, 'Timur agree. He make Kamal's arm strong!'

Linking his name with the cult of Over-Malik Timur was a clever idea, but it raised an important question.

He was ready with the answer.

'But where Timur go?' he asked the crowd staring up at him. 'Kamal, your new Malik, tell you now.'

Two hundred Zed faces gawped in open-mouthed anticipation.

'Flabtoads steal Timur!' shouted Kamal. 'Kogon flabtoads take Timur prisoner!'

Howls of fury echoed around the ruins.

'Listen, Zeds of Grozny and Gurkov,' Kamal continued. 'Malik Kamal now give Zeds what they want. He lead to find Timur – and Kogon flabtoads! Timur come back – and plenty flabtoad breeding slaves for you!'

The promise of such rich prizes, reinforced by a series of harsh punishments, cemented Kamal's authority. In two days, he was ready for his first campaign.

The mettle of Tarangala's command was about to be tested sooner than she imagined.

Far away, another Zed tribe was on the move. These were the Murax. Ferocious rivals had recently driven them from their native woodland into an unfamiliar landscape of hills and pasture.

Malik Eziz, the Murax's semi-educated chieftain, established his base in a wrecked hydroelectric power station at the foot of a steep cliff. From there he sent out patrols to locate signs of nearby Constant activity. Many of the tribe's flabtoad breeding slaves had died recently and Eziz needed to replace them. The principal task of all Zed leaders was maintenance of tribal numbers. Given their murderous way of life, this was not always easy.

Eziz had given the leadership one of the search parties to Captain Kemran. Had he been able to count, the Captain might have worked out that he was no more than fifteen years old. This was unusually young for a Zed officer; he owed his position to his exceptional strength. To maintain discipline, Kemran simply wrapped his arms around those who disobeyed him and crushed the breath out of them like a boa constrictor.

Unfortunately, Kemran's brain had not developed at the same pace as his body. Having wandered aimlessly up and down the mountainside for three days, it dawned on him that he was lost. He was saved by a stroke of good fortune. At dusk on the third day, as they neared the crest of a slope, they found the remains of the goat Cyrus had killed the previous week. Carnivorous birds and mammals had carried off most of the flesh, but the skull and several bones remained.

'Birds eat dead sheep,' said one of Kemran's men, eyeing the remains.

'Goat,' corrected the Captain in his bizarrely high-pitched voice. 'Englebirds eat dead…' As he examined the bones more carefully, a puzzled look came over his face. Strange. What animal would take just the ribs and legs…?

Kemran gave a self-satisfied sigh. Turning to the man who had first seen the carcass, a thin fellow with a face like a stoat, he poked him sharply in the ribs.

'Argh! Why Captain hit Lopz?'

'Kemran thinking. Lopz have ribs; goat have ribs.' He pointed to the carcass. 'Where ribs of this goat?'

Lopz and the rest of the patrol shrugged and glanced around as if half expecting to see the missing bones floating somewhere in the sky.

Kemran laughed. 'Ha-ha! Ribs not clouds, rockheads! Ribs taken by wolfs or...' A crafty grin spread upwards from his smooth, heavy jowl to his piggy brown eyes... 'or Constants!'

His men broke into spontaneous applause. 'Constants!' they choroused. 'We find Constants!'

'They are near. Kemran smell them,' the Captain lied. 'We go hunting.'

It was a foolish idea, but fortune continued to smile on the dim-witted Captain. The moon and stars gave sufficient light for his patrol to continue along the meadow, and in a short time they came to an overgrown path between ruined stone walls. Kemran summoned his men to him. 'If Zeds make noise,' he threatened, 'Zed ribs crack – like goat.'

His men, terrified into unusual stealthiness, followed him up the path until they reached the outskirts of the village. Ahead of them stood a narrow bridge. Beyond that, they could make out the silhouettes of a dozen houses. In the window of the one furthest from them, high up at the far end of the village, shone a light.

Kemran shivered with delight. 'Constants,' he hissed. 'Only Constants have light in night. Kemran and Zed men attack.'

He was about to advance when Lopz asked in a hoarse whisper, 'What plan, Kemran?'

'Attack!' responded the Captain without thinking. He

stopped. Ah yes! Malik Eziz had said making plans was important, so maybe he should make one now. He wasn't too sure what a plan was, but he understood it involved thinking about what was going to happen. Well, he was going to charge up to the house, rush inside, kill all the male Constants except one, and capture their flabtoads. That was his plan.

But what if the door was locked shut and he couldn't get in? Mmmm. He needed the Constants outside. That's when he had the idea of throwing stones through the window. When they came crashing in, he reasoned, the Constants would come crashing out to see what was going on – and he and his men would be waiting for them. Ribs would crack! Ha! Ha! Ha! Ha!

If the Constants had left the house as Kemran anticipated, his strategy might have worked. But immediately the first missile hit the floor, Cyrus dived for the light switch. 'Get down!' he yelled. As he extinguished the lamp, a second rock smashed into the room.

'Bring the laptop and the cable, Sammy. Upstairs. Quick! And make sure Corby's with us!'

He checked the bolt on the front door and followed his friends out of the room. On the landing, he switched off the power supply so it was darker inside than out. They now had a clear view of their enemy. Kemran and three of his colleagues, clubs and gut-rippers at the ready, stood in a row before the front door. Round at the back, the other two members of the troop continued to bombard the windows with stones.

The house, like most in the village, stood on a steep slope with its upper part set into the hillside. Here the bedroom windows were only six or so feet from what had once been a gravel path. The three Constants quickly filled sturdy plastic bags with all the food and possessions they could carry. They then lowered their baggage before them, slipped noiselessly out of the first-floor window, and signalled for Corby to join them. When he was safely down, they escaped into the night.

By the time Kemran and his gang had battered down the front door, the Constants were over a mile away. Finding their prey had vanished, the frustrated Zeds gave vent to their anger by spending the next few days trashing every house in the village.

Malik Eziz was not best pleased when, a week later, Kemran and his troop stumbled into his tribe's headquarters empty-handed. Having listened to its leader's garbled report with a mixture of anger and contempt, he stared at his incompetent Captain for a long time without uttering a word.

The muscly oaf gazed blankly back. Eventually it dawned on him that all was not well, and he asked in a voice made shriller than usual by his nervousness, 'You not happy, Big Malik?'

Eziz fingered the blade of his gleaming scimitar. 'Does Malik cut off Kemran head? Would Kemran enjoy?'

The giant instinctively placed a hand on his thick neck. 'No, Big Malik! No!'

'Don't call me "big"! You are big man, Kemran. Big fool!'

Hoping agreement might lighten his sentence, the Captain nodded slowly, like an elephant.

'Kemran deserve die, but Malik not kill Kemran. Malik not even cut off bit of Kemran.' The Captain grinned like a gorilla. 'One last chance, Kemran: go find Constants you lose!'

Disbelief mingled with incomprehension on the officer's pear-shaped face. 'Find Constants?' he squeaked.

'Yes, big fool! Take one man and go find Constants you lose. Go!'

And so it was that Captain Kemran and the puny Lopz left the power station to look for the Mission. As they set off in completely the wrong direction, their quest was doomed from the outset. But as chance would have it, their route brought them into contact with another party of Zed searchers. From Kemran and his diminutive crony, this party would gather information that would prove very useful indeed.

8
Pursuit

It was a strange procession. First came Pram, square-jawed and sweating as he struggled to hold on to the leashes of his powerful hounds. Giv walked two steps behind, proudly holding aloft the swaying Head of Timur. The fair-haired Xsani, with Jinsha at her side and overshadowed by the six bare-chested eunuchs of the bodyguard, brought up the rear.

Watching Giv strutting ahead of her, Xsani tried to work out what she made of him. In a way, he had served his purpose: he had brought the male Zeds under her control, confirmed Cyrus' escape from Alba, and provided Pram and the tracker dogs. But she couldn't get rid of him yet. He was needed to keep Pram and his dogs under control – a Grozny Captain could not be trusted to take orders from a Malika without the backing of Giv and his totem.

Nevertheless, Giv's obsession with that smoked and shrunken head irritated her. The Timur cult had been her idea, a brilliant way of getting the Grozny and Gurkov to accept her leadership. But Giv had taken it a step – no, several steps – further. He was bewitched. The way he spoke with Timur's voice was uncanny. The poor man was almost unhinged.

Poor man? What was she thinking? Her entire upbringing had warned her against showing any sympathy for a dumbman, least of all a Zed. Recently, however, so many of the foundations of her education had started to crack. A year before, she would never have dreamed of leaving her tribe to look for a Constant, especially a male one. Yet here she was doing precisely that, and in the company of two Zed men.

The world in which she had grown up was simple and clear: female v male, Zed v Constant. From the moment they were born, everyone knew where they were. Maybe that was why the divisions had persisted? All they required was unthinking obedience.

But Xsani was no longer unthinking. She had learned too much. From Sakamir and Giv she had seen a blurring of the boundaries between Constant and Zed: Sakamir had willingly become a Zed, while Giv's extraordinary respect for her was the sort of conduct one might expect of a Constant. And her own longing for the secrets of the Soterion, for a return to the world of the Long Dead? Wasn't that precisely what Cyrus and his Constant accomplices were hoping for too?

Xsani was also perplexed by her feelings for Jinsha. It was like the behaviour she had witnessed between male and female Constants when attacked by Zeds. The man or the woman, using words Xsani did not usually understand, would sacrifice themselves to save the other. It seemed so stupid – yet Xsani felt she would happily do the same for Jinsha.

What weakness! There were times when she hated herself for allowing such thoughts to cross her mind. And yet... in Jinsha's arms she felt peaceful and complete, a human being without the label of Constant or Zed. As the Long Dead had been... as the Man in the Yellow Hat had been.

The stars gave sufficient light for Xsani and her party to locate the well-worn path down to the Soterion, and they were soon standing before the sealed door of the vault. The Malika traced the writing on the door with her finger. An S and an O and a T – she immediately recognised the letters that Sakamir had taught her.

'Tho thith ith where it wath thtored,' she lisped quietly to herself. 'The Thoterion.'

She examined the trampled grass nearby. 'And thith ith where they came,' she announced, speaking louder. 'Find a thent the dogth can follow.'

The Constants had left nothing on the ground. Xsani was thinking they would have to make do with a trail of footmarks and damaged vegetation, when she glanced again at the door. The hands of whoever had opened and closed it must have rubbed against the metal. If those hands were dirty or sweaty...

Pram brought the dogs over to the door and lifted them one at a time on to their hind legs so their noses were level with the keyhole. Yes, there was a scent, and when he lowered the hounds to the path, they identified it easily.

And so the pursuit began.

From resting place to resting place, guided by the trail of ashes, broken branches, bones and other debris, Xsani and her posse tracked the Constants through the wilderness. When the dogs lost the scent on rocky soil, the Malika always knew by instinct where to go. It was almost as if she were inside Cyrus' head, Jinsha thought.

The Mission, normally even-tempered in the most testing situations, were in a tetchy mood after they fled the mountain house. Their joy at finally finding a working panel had turned to bitter disappointment when they failed to learn whether their computer worked and, if it did, what it contained.

Cyrus led the way on his own, navigating by the stars. Miouda could tell he was annoyed by the way he cracked his fingers, and she hung back with Sammy. 'Don't worry,' he whispered. 'It won't last long.

'I don't blame him,' he added later as Cyrus was clambering over the tumbled remains of a stone wall. 'He's made this Mission his whole life.'

'I think we all have, Sam,' replied Miouda, grimly serious. 'None of us can return to our homes, can we?'

They continued briskly across wildly overgrown farmland for a couple more hours. Cyrus finally agreed to stop for a rest when he was sure there was no chance of the Zeds catching them up.

Miouda slumped wearily down on the damp grass. 'So near yet again.'

'You ok?' asked Cyrus. He sat beside her so she could lean her head on his shoulder. 'Sorry I've been a bit grumpy.'

'It's alright, Cy. I understand.'

He laid a hand on her knee and sighed. 'If only you had

managed to press…' There was no point in finishing the sentence. Her finger hadn't reached the "On" button, and that was that.

Sammy plonked himself down heavily next to them. 'We'll just have to carry on looking, won't we?'

'Sure. There must be hundreds more panels out there that work,' said Cyrus. 'All we have to do is find one.'

Miouda laughed quietly. 'That's what's so amazing about you, Cy!' She reached up and kissed him on his stubbly cheek. 'I don't think you'd know how to give up even if you wanted to.'

'Oh, I don't know,' he muttered, taken aback by his own embarrassment. 'Anyway, don't you want to see what would've happened if that stone hadn't come through the window?'

'Of course I do. As much as you, Cy.'

'Me too,' said Sammy. 'It's what we're all about, isn't it?'

'Sure is,' said Cyrus. 'Look at it this way,' he added, climbing to his feet. 'Back there we were really lucky. We could easily have been trapped in the house and killed. Instead of that, here we are. So let's go!'

His renewed enthusiasm was infectious and they were soon on their way once more.

As dawn broke, they were following the course of a river along the bottom of a broad valley. By day, afraid of Zeds, they stayed in what had been fields beside a winding road; by night, when the world was cloaked in silence, they felt safe to use the ruins of the road itself.

They examined the solar panels in every settlement they entered, but none were intact. Nor did they meet with a single person, Constant or Zed, although there were signs that both had been in the district at some time in the past. On the outskirts of a small village whose wooden houses had long ago burned down or rotted to ruin, they found the remains of a Constant settlement.

At its heart lay a Long Dead farmhouse surrounded by a low stone wall. The settlement had clearly fallen to a Zed attack many years previously, for the skeletons of the inhabitants, most of them children, had been picked clean by predators. One little girl had died holding a small china doll. Its smiling painted face was still visible between the clawed bones of the fingers wrapped around it.

Cyrus tried to block the scene from Miouda, but he was too late and she stood staring at it for a long time. When she turned away, Cyrus reached out for her, expecting to see her eyes filled with tears.

'Don't worry,' she said, taking his hand and leading him away, 'I saw enough in Alba. I don't think I've got any tears left. Sights like that make me stronger now, more determined for the Mission to succeed.'

Sammy was right, Cyrus said to himself. She really does resemble Roxanne more with every day that passes. He remembered reading one of the Soterion books that told how some of the Long Dead said women were weaker than men. Strange idea! What sort of culture could have believed that? The more he turned it over in his mind, the more complex the civilization of the Long Dead became.

The valley became narrower as they advanced, until its towering sides pressed in on them like a vice. The only way was forward. But how? A massive rockfall had blocked the tunnel that had taken the highway through the mountains. To the right of the entrance they could make out the old road. In places, the rain had washed it away completely. Where it remained, it was strewn with broken boulders and insolent ash trees that had pushed their way up through the grassy tarmac.

Sammy examined the track zigzagging above them. 'Is that where we go?'

'Unless you want to turn back,' said Cyrus.

There was nothing more to say. Towards evening, they camped under a rock face and lit a fire with the flint and steel Cyrus had brought from the mountain house. Sending a shower of sparks on to dry tinder was one of the skills he had learned as a child in Della Tallis.

How far away that life now seemed! Gazing out over the valley as night closed in, he suddenly saw clearly what he had known for a long time: with most of his life spent, he would never see his home again.

It was very cold during the night, and for warmth the friends huddled close together beneath a covering of dead leaves. They awoke at dawn, shivering and eager to get going. When in the middle of the morning a light rain began to fall, Cyrus wrapped a plastic bag around the laptop to protect it. By noon, the drizzle had increased to an icy downpour, soaking them to the skin and bringing streams of yellow-brown water cascading across their path.

A number of the ancient bridges had been carried away by storms, and crossing the swollen torrents was difficult and dangerous. After a couple of near disasters, they let Cyrus go first with a creeper rope tied around his waist. The others held the free end, ready to pull him to safety if he slipped or was swept off his feet. Once he was over, Miouda followed with two ropes attached to her, Cyrus' and a second held by Sammy. The youngest of the party crossed last, as Cyrus and Miouda held his safety line and Corby splashed over at his side.

The system may have saved their lives, but it was time consuming and tiring, especially in the driving rain. On the third day, the clouds descended to ground level, blotting out the valley and driving the chill deep into their bones. Slipping and sliding on the muddy track, struggling over flooded gorges, sitting in the dark beside miserable fires of damp leaves and brushwood, and sleeping in cold caves, they slowly, painstakingly, made their way up the mountain.

Miouda's pregnancy was now showing clearly and she found the climb tough going. Several times, realising she was no longer at his side, Cyrus looked back to see her sitting on a rock at the roadside, pale and breathing heavily. Although she never complained and said she felt fine, he was increasingly concerned for her welfare and that of their unborn child. He tried not to think what might happen if she fell.

Mercifully, after days of toiling uphill, the track levelled out and they entered upon a broad, green meadow. At noon, the clouds lifted to reveal a small stone hut a hundred or so paces to their right.

Shepherds had built the shelter to withstand the fierce mountain weather and it was in better condition than most lowland dwellings. The front door had fallen from its rusted hinges, but the roof was undamaged and the interior was dry. Better still, in one corner stood an ancient iron stove. By nightfall, Cyrus had lit a fire from scraps of timber and the dried sheep droppings that littered the floor. The smell was a small price to pay for the luxury of warmth.

A Zed tribe on the move was something to behold. Kamal did his best to adhere to the pattern established by Timur. The bulk of the warriors loped along in a column headed by the dog-handlers. Next came the boys, leading donkeys laden with equipment. The heavily guarded infants and flabtoad breeding slaves brought up the rear.

In practice, the column was never as neatly organised as that. The dogs would pick up the scent of a wild animal and bolt off left or right, taking a contingent of handlers with them; or a fistfight would break out in the ranks, leaving its participants rolling in the dirt as their jeering, cheering colleagues passed by. The sick or injured soon fell back, too, and mixed with the boys and females.

Kamal and his Captains rode the only horses, moving up and down the line shouting orders. They used whips with equal harshness on their mounts and their men. Progress was never swift. On a normal day's march – if there was such a thing as a normal day in the life of a Zed – the warriors pulled ahead of the boys and females, then hunted or scavenged for food while the rest of the column caught up.

Kamal had once come close to being murdered by mutinous Grozny and he had learned from the experience. He remained as ruthless and, when necessary, as cruel as he had ever been, but he was less impetuous now and explained his decisions with care.

Before a man was flogged for molesting a pregnant breeding slave, for example, he told the spectators – there was always a good crowd to watch punishments – that the offender had committed three crimes. (Kamal prided himself on his ability to count.) First, the reprobate had reduced the chances of another Grozny being born. Second, he had disobeyed the order of a Malik. Third, and most heinous, he had gone against the express command of the Mighty Timur.

'Man lucky,' Kamal explained, glowering at the crowd. 'Man lucky not die. One, two, three crime and only thirty stickhits? Man much lucky!'

As the onlookers grunted and nodded in agreement, Kamal signalled for the lashing with a spiky thornbush rod to begin. He counted the number of strokes out loud until, unsure what came after twenty, he jumped straight to thirty and ended the ordeal.

The Zeds took a while to locate the abandoned site of the Kogon camp outside Alba. Thereafter, the trail was easy to follow. But the more they advanced, the further away the Kogon appeared to be. When two moons had come and gone, it finally dawned on Kamal that his quarry was moving faster than him.

The realisation led him to make one of his more sensible decisions. Leaving the bulk of his column to follow as quickly as it could, he pressed on with a small contingent of his strongest and fittest warriors. They covered more ground in a day than the full column did in four, and they soon found a deserted Kogon encampment where the ashes of the previous night's fires were still warm.

'Flabtoad Zeds near,' muttered Kamal, using his left hand to climb into the saddle with surprising agility. 'What dogs say?'

'Sniff flabtoad strong!' grinned the leading dog handler, who was struggling to restrain a pair of slavering hounds.

'Near?'

'Near?' the man repeated. He was unsure whether or not he had been asked a question and, if he had, what it meant.

'Are flabtoads near this place, fool?'

'Ah! Understand. Yes, Malik. Flabtoads near.'

'Good. Let hounds go – and follow. Flabtoad hunt start now!'

The hunt was over almost as soon as it had begun. To cover her retreat, Tarangala had set a number of scouts, known as "Eyes", as a screen. They were to report back the moment they noticed any human activity.

One of these watchers had positioned herself in a tree overlooking the stretch of barren scrubland. Although well placed for observation, she had given little thought about how she would report back to the Malika. She began clambering down from the tree as soon as the distant cloud of dust materialised into Kamal and his war band, but she was too slow. The hounds seized her before her feet touched the ground.

Kamal would normally have enjoyed the spectacle of a flabtoad being torn to pieces. But this was not an occasion for frivolous amusement. Lest the Eye's screams alert the rest of her tribe, he jumped down from his horse, kicked aside the dogs, and ended her agony with a thrust of his long-bladed knife. Job done, he wiped the blade on his horse's mane and stood listening.

Apart from the sound of the hounds feeding on the woman's corpse, all was still. Kamal's mean features relaxed into a rare smile. He now had every chance of sneaking up on the rest of the traitorous flabtoads unnoticed.

9
Into the City

The Mission stayed in the mountain hut for three days. A nearby stream provided water for drinking and washing, and they dined off edible plants, pinecones and the meat of a sheep killed by Cyrus. From a box alongside the stove, they drew out a bundle of sheepskins preserved in plastic wrapping. The ancient garments insulated them from the cold by day and made a warm bed at night.

They would have stayed longer, but on the fourth morning they woke to an eerie silence. Rising and looking outside, Cyrus screwed up his eyes against the glare. Snow had fallen during the night, covering the meadow with a blanket of crystal white. None of them had seen snow before and they were stunned by its beauty. But the price was a sharp drop in temperature.

Cyrus leaned on the doorpost while Corby nuzzled his leg, and gazed out over the snowfield. 'Quite a sight, isn't it old thing?' he said quietly, stroking the dog's ears. 'Magical. But we'll freeze to death if we stay up here. I can't see any sheep, either, can you? If they've got any sense, they'll have gone lower down to get something to eat. I think we should do the same.'

They had not gone far over the snowy plateau before they realised they were on a pass between jagged peaks. Where the ground started to slope downwards, they located a continuation of the old road they had used on their way up. The snow soon disappeared, and although the path was rough and broken, their mood lightened with each step they took.

On the second morning, after they had heaved themselves across another torrent and were back on the road, Sammy suddenly said, 'I've got a good feeling!'

Cyrus turned and smiled at him. 'Oh yes?'

'Yeah. It's nicer on this side of the mountains. I can feel it in the air. I know we're going to find a panel somewhere and get our computer working. I know we are!'

'We'd better,' said Miouda, who was at Sammy's side. 'It'd be pretty heartbreaking if we've come all this way for nothing.' And I also need to get to a Constant settlement soon, she thought. I really don't want to give birth out here.

Hearing his friends chatting, Cyrus dropped back to join them. 'It won't be for nothing, Miouda,' he said. 'One day, the child you're carrying – our child – will reap the benefits of this.' He patted the bag containing the laptop. 'He or she—'

'I think it's a she.'

'Really? That'd be lovely – I hope you're right. I was thinking that one day she'll live as the Long Dead used to because someone – maybe even Sammy—'

'What do you mean "even Sammy"?' he said with a laugh.

'Of course it'll be me!'

'You don't know what I was going to say!'

'Go on then. What am I going to do?'

'Sammy, or someone his age, will be able to read the work of the Salvation Project and finish it so that we no longer die at eighteen!'

Sammy punched the air. 'That's me!' He turned to Miouda. 'And then, Miou, we can start being like the Long Dead.'

His words made Cyrus feel strangely uncomfortable. 'Sammy, I wish you wouldn't call her Miou,' he said.

'Why not?'

'It makes her sound like a cat!'

When Miouda confessed that she too preferred her full name, and Sammy agreed with Cyrus that the shortened version did sound a bit feline, he laughed and said he'd drop it.

Cyrus thanked him. However, at the back of his mind he knew it was not really the "Miou" that worried him. It was what Sammy had said immediately afterwards, about being like the Long Dead. Like the people who cured sickness, yes. But not those who said women were weaker than men and shot tigers for sport.

By the time Xsani and her small troop reached the carcass of the tiger, its grandeur had long gone. Lesser creatures had eaten the flesh and the once beautiful hide, torn and riddled with a thousand gnawed holes, was a shabby tent over the clean bones. To the Malika, the wreckage signified only that she was on track and must press ahead as swiftly as possible.

But the jungly forest took its toll on the pursuers as it had on the pursued. When they reached the river, a dog and one of the eunuch bodyguards had died of snakebites. A second guard, whose fever-ridden body was trembling as if in terror, would shortly join them. Giv was as lean as the creepers hanging like gallows' ropes from the giant trees. Pram and Jinsha, drained by the unrelieved heat and humidity, hardly spoke. At times, even Xsani's head drooped.

Giv stuck his totem pole in the mud and stood surveying the dirty brown stream. 'No-Man,' he said enigmatically.

Xsani asked what he meant.

'Giv see this river in time of Mighty Timur,' he replied, eyeing the shrivelled skull beside him. 'No man cross. Impossible. Crockendiles eat them.'

How did he know this? questioned Xsani. Giv told how, in the time of Timur, the Grozny had chased the original Mission as far as the river No-Man before losing them as they escaped over a collapsing bridge.

'Tho they crothed thith river by a bridge?' suggested the Malika.

Giv twitched nervously and a glazed, far-off expression came into his bloodshot eyes. 'Ti-mur see,' he chanted, swaying slightly on the balls of his feet. 'Batpiss flee, flee, flee—'

'Shut up!' snapped Xsani. Giv stared at her in bewilderment. 'If Thyruth crothed a bridge,' she went on, looking at Jinsha, 'then tho shall we.'

She was right. A day's march beyond the boathouse used by the Constants, they found a concrete road bridge whose cracked and crumbling spans were still passable. Once safely over, Xsani had another difficult decision to make.

The Long Dead highway led directly from the bridge into the jungle. It would be much easier to follow it than go back up the riverbank in search of the Constants' trail, Xsani thought. But was there a trail? She could only assume Cyrus had crossed the river; she had no evidence that he had.

She glanced at her dwindling band. The fevered bodyguard had died before he reached the bridge. Two of his colleagues were showing similar symptoms and were unlikely to last long. One of the dogs was clearly sick, too. Pram was flagging, his energy sapped by continual diarrhoea. Her beloved Jinsha was tired and wan.

But if the jungle trek had taken its toll on her party, Xsani realised, then surely it had done the same on the Constants? If she were Cyrus at this point, she asked herself, what would she do? Obviously, try to locate the shortest route out of this foul swamp before it killed them all. And the shortest route? Xsani gazed up at the treetops high overhead...

Not for the first time, the former Malika of the Kogon Zeds read the mind of the man she was pursuing. Clinging to the uppermost branch of a tree, the fittest of her bodyguards saw what Sammy had seen, and it was towards the same distant mountains that his mistress led the way.

Through the strangling heat and humidity they pressed on, day after day, along the course of the overrun highway. The two fevered bodyguards died on the same night and their bodies were left to rot. The following day, the sick dog slipped and fell into a miry pool. It swam a few hopeless strokes then disappeared noiselessly beneath the green slime.

Undaunted, Xsani drove her team on until the road rose, the

undergrowth thinned, and they found themselves breathing the clear air of the grassy foothills. They were alive, yes, but where was the trail? Where had the Man in the Yellow Hat gone?

They rested for two days. On the third, Xsani told Pram to comb the hillside with the one remaining hound. Standing with an arm around Jinsha, she watched as the dog, nose in the grass, scampered across the slopes above them. Every now and again it stopped and set off in a new direction. The result was always the same – sheep and goats aplenty, but no sign of any human, Constant or Zed.

The relationship between Xsani and Jinsha had changed over the course of their journey. Daily discomforts and little humiliations had stripped away much of the former Malika's mystique. The younger woman was no longer her kumfort; she was more of an equal, a friend.

Jinsha stroked the back of Xsani's head. 'Dog will find them, I know it will,' she said. 'We have come so far—'

Her sentence went unfinished. The dog had stopped running about and stood stock still, ears pricked. It had heard something.

Moments later, with the hound dragging behind him, Pram bounded down the slope. 'Dog hear!' he panted. 'Dog hear voice. Pram hear – people come, Malika! People come!'

On reaching the bottom of the mountain, the Mission abandoned the road and skirted through the wooded countryside on either side of it. In farms and villages the story was always the same: plenty of panels, but all overgrown or broken when the roofs beneath them collapsed. Once, they ran into what had been a whole farm of panels, lined up in ranks like soldiers smiling at the sun. But they had been neglected for over a century. Trees had sprouted up in the fields, and the equipment was useless.

Even Cyrus' optimism was bruised by these disappointments and he was forced to consider a change of plan. Until now, as on the original Mission from Della Tallis to Alba, they had deliberately steered clear of Long Dead conurbations. It was one of a Constant's earliest lessons: cities were dangerous places.

Zeds and wild beasts dwelt among the ruins, and although the crumbling buildings offered hiding places, they were also traps. The Tallins, among whom Cyrus had grown up, had frequently visited the town near their settlement to salvage tools and other useful bits and pieces. But no Constant ever stayed overnight. The only patrol that said they were going to try never returned.

Cyrus mentioned this as they were standing on top of a wooded hill overlooking the sprawling ruins of a huge city. The panorama of tumbled concrete and brick, interspersed with swathes of greenery, stretched into the distance like a gigantic rockery, a spiteful distortion of what the Long Dead had called a "garden city".

'Well,' said Cyrus, 'what do we do? It'd be quite a risk going down there.'

'Yes, but all those buildings…' said Miouda. 'There's got to be a panel on one of them. If we're really careful—'

'What if I go in on my own to look about?' interrupted Sammy. 'And when I find—'

Cyrus cut him short. 'No! Absolutely not, Sammy. Sorry, but it's everyone or no one. That's how it's always been and that's how it'll stay.'

Miouda agreed, and they decided to remain where they were for the night and venture into the city at dawn. Zeds rarely stirred at that time of the morning, Cyrus assured them.

A warm rain was falling when they entered the suburbs. Sammy led the way, with Corby trotting at his side. The dog's acute hearing and sense of smell would detect danger long before any human. To keep his hands free, Cyrus now carried the laptop in a rucksack Miouda had made from leather and plastic sheeting. The couple walked side by side behind Sammy, staring about them in fear and wonder that so much endeavour could have come to such a tragic end.

They kept out of the middle of the roads, advancing quickly from shelter to shelter along the sidewalks like street fighters. Except there was no enemy. Not yet, anyway.

The city's outskirts were similar to the several towns they had already passed. The streets, dotted with rusted hulks of vehicles and strewn with fallen cables, were overgrown with vegetation. Most of the wooden single- or two-storey houses had either collapsed or burned down. The clusters of brick and concrete that had formerly been shops and businesses were now no more than drab, roofless husks. The only sounds were the occasional cry of a bird and the patter of rain dripping from the ruins.

Block by block, they advanced steadily nearer the city centre without finding a single undamaged panel. By late afternoon, it had stopped raining and they slipped into a shop front to

106

take stock of their position.

It was not too late to go back, Cyrus said. Miouda shook her head. As soon as they discovered a building with a working power supply, she pointed out, they would have to stay there for some time. So they might as well get used to the idea now.

Cyrus and Sammy agreed. There could be no retreat.

In the early evening, they reached a precinct where the buildings were taller, some rising to twenty or thirty storeys. If they had solar panels, they would be on the roofs. Cyrus singled out an office block on the opposite side of the street that looked less dilapidated than most. The glass in a number of windows was unbroken. Whether or not it had panels, it would be a safe place to spend the night.

Weaving between wrecked vehicles and bushes that had forced their way through the cracked tarmac, they crossed the darkening street. A rusted iron grill closed the entrance to the building. Cyrus tugged at it with little effect.

'Here, Sammy, give us a hand,' he called.

As Sammy stepped forward, he noticed that Corby was standing stock-still, ears pricked.

'What is it, old thing?'

'Shh!' said Miouda, lifting her hand. Cyrus stopped tugging at the grill. 'Corby can hear something.'

They stood and listened. At first, there was nothing. Then, echoing through the deserted streets, came the unmistakeable howl of wolves.

10
The Scattering of the Kogon

The Kogon tribe of female Zeds had learned to survive by stealth in a cruel and violent world. As movement attracted attention, they chose to dwell in forests or on remote hillsides. In this, their quest for security made them more like Constants than the nomadic male Zeds.

Their attitude to fighting was also more Constant than Zed. Whenever possible, they avoided conflict. If danger threatened, the reaction of a Kogon was to slip quietly away unseen. Battle was anathema to them. Indeed, they regarded it as a failure just to be seen by a male, Constant or Zed.

They could fight, of course; in some situations, they had to in order to stay alive. Discipline, speed and surprise were their strengths. Wielding their long spears with extreme dexterity, their chosen tactic was what they called a "hojoom" – hissing like geese, they left their cover and darted swiftly forward, inflicting as much damage as possible before disappearing whence they had come.

Xsani's decision to join with the Grozny and Gurkov in an open attack on Alba had broken with all these traditions, and its repercussions for the Kogon were disastrous. At first, all had gone well after Xsani's sudden and secret disappearance. Tarangala, aided by the Zektivs, Zilna and Yalisha, had taken on the mantle of Malika and led her tribe out of Alba unnoticed. She easily found the hidden camp where the youngsters, the infirm and the male breeding slaves had been left, and she got the whole tribe on the march well before midday.

It was then that her difficulties began.

When told they were being moved on, the half-dozen male captives started causing trouble: swearing, making obscene gestures, and deliberately tripping over their chains. Tarangala had to resort to the public castration of their ringleader to restore order. It was not a punishment she wished to use too often: male breeding slaves were hard to capture and useless if incapable of fulfilling their purpose.

Once under control, the men walked quite quickly. But the sick, the very young, the heavily pregnant, and those in their Death Month, could not be hurried. Nor could they be sacrificed for the sake of speed; abandoning the children and the pregnant jeopardised the future of the entire tribe.

The Kogon moved through the wooded terrain at the pace of the slowest, and were safe as long as the gap between themselves and their pursuers didn't narrow. But now Kamal had divided his forces and ridden ahead with his war band, the women were hideously exposed.

'Zed blood! Zed blood! Kill! Kill! Kill!'

Tarangala heard the chant long before she saw who was

making it. Once the dogs had picked up the scent of the Kogon column, the Malik ordered his Zeds to charge. Through the trees they ran, brandishing rusty gut-rippers, swords and spears.

'Zed blood! Zed blood! Kill! Kill! Kill!'

The steel hand of panic seized Tarangala and crushed the breath from her lungs. Her throat went dry. The Kogon never fought battles in the open. They had no experience, no tactics. They would be massacred – and it would be her fault. Oh Xsani! Why did you leave us? What will—?

'Malika! Malika! Can you hear? What we do?' Zilna's urgent pleas brought Tarangala back to the present. It was going to be terrible, yes, but she had to save as many as possible.

'Zed blood! Zed blood! Kill! Kill! Kill!'

The chant was louder now, accompanied by the ominous thunder of hooves.

'Scatter! We must scatter!' Tarangala shouted, gazing wildly about her. 'Zilna, take ten children! Go there!' She pointed to the thicket to her left. 'Run! Fast!'

She turned to the younger Zektiv. 'You take more children, Yalisha. Carry them. Go to the hill!' she yelled, indicating the rising ground beyond the trees.

There was no hope for the infirm, but the children were her people's future. She had to save as many as she could. Shaking with fear, she ran to the rear of the column. Zilna and Yalisha, each leading some twenty warriors, were already grabbing children and carrying them off.

'Kogon warriors come to me!' the Malika cried at the confused mêlée of women who were left. As a band of about fifteen warriors gathered around their commander, Kamal came thundering into view.

'Zed blood! Zed blood! Kill! Kill! Kill!' The ghastly chant mingled with the baying of hounds and the screaming of children.

Tarangala checked over her shoulder to see Zilna and Yalisha disappearing into the trees. To buy them more time, she had to do something to draw the attackers' attention. The male breeding slaves… Despite being shackled hand and foot, they were keeping their guards fully occupied by throwing themselves about and shouting to the Grozny tribesmen emerging from the trees.

Tarangala needed every available able-bodied fighter. 'Guards, kill slaves!' she yelled. 'Kill slaves and come to me!'

The execution was quickly done and the guards ran to join the circle of fighters gathered about the remaining children. Seeing what was happening, the ill, dying, and pregnant took up weapons and hobbled to their leader's side. It was a brave but futile gesture.

The killing of the male breeding slaves had its intended effect. Kamal slowed his horse to a walk and shouted furiously at his men not to pursue the 'running flabtoads'. He then rode slowly round what was left of the Kogon column. A puzzled look came over his face. There was the Malika in the blue robe, but she was not the Malika he knew.

On completing the circuit, Kamal brought his horse to a standstill and gave a loud, shrill laugh.

'Flabtoads run away!' he cackled. 'But Grozny faster!' His eyes narrowed. 'Flabtoads kill prisoner Zed men – now Zed men kill flabtoads! Ha! Ha!'

His men, some fifty in number, had spread out to encircle their enemy. An eerie quietness fell on the scene, broken only by the whimpering of children. Then, slowly and quietly, the Grozny chant began once more.

'Zed blood! Zed blood! Kill! Kill! Kill!'

'No!' yelled Kamal suddenly. 'Listen to Malik! Not kill all flabtoads.' His thin lips parted in a hideous grin. 'Grozny need breeding slaves, yes?'

The Zeds, some nodding furiously, others leaping up and down in excitement, uttered a sound that was part howl, part lascivious cheer. Tarangala eyed the surrounding trees, wondering whether Zilna or Yalisha might come to her rescue. There was no sign of them. No, they wouldn't disobey orders and risk extinction. She was on her own.

Kamal was speaking again. 'Kogon flabtoads, Malik Kamal kind man.'

At this, his men burst into a chorus of crude laughter. 'Silence!' he roared. 'Kamal have power kill all Kogon. Kamal have power make all Kogon breeding slaves. But no! Kamal kind man.'

More howls of coarse laughter.

The Malik's face darkened. 'Flabtoads steal Over-Malik Timur,' he said with deliberate menace. 'Where Head? Where Malika Xsani? Where Giv?'

Tarangala stared back at him but said nothing.

Undaunted, Kamal continued, 'Flabtoads give Kamal Head of Timur, Kamal let flabtoads go free as dancing birds!'

Tarangala gave a scornful snort. She couldn't hope to defeat the stronger, more numerous force, but at least she and her women could die bravely and take a few despised dumbmans with them.

She took a deep breath. 'Kamal lie!' she cried. 'All dumbmans lie! Giv gone! Malika Xsani gone! Dead head of dead dumbman Timur gone! Gone! You hear me, mudbrain dumbman? Gone! And you too stupid to find them!'

Kamal stared as if struck by a physical blow. Only Timur had ever addressed him like that. And now this flabtoad had dared insult him! In front of his men, too! It was… It was… He had no thoughts, let alone words, to describe his fury.

'Flabtoad bitch!' he screamed. 'I get you now! You not long live – but before die, you tell me WHERE IS OVER-MALIK TIMUR?'

Although neither Tarangala nor Kamal could possibly have known it, Over-Malik Timur was at that moment lying face down in a pile of sheep droppings.

When Pram said he heard voices coming along the hillside, Xsani had ordered him to bring his dog and hide behind a rocky outcrop alongside Jinsha, Giv, the two eunuchs, and herself. There was no point in giving away their presence until they knew who was out there.

It was only after he had dived to the ground and placed the smoked and blackened Head of Timur beside him that Giv realised what he had done. The proximity of animal excrement to the adored relic was sacrilege. But he still revered Xsani almost as much as his totem, and he opted not to offend her by moving. Instead, he watched in silent anguish as inquisitive

114

flies buzzed between the droppings and the empty eye sockets of his dead hero.

Two voices became audible – one squeaky and authoritative, one whining.

'Lopz say never find,' said the whinger.

'Huh!' retorted the squeaky one. 'Captain Kemran of Murax more brain than Lopz. He know where Constants go.'

Xsani tensed and glanced towards Jinsha. Constants? Surely these people, whoever they were, were not looking for Cyrus too? She didn't have long to wait for the answer.

'So where Constants go?'

'How many times Kemran tell you? Kemran see man Constant, man Constant, woman Constant in house' – the Captain had never mastered the art of counting – 'then window open, Constants gone.'

After a long pause, Lopz asked, 'So where Constants?'

'Dumbhead! Out of window into mountains!'

At the end of another long silence, Lopz said, 'We not in mountains, Captain.'

The remark prompted what sounded like a slap and a squeal. As the pantomime was getting interesting, it was interrupted by an extraordinary spectacle. A blackened head gradually emerged above the rock beside the astonished Murax patrol. As it did so, a disembodied voice began to screech.

'Vermin! Volepizzle scum! Bow before the Head of the Over-Malik of all Zeds, the Mighty Timur! Fail, and you will be pounded to dust and your blood fed to flabtoad breeding slaves!'

It was Giv. Driven to distraction by the antics of the flies and the stench of the sheep droppings, he had decided it was time for the strange Zeds – it was clear from their conversation that they were indeed Zeds – to be brought under the command of his master.

Kemran, who had never heard of Timur, stared in disbelief for a few seconds before raising his gut-ripper and rushing round the rock to see what was going on. Lopz, armed with a spike tied to the end of a pole, followed a safe distance behind.

Pram's hound sprang at Kemran the moment he appeared. The giant swatted it aside, and with a single blow sliced the head off one of Xsani's two bodyguards. The other lunged forward with his spear, piercing Kemran in the side.

Lopz decided it was about time he joined in. He finished off the hound with a neat spike thrust and turned the bloody weapon on the man who had stabbed Kemran. The eunuch didn't stand a chance. As the Captain grasped his spear and broke it in half, Lopz dispatched him off with a shrewd stab in the throat.

By this time, Giv, Xsani, Jinsha, and Pram were all on their feet. Dribble ran down Giv's bony chest as he stood, totem in hand, staring in bewilderment. Jinsha had snatched up her spear and slipped left to outflank the attackers. As Pram lurched at the assailants with a primitive roar, Xsani drew a gleaming knife and waited.

Lopz fell first. Distracted by Pram, for a fatal instant he took his attention off Jinsha. The tip of her spear impaled his heart. To her left, Pram and Kemran met head-on in a mighty collision that sent them both reeling to the ground, bleeding heavily.

Kemran had just enough strength to hurl his gut-ripper at

his dying foe, embedding it in his skull, before Jinsha's spear claimed its second victim.

Xsani turned to face Giv. 'You are the motht thtupid dumbman I have ever theen,' she lisped. 'Why did you do that?'

Giv quivered in terror. His totem fell from his hand and landed with a thud on the grass. Tears streamed from his sunken eyes. 'O Malika!' he whispered. 'Giv wor-ship you.'

The blade of Xsani's knife gleamed in the sunlight. 'Wor-thip?' The word was new to her.

'Giv go anywhere, do anything for Xsani, beautiful Xsani!'

Jinsha came up and stood by her kumfort's side. 'What do we do with him?'

Giv looked desperately from one to the other. 'Giv help find Man in Yellow Hat. Three better than two. Please! Please!'

Xsani sighed and put away her knife. There had been a time when she would have killed Giv without a qualm. She might even have enjoyed it. But now…

'Yeth,' she said, smiling at Jinsha, 'three ith better than two. And now we know where to go, don't we?'

'To the mountains?'

'Yeth, Jintha. We three shall go to the mountainth.'

11
Metro

All day, Cyrus had wondered vaguely why the abandoned city they had been exploring showed no sign of human habitation. Apart from the occasional bird and scuttling rat, they had seen no animal life, either. The place was more than deserted – over the bleak ruins a deathly stillness hung like a pall.

They knew why. The city was overrun by huge wolves. Wild creatures, released from captivity at the time of the Great Death, had mated with Long Dead guard dogs to produce an urban animal the size of a wild boar and equally ferocious. They were creatures of darkness, lying low during the day as unsuspecting prey wandered into the empty streets.

At night, when it was too dark for their prey to find a way out, the beasts emerged. They hunted in packs. Deer, wild horses and other animals were chased down mercilessly. So were humans. If they managed to barricade themselves in a building, the wolves waited patiently until hunger and thirst forced their victims to make a run for it. They never got away.

Legend said the larger female wolves, eager to take home food for their cubs, chewed through wooden doors to get at the flesh inside.

Alerted by Corby, Cyrus and Sammy had stopped pulling at the rusty grill blocking the entrance to the office block.

'Is that what I think it is?' asked Miouda.

'Yes,' said Cyrus. 'Wolves.' He was staring anxiously up and down the street, searching for something.

Corby, hairs bristling, whined pitifully. Miouda reached down and patted him reassuringly. 'It's alright, old boy. It's our turn to save you, remember?'

'Easier said than done,' muttered Sammy. 'Don't fancy taking on a whole pack.'

The howling was much louder now and mingled with savage barking. The wolves could be no more than a couple of blocks away, thought Miouda. She shivered and turned to see what Cyrus was doing. He had gone to the porch of the shop next door and, kneeling amid a pile of leaves and rubbish in the doorway, was furiously striking steel against flint.

'Here!' he said urgently. 'Quick! Come and lend a hand!'

Miouda and Sammy exchanged a puzzled glance as they hurried to his side.

'Fire,' he muttered. 'I'm sure it's the only thing they'll be afraid of. Get hold of some wood – a stake, a plank, anything!'

As he was speaking, a shower of sparks fell on to the dry leaves in front of him and they started to smoulder.

'Come on!' he urged, blowing gently until small flames appeared. 'Right. Now the wood.'

He looked up to see a shadow gliding across the end of the

street. The wolves had arrived. Seeing the blaze in the shop front, the leader of the pack hesitated before slinking forward, its belly close to the ground. Another wolf emerged, then another and another until the entire road was blocked by a grim barricade of malevolence.

The length of rotten doorpost that Sammy pushed into the flames had immediately caught fire and was burning brightly.

'Great,' said Cyrus. 'Shove a bit of wood in for me, too. How about you, Miouda? What've – Miouda? Miouda!'

Spotting a length of wood beside the doorway of a former bar, Miouda had crossed the street to get it as the wolves came into view. The pack instinctively recognised an easy prey.

Those in front advanced in stages, making short, loping runs before crouching down with their eyes fixed on their target. With shaking hands, Miouda raised the pole she had collected and prepared to defend herself. She didn't stand a chance.

Cyrus swore under his breath. Snatching Sammy's post from the fire, he sprinted across the road. He reached Miouda as the first wolf was preparing to pounce. Holding the flaming brand with one hand, he jabbed at the beast's face. It fell back with a snarl.

He put his spare arm around Miouda's waist and, fending off the wolves with the fire, guided her to the other side of the street.

'Thanks Cy!' she gasped, plunging the pole she had brought with her into the fire. 'I'm sorry—'

'You're sorry?' muttered Cyrus as he and Sammy stabbed and waved to keep the wolves at bay. 'I brought you here.'

Without taking her eyes from the fire, she said firmly, 'Uh-huh, Cyrus. It was my choice.'

He flashed her a grin and, when her brand was well alight, cried, 'Right, Mission! Let's get out of here.'

About twenty paces away, he had noticed the dark outline of a stairway leading into some sort of tunnel. The entrance was festooned with rusted ironwork. Whatever it was, it'd be easier to defend themselves there than in the open street.

'Wave the flames in their faces,' he commanded. 'They hate it, and the movement keeps the wood alight. Whatever you do, stay in line.'

Brandishing their fiery torches, the Mission backed slowly down the street towards the tunnel. Corby chose discretion over valour and led the way. The wolves followed patiently. They were in no hurry.

When they were a short distance from the steps, one of the wolves made a dash to get behind them. Corby bared his teeth and growled. Unsure what to make of this, the beast lowered itself to the ground and eyed the dog suspiciously. By the time it decided Corby was no serious threat, the Mission had reached its destination.

'Give me your torch, Sammy,' said Cyrus. 'I'll stay here and hold them off while you two take Corby and see what's down there.'

Cyrus stood astride the top of the stairway, a flaming brand in either hand. Before him, the wolves circled and snarled. Above him, entangled by creepers and lit by the orange glow of the flames, the wrought iron letters TRO hinted at the entrance's former purpose.

Checking that Cyrus was alright, Miouda and Sammy followed Corby down the steps. It was almost dark, and the flickering shadows thrown up by Miouda's torch danced on the concrete walls on either side. Although the descent was overgrown with bushes and briars, a well-worn path zigzagged between them. Corby sniffed at it suspiciously.

The two friends looked at each other and nodded. Humans. Take care!

At the bottom, the tunnel swung to the left and shiny tiles replaced the bare concrete of the walls. A few steps further on they found their way blocked by a metal lattice.

Sammy groaned. 'Now what? Trapped in a dark hole with a load of howling wolves waiting to rip our guts out!' Corby let out a long, dismal whine. 'I agree, old thing. We're really in it this time, aren't we?'

Miouda shook her head. 'Hang on. Hold my torch a second.'

Handing him her brand, she approached the frame of steel and tarnished brass. 'You saw the path. Someone comes down here quite regularly.' She examined the lattice. Grasping it firmly with both hands, she tried to slide it to one side. It wouldn't budge.

'Can you shine the light a bit more over here?' she asked, peering at the place where the end of the grill slotted into the wall. 'That's better. Thanks.'

She put a hand through one of the lattice triangles and raised a metal catch. 'I think that's done it. Let me try…'

She grabbed the handle on the end of the grill and, leaning back to give herself leverage, heaved to the right. The barrier opened enough for her to squeeze through.

'Wow!' cried Sammy. 'No wolf's going to break that thing,' He looked down at Corby. 'Cheer up! We're going to be safe after all, old boy!'

Miouda rejoined Sammy. 'I'll go and get Cy. You and Corby wait here. Get ready to shut it as soon as we're in, ok?'

'Will do.'

Miouda hurried up the steps to Cyrus, patting him affectionately on the backside as she arrived. 'We're in luck,' she said. 'Give me one of the brands and I'll explain.'

She took the torch and thrust it towards the nearest wolf. The beast snarled and withdrew into the darkness.

'There's a sort of sliding metal door down there,' she said. 'It's pretty worn but it still works. We've got it open, and Sammy will shut it as soon as we're safe inside.'

'Safe?'

'Well, safer than out here.'

'Not difficult. You lead. Take my hand and guide me. I need to keep an eye on this lot.'

The retreat into the metro station was easier than they had anticipated. It was as if the wolves had seen humans escape this way before. As Cyrus and Miouda backed down the steps, only two of the pack came after them. Cyrus held them off, and when he reached the foot of the stairs, they turned and slunk back up to the street.

'Phew!' he exclaimed as Sammy closed the lattice and dropped the catch. 'Wouldn't want to do that again!'

'Me neither,' echoed Sammy. 'Nor Corby!'

Miouda laughed. 'Sure, but what is this place? We've not much chance of finding a solar panel underground, have we?'

Cyrus took her hand. 'No. But at least it's safe. We can carry on exploring the city in the morning. We'll find a panel, don't worry.'

'There you go, Cy! Mister Optimist! Well, you've been right so far…' Her voice trailed off. Now the immediate danger had passed and they had time to reflect, it was dawning on all three of them just how desperate their situation was.

Sammy spoke first. 'Course it's tough,' he said, putting into words what they were all thinking. 'But we knew it would be, didn't we? We're pioneers – one day they'll sing songs about us!'

'Or even write books,' added Miouda wryly.

'Hang on! Let's not get ahead of ourselves,' said Cyrus. 'Don't forget the path leading down here – we're obviously not the only ones using this place.'

Sammy exhaled loudly. 'Zeds?'

'Doubt it,' said Miouda. 'They don't like being penned in.'

'Not the men, anyway,' said Cyrus. 'Look, I don't know about you, but I'm starving and tired out. Let's find a safe corner, have something to eat, and get some sleep. We can plan what to do next in the morning, ok?'

No one objected.

When Miouda awoke, it took her a few moments to work out where she was. It was dark, so dark she could barely make out her own hand before her eyes. The air was damp and musty, and the floor as hard as concrete…

It was concrete.

Then she remembered… The decision to go into the city, the

fruitless trudge through the rain in search of a working panel, the wolves, Cyrus saving her life...

Cyrus. She could feel his warmth beside her. He was still asleep, breathing peacefully and evenly. She admired him so much – his strength, his determination, the way he cared for her. Never before had she met anyone with these qualities in such abundance. And yet it was also frightening.

He hadn't hesitated to rush to her rescue in the street. But what if he ever needed to decide between her and the success of the Mission? If she had fallen on the mountainside and been unable to go on, what would he have done?

She was fairly sure his priority would be saving her and their child. But could she blame him if he chose otherwise? Like all Constants, he had been raised to prize the community over the individual. It had to be, they were told. If people thought only of themselves, society would collapse and everyone's life – if they still had one – would be nasty and brutish.

Sometimes she longed for Cyrus to take her in his arms and tell her that he had seen through the frailty of this argument; that without individuals there could be no society, so we protect everyone by caring for each person separately. Yes, she wanted to hear him say, you and our child are more important to me than anything in the world; more important even than the Salvation Project.

But she knew Cyrus was not one for grand pronouncements, and her thoughts moved on to what would happen when they got the laptop working and discovered its secrets. How the world would change! The division between Constants and Zeds would disappear; with the effects of the Mini-Flu cured, everyone would live as long as they had in the time of the Long Dead.

When people stopped dying after eighteen winters, death would no longer hang over their relationships like a sword on a thread. They would make families and care for their children over many years as they guided them into adulthood.

She rested a hand on her swollen stomach. 'Yes, little baby,' she whispered to herself in the dark, 'we are doing this for you. I will not live to see you grow up into a woman; but if we succeed – when we succeed – you will see your children develop into adult men and women. You will live in a brave and lovely new world—'

'Miouda?'

'Oh, Cy! You're awake?'

'Yes. Who were you talking to?'

'Our baby. Telling her how happy her life will be because of us, because of you.'

He paused. 'Aren't you happy now, Miouda?'

'Yes, of course I am. But…'

'But what?'

She leaned over and, feeling for his face in the dark, kissed him with a sudden intensity. 'Oh Cyrus,' she said, trying not to cry, 'do you love me?'

'Love? It's a Long Dead word, isn't it? But yes, I love you.'

She kissed him again, more tenderly. 'And do you love me more than anything else in the world? More than the Mission? More than the Salvation Project?'

Before he could reply, they were interrupted by the sound of voices far below. They instinctively reached for their weapons.

Cyrus woke Sammy and told him to keep Corby quiet. If they stayed where they were – in some sort of kiosk at the top of a long flight of unusual-looking stairs – they should be safe.

The voices drew nearer, and beyond the blackness of their hiding place a yellow light threw strange shadows on the tunnel wall. Footsteps echoed towards them up the stairway. If whoever this was suspected intruders, Cyrus reasoned, they wouldn't be making all that noise. It was now daylight up in the city and they must be heading for the streets.

Individual voices became recognisable.

'Sure it's daylight?' The tone was that of a young woman. At least they're not Zeds, said Cyrus to himself.

'Don't be silly, Olo! Are you really thinkin' we'd take you out there in the night?' That was a man's voice.

'I was only checkin',' said the young woman. 'I don't fancy gettin' eat up.'

She was answered by an older woman. 'Us neither, Olo. Our job's feedin' the Safids, right, not the wolves.'

'Sure thing,' said the man.

The group said nothing more as they passed in front of the kiosk and disappeared along the passage. Shortly afterwards, Cyrus heard the grill creak open and clang shut. Then silence.

The Mission were wary of a trick and waited a while before moving. To be on the safe side, Sammy went to examine the sliding lattice. 'All clear,' he called. 'They've gone. We going to follow them, Cyrus? I don't want to live like a mole.'

Cyrus agreed. He wanted to return to street level straight away. They needed food and he was keen to resume their search.

Miouda had other ideas. 'Listen,' she said. 'Those people who came by just now, men and women chatting together, were obviously Constants. The chances are they're going to be friendly, even helpful. They obviously know this place and maybe they can help us find a panel.'

'Makes sense,' said Cyrus. 'What do you propose?'

'Before we go back up, let's take a look at where they came from.'

After talking it over, they accepted Miouda's suggestion to go deeper underground and make contact with those Safids, or whoever lived down there.

They re-lit their brands from a fire of dry leaves and set off down the long staircase. It was the weirdest place they had ever seen. On the arched walls, faded images of the Long Dead and their lost world stared out from beneath a century of mould and fungus. At the foot of the steps, their torches shone upon meaningless maps and diagrams, all distorted by rust and decay.

'Spooky, eh?' said Sammy. 'Think it was a kind of prison?'

'Unlikely,' said Miouda. 'With all these pictures and things, maybe it was some sort of home.'

While they were talking, Cyrus had gone ahead. He took a tunnel to the right, went down some more steps and…

'Hey! Miouda! Sammy! Come here! Quick!'

'What is it, Cy?'

'Am I going crazy, or can you see what I see?'

His friends lowered their torches.

'Oh wow!' gasped Miouda. 'Yes, it's incredible, Cy! They're lights – a whole row of bright, burning, electric lights!'

12
Living in Darkness

The Kogon were not wiped out. The groups led by Zilna and Yalisha escaped into the woods, wading through streams to throw Kamal's dogs off the scent. United under Zilna, their new Malika, they settled in a hilly region where they were comparatively safe from further harassment.

For Tarangala and the rest of the tribe, there was no such happy ending.

Kamal was infuriated by her insolent rejection of his offer of a free pass in exchange for information about the Head of Timur, and came close to launching an immediate and total massacre. Just in time, as his men were starting their battle cry, he realised that if all the Kogon died, he would have no way of finding what he was after.

'Stop!' he yelled. 'You move, you die!' He rode scowling among his men to make sure they obeyed. 'Here is command of Malik Kamal: kill old flabtoads!'

To make sure his audience understood him, he insisted they

repeat his order. 'Kill old flabtoads!' they roared, waving their weapons in the air.

'Kill child flabtoads!' bellowed Kamal.

'Kill child flabtoads!' echoed the Zeds.

Kamal paused and glared about him. 'NOT kill big flabtoads!' he screamed.

After a slight hesitation, the order was repeated, but with rather less enthusiasm.

Kamal explained. 'Big flabtoads wanted for breeding slaves! Fun breeding slaves!'

The tribe pointed at the Kogon, made obscene gestures and squealed like pigs. 'Bree-ding!' they chanted. 'Bree-ding! Bree-ding!'

Tarangala looked at the grim faces of her women and wondered whether the kindest order would be for mass suicide. Horrific, yes, but capture… Before she could make up her mind, however, a more deadly chant arose.

'Zed blood! Zed blood! Kill! Kill! Kill!'

With each repetition, the stamping, screaming mob took a step closer to the ring of doomed women. Finally, when they were no more than five paces away, they howled one last 'Kill!' – and charged.

The outcome was never in doubt. Kogon spears accounted for a number of attackers before the defensive circle gave way and the slaughter began. Not one got away. As Kamal had directed, the children, the infirm, and those in their Death Month were hacked to pieces. Several able-bodied fighters died, too, either mortally wounded or killed by men who, carried away by the sights and sounds of carnage, forgot

Kamal's orders. The remaining women were pinned to the ground, violated and chained.

Kamal made straight for Tarangala. Tall and conspicuous in the blue gown of the Malika, she stood at the very centre of her tribe, commanding and encouraging to the last. From time to time, tears streaming down her handsome brown face, she used her spear to dispatch one of her own fighters in order to prevent their being dragged away to cruel captivity. She might have turned the weapon on herself had not Kamal, his horse slipping and sliding on the blood of massacre, ridden through the mêlée and knocked her down.

Leaping from the saddle, he was on her before she could recover. 'Flabtoad bitch!' he screamed over the noise of the carnage. 'Where Over-Malik Timur? Tell Kamal!'

Tarangala said not a word. When the fighting was over and the other captured women had been led away, she was stripped and paraded before his laughing, leering warriors. Torture and unspeakable indignities followed, but still she did not tell him what he wanted to know. To his increasing fury, she said only, 'I do not know. Malika Xsani is gone. Gone. Gone.'

She spoke the truth, and it was all Kamal ever learned. That night, though chained and closely guarded, she used a fragment of flint to open a vein in her wrist. When morning came, her captors found just one more lifeless body on the rough and bloody floor of the forest.

The Mission stared in amazement. They had emerged from a smaller tunnel into an enormous underground hall, rounded and as tall as a tree. Black mould disfigured the roof and dripping walls, and a gap like an empty canal divided the platforms. Enamelled signs, corroded into illegibility long ago, lay flat on the walls or hung lifeless from rusty gantries. The pale yellow light of twelve electric lamps, suspended from the roof on a wire, filled the cavern.

'Lamps!' gasped Miouda. 'Electric lamps!'

'It's impossible,' said Cyrus. 'There's no panel, no sunlight… Who could've set them up? When?'

'Excuse uss,' hissed a strange voice from the void between the platforms. 'We might answer all your questionss. But first, extinguissh your torchess. They are sso bright!'

Cyrus peered in the direction of the sound. Nothing. Then something moved, something black and white. He raised his torch to get a better look.

'Sso bright!' begged the voice. 'Don't do that! It'ss sso hot!'

Cyrus lowered his burning brand. 'The torches? Alright, we'll put out two of them. But we'll keep one alight till we know who you are.'

There was a scuffling and a whispering. 'That animal – iss it a wolf?' asked the voice.

Cyrus laughed. 'You mean Corby? No! He's just a dog, as friendly as the man who owns him.'

There was more whispering. 'It lookss like a wolf. The Meshkiss have described them to uss. You must tie it before we come out.'

As Miouda and Sammy placed their torches on the ground and stamped out the flames, Sammy got Corby to lie down, took off his belt and passed it through the dog's collar. 'Ok now?'

'Yess. We will greet you.'

The Mission grasped their weapons and watched as half-a-dozen of the strangest-looking people they had ever seen climbed with a slug-like slowness out of the void and on to the platform. When they were all safely up, they stood in a row and bowed.

'Welcome sstrangerss,' hissed the woman in the centre, who was clearly some sort of commander. 'Our pleasure iss your good fortune.'

The Mission could hardly believe their eyes. The apparitions from the dark were certainly human, and their lack of tattoos showed them to be Constants. But that was where any resemblance to Cyrus, Miouda and Sammy ended.

The creatures from the pit were short – no more than four feet tall – plump, bow-legged and astonishingly white. They looked, Cyrus thought, as if they had never seen daylight. And as he would learn, he was entirely correct. Males and females, both equally shapeless, wore nothing but a short, black cloak draped around their sagging bodies.

The most peculiar feature of these washed-out dwarves was the head. They were all bald and had ears that stuck out like large shells. Their noses were long and pointed, their mouths grey-lipped and small. Two enormous eyes, brown-green and unblinking, stared at the visitors with a mix of politeness and conceited pity.

'Oh dear,' continued the Leader when she had finished staring at their visitors, 'you are sso dark, aren't you? Like Meshkiss.'

'Perhapss they are Meshkiss,' said a man to her left. He

waved a fleshy white hand in Miouda's direction. 'Sspeak! Are you Meshkiss?'

'Meshkis? I'm afraid I don't know what you mean,' said Miouda, ignoring the man's rudeness and his strange, hissing speech. Whoever these people were, they had electricity and it would not do to fall out with them. 'I'm from the Constant community of Alba,' she continued. 'My name's Miouda. My friends are Sammy, from the Gova people, and Cyrus, my copemate. He was born in Della Tallis.'

'And this here animal, who is definitely not a wolf, is my dog Corby,' added Sammy.

'Yess,' replied the Leader with a sigh. 'I ssee. But it iss sso tiring sstanding here, and that torch iss sso hot. Put it out, please, and we will talk to you ssomewhere more comfortable. Come!'

When Cyrus had extinguished his torch and Sammy had tied Corby to a corroded bench, they followed their pale hosts down a ladder into the pit. Here they found dozens of similar creatures, white, slack and owl-eyed, lying on mattresses and eating. The Leader pointed to a couple of empty mattresses and told them to relax.

'Sso,' she began, helping herself from a plate of cold meat, 'you have not had the pleasure of knowing about uss. Too bad. And we don't know about you, either. Please tell uss why you are here.'

The pallid dwarves lay back and, munching ceaselessly, listened attentively as Cyrus explained about the Soterion and the Salvation Project, and their Mission to recover them.

'And that's who we are and how we came to be here,' he

136

concluded. He pointed at the lamps. 'You can understand why we're excited.'

The Leader wiped her mouth with a limp hand and nodded. 'Mmm, interesting. It'ss just ass we feared. Yess, just as we feared. The world up there, the one you come from, iss uncivilised, positively barbaric. It iss what makess uss sso sspecial, iss it not?'

Sammy coughed politely. 'Excuse me,' he asked, 'but I don't get it. I mean, what makes you so special?'

The Leader stared at him with her huge, watery eyes. 'Oh dear, oh dear!' she said with a long, slow, exasperated sigh. 'I ssuppose you can't ssee, can you? Although you come with newss of a remarkable machine, you are brown, polluted by the ssun and cursed with ssmall eyess that cannot ssee ass we ssee.'

During this bizarre speech, Miouda became more and more agitated. Yes, these troglodytes had electricity and she probably needed to remain on good terms with them. But some of the things the woman was saying...

'Do you mean,' she said, sitting bolt upright on her mattress, 'do you mean you are special because you are whiter than us and have bigger eyes?'

Cyrus tapped her on the knee and frowned. 'No Cy,' she said. 'This is important.'

The Leader nodded and gave a thin-lipped smile. 'Yess. Sshe iss correct. It iss important. Listen, and my closse friend Flossco will explain.'

The man who had spoken to them earlier leaned over to his partner, placed a limp hand on her thigh and gave her a soggy kiss that sounded like a fart. 'Delighted, my ssweetest mattress-consort,' he said, stuffing another piece of meat into his mouth.

From Flosco's explanation, and from what they had learned from the books in the Soterion, the Mission were able to piece together the story of these extraordinary people. At the time of the Great Death, as violent chaos swept the planet, a group of adults had created a refuge for their children in their city's metro system. Deep beneath the city streets, they set up a community and stocked it with years' worth of food in tins and freezers.

The Safids – as they called themselves – lived below the city in peace and security for several decades. A subterranean stream provided them with drinking water and powered what Flosco called the "Wheel" – a device that generated their electricity. However, the freezers and other electrical goods had inevitably failed and the supply of tinned food ran low. In Safid mythology, this was the Time of Peril.

Over the generations, the Safids had adapted to their environment. Without exercise, their bodies grew weak and slack. Never seeing sunlight, their skins bleached pearly-white and their bones became feeble and bent with rickets. Their eyes grew larger and larger, enabling them to see in the semi-darkness of their underground home.

When the food ran out, scouts were sent to the surface to bring back fresh supplies. Not one returned. Week, feeble and blinded by sunlight, they were easy prey for Zeds by day and wolves by night. Yet, by accident, these martyrs saved the Safid community. They left the sliding lattice door at the entrance to the metro network unlocked.

Shortly afterwards, a small band of Constant men and women, fleeing the gigantic wolves that had taken over the city, stumbled down the steps and came face to face with the Safids. They begged to be allowed to stay in their dark but secure world. The Safids agreed, on condition that the new arrivals – the Meshkis – went up to the surface from time to time to gather food.

The Meshkis gratefully accepted the offer, and a station down the line was found for them to live in. They accepted their inferior status without question: they were the brown- and black-skinned labourers who, in return for safety, kept their lilywhite superiors well supplied with meat, fruit and other food from the upper world.

The peace-loving Meshkis were so brainwashed into accepting their status that they failed to see they were more powerful than the Safids. And their grateful innocence fed Safid arrogance. The more the Safids heard of the city, the more special they thought themselves. Living beneath the world, they believed themselves above it. Their electricity, a direct link with the Long Dead, they proclaimed to be a sign of their superiority. Their whiteness and their lack of muscle tone were not weaknesses but badges of dominance.

The flaccid Flosco explained all this, pausing every now and again to eat. But he gave only the Safid side of the story, as the Mission were quick to realise. On several occasions, Miouda was tempted to intervene. Cyrus' firm hand on her arm cut her short, reminding her that there were more important issues at stake. The glow of the lights reminded her what they were.

When Flosco had finished, the Mission sat for a while and listened to the sounds of munching and flabby fondling going on around them. Eventually, Cyrus put the question they all wanted to ask.

'Very interesting. Thank you. But where do we fit in? We are brown and we have lived in the world above, so are we inferior to you, like the Meshkis?'

'Of coursse,' replied Flosco quickly, rubbing his fleshy hands together. 'It iss not your fault, but you have been burned, polluted by the ssun.'

'And yet,' cut in the Leader with a tight smile, 'there iss hope for them, isn't there, my dearesst Flossco?' She danced her fingers on his bare, hairless knee as she spoke.

'Whatever you ssay, my honeyed mattress-consort,' he replied, sliding a hand inside her loose, black gown. Cyrus looked away in disgust.

The Leader's eyes opened wider. 'If you sstay here and help uss,' she explained, 'your descendantss will grow whiter. It'ss happening to the Meshkiss – gradually – sso it will happen to you. If you sstay out of the ssun.'

Cyrus sensed Miouda and Sammy were about challenge this preposterous statement and said quickly, 'Yes, if we are lucky. But what about this?' He pointed to the rucksack containing the laptop. 'If we connect our computer to your electricity supply, we'll all be able to share in the riches of the Long Dead. The Meshkis bring you food in exchange for safety. We'll bring you knowledge in exchange for electricity. Is that a fair bargain, Safids?'

The guzzling and fondling had stopped while he was speaking and Cyrus was aware of dozens, perhaps hundreds, of saucer eyes staring at him in the gloom. He saw Sammy glance up at the platform where they had left their weapons.

If it came to a fight, they'd have no difficulty escaping these colourless slugs. But if the Meshkis hunters remained loyal to the Safids, they'd be a much tougher proposition. For the time being, Cyrus concluded, diplomacy was the best option.

'Sstrangerss from above sseek to bargain with uss?' hissed the Leader, spreading a sickly smile in Flosco's direction as she removed his hand from the front of her gown.

'Irregular,' muttered Flosco. 'Ssafidss do not bargain. We decide becausse we are sspecial.'

'Yess!' echoed a chorus of voices. The sound was like rain on water. 'Sspecial.'

Miouda couldn't let this pass. 'Alright. You are special – in some ways – but maybe we are too? We can read. We have a machine left to us from the Long Dead, full of their information and ideas. Isn't that special?'

The Leader looked her up and down. 'Perhapss. But you are hard and brown, not ssoft and white like my mattress-man Flossco.' She leaned across to him once more, this time wrapping her pale arms around his neck and pulling him towards her.

Miouda sat back and waited for the sordid show to finish. 'So are we special enough to use your electricity?' she asked when the couple's sloppy embrace had ended and she had their attention.

The Leader blinked and slid a meatball into her mouth. 'We musst discuss,' she said, rising slowly. 'Come Flossco, we must discuss.'

While the Safid commander and her partner were away, the Mission took stock. Revolting though their hosts were – Miouda said they made her feel sick – they had to avoid confrontation.

Cyrus said he was sure that when the laptop was up and running they could influence the Safids' ideas. As they had seen in Alba, the knowledge of the Long Dead brought great power.

'As long as the laptop really has got all that stuff in it,' commented Sammy ruefully.

'Only one way to find out,' said Cyrus. 'One step at a time.'

'And the first is getting to use this lot's electricity,' said Miouda.

'And if they don't agree?' said Sammy. 'Things might turn a bit nasty, eh Cy?'

'Maybe. If they did, we'd have to get the Meshkis on our side. That shouldn't be too difficult, seeing how they're treated. But I hope it doesn't come to that.'

'You can say that again,' said Miouda with a shiver. 'This place is horrible. The sooner we're out of it, the better.'

'It won't be long,' said Cyrus. 'Promise.'

The Safids, continually side-tracked by eating and cuddling, never did anything quickly. But when the Leader and Flosco waddled back between the mattresses, their faces shone with greasy smiles. It was the duty of the Mission to share the secrets of the Long Dead, the Leader said, and as a reward she and her people would give them 'Ssemi-Sspecial sstatuss': they could use the electricity for their machine.

The Mission's delight was interrupted by the sound of

footsteps approaching down the steps at the end of the hall.

'Excellent!' grinned the Leader. 'The Meshkiss are here. Bringing food, I trust.'

'Yess,' hissed Flosco, looking straight at Miouda. 'They understand how important it iss to sserve uss.'

As he was speaking, a troop of half-a-dozen Constants, three men and three women, came into view at the end of the platform. Brown-skinned, black-haired and athletic, they were led by a young woman bearing a burning torch. She could not have been more than thirteen, Miouda reckoned, and was probably the person they had heard referred to as Olo. Her colleagues carried baskets of fruit and the carcass of a freshly slain deer.

When they noticed the Mission, they stopped and reached for their weapons.

'Sstop, idiotss!' the Leader cried in something between a hiss and a scream. 'Are you sso blind you can't ssee our Ssemi-Sspecial visitorss come in peace?'

'We's so sorry, Leader,' said the tallest of the men. 'We's not knowin' what they is.'

'Oh sstop whining!' spat the Leader. She turned to Cyrus and waved a limp hand in the direction of the Meshkis. 'Sso sstupid!' she sneered.

When Cyrus did not reply, the Safid gave a sickly shrug and switched her attention back to the new arrivals. 'What have you brought uss?'

'Successful huntin', Leader,' said the tall man. 'Food for all.'

The Leader ignored him. Glaring at the torchbearer, she said, 'Lower that brand, sservant! How many timess do I have to tell you? It'ss too bright for ssensitive eyess.'

The embarrassed girl did as she was told.

'We's sorry, Leader,' said the man. 'It's the first time Olo's been out with us. We'll go and get cookin' right away.'

'Good. And when you get to your sstation, ssend a guide to take our Ssemi-Sspecial visitorss to the Wheel Housse.'

'Yes Leader.'

With that, the Meshkis picked up their booty and disappeared into the tunnel at the end of the platform.

I don't believe it, thought Cyrus, turning to his friends with a shake of the head. A single one of those hunters is worth ten of the selfish, idle Safid slugs. Lounging around on their mattresses all day, wallowing in self-importance, they haven't even bothered to ask our names. Just because they have inherited technology, they think they're special. Huh!

For a few seconds he allowed his mind to wander back over the bizarre array of human beings he had encountered since that fateful day in Della Tallis. Roxanne, the noblest of all; Ozlam, the perverted High Father of the Children of Gova; Sammy, so honest, so kind-hearted; the vicious and twisted genius of Timur; the tragedy of Yash, seduced by the power of knowledge; dearest Miouda, his copemate and the hope for a brighter future, and that fair-headed Zed woman who had spared his life before the burning Ghasar.

What strange creatures we are! he said to himself. What a piece of work! And the Long Dead – as far as he knew – had been the same, a painful mix of kindness and cruelty, Constant- and Zed-like at the same time. The Salvation Project would allow them to live as their ancestors had done, but would it really be salvation...?

Flosco's voice intruded upon his musing. 'visitorss, a Meshkiss will take you to ssee our Wheel. It'ss what makess uss sspecial, you know.'

'Yes, I know,' said Cyrus, doing his best to sound civil. 'It's kind of you. And there is a plug socket?'

Flosco and the Leader stared at him blankly.

'You have other electrical machinery,' explained Cyrus. 'Where is it?'

The Leader dismissively waved a feeble white hand. 'Oh! Ssomewhere in the Meshkiss sstation. They will sshow you.

'Now, we need to press on with our busy lives. If you climb on to the platform, a guide will collect you ssoon.'

Stretching back on her mattress, she opened her mouth for Flosco to drop in a piece of honeycomb. 'And don't forget to come and tell uss when your machine iss working,' she added, her lips sticky with sweetness.

Not long afterwards, the cheery-faced Olo came running out of the tunnel and led the Mission away. Corby, who had lain patiently on the platform all the while, trotted along eagerly at their heels. He disliked the atmosphere in the Safid station as much as they did.

When they were out of earshot, Sammy fell into step beside their guide. 'Weird lot back there, eh?'

Olo lifted her torch and gave him a strange look. 'Weird?'

She just doesn't get it, he thought. 'Doesn't matter, Olo,' he replied, giving her a friendly grin. 'One day I'll explain what I mean.'

The day came sooner than either of them expected.

13
Sammy's Friend

The Meshkis station was laid out like that of the Safids. There the similarity ended. Lit by torches burning on the walls, the place bustled with cooking, cleaning, weapon-making, and military training. Near the entrance, a second food patrol was preparing to go up to the surface.

In place of the Safids' loose black cloaks, the Meshkis were dressed in leather and furs. Looking at the kilts and jerkins more closely, Cyrus realised that they were all made from wolf hide. His respect for the supposedly inferior people of the underground increased: to kill and skin one of those ferocious beasts required considerable skill and courage.

Olo passed along the platform, exchanging greetings with all she met, and led the Mission through a door, through a long, narrow tunnel, and down a flight of steep, concrete steps. 'Be takin' care,' she called over her shoulder. 'Slippery.'

The vaulted ceiling was low and damp. By the light of Olo's torch, Cyrus noticed electricity cables fixed to the walls. From somewhere ahead of them came the sound of running water, and at the foot of the stairway the passage broadened into another platform overlooking a dark pool.

On the far side, driven by a stream falling from a ceramic pipe, a large wheel revolved slowly. Its axle ran to a series of gears that turned a spindle in a rusty, barrel-shaped box.

The Mission stood for a few seconds taking in the scene. Cyrus spoke first. 'And all that time we were searching for solar panels!' he laughed.

'What's this, Cy?' asked Sammy, following the wires from the box, across the pool and into the tunnel.

'Some sort of generating machine. When it turns, it makes electricity.'

'Only just,' said Miouda. 'Listen! Doesn't sound like it's working too well.'

Beyond the rush of water, they heard the high-pitched screech of metal on metal.

'Not surprising,' laughed Sammy. 'I reckon I'd be pretty worn out after spinning round for a hundred years.'

Cyrus smiled. 'Been going even longer than that, Sammy. It must have been specially made, like our laptop. We might be able to mend it if it goes wrong, but I say we connect up the computer straight away, just in case.'

The others agreed. Olo took them back to the Meshkis station where they had seen the rusted hulks of old freezers. Although the damp had corroded most of the sockets, those where the plug had been left in were still usable.

Olo brought over a small stool, Cyrus placed the laptop on it, and a crowd of excited Meshkis gathered to watch the show. In contrast to their dangerous exploits in the city, their underground routine was normally rather dull.

Olo leaned forward and held on to Sammy to get a better view. 'What's we lookin' at'?' she whispered.

Turning around quickly, his nose almost bumped into hers. 'Sorry!' he said with a grin. 'We're going to get a message from the Long Dead!' The news flew around the station, bringing more and more Meshkis to see what was happening.

Miouda weaved her way through the crowd to run the cable from the wall to the socket on the computer. When all was ready, Cyrus stood up and spoke to the crowd.

'Friends, this is an amazing moment! It may change our lives – the lives of all of us – for ever.' He pointed at the computer. 'We think this machine holds the knowledge of the Long Dead.'

Waiting for the rustle of voices to die down, he went on, 'We have been searching a long, long time for the electricity it needs. Now we have found it. We can't be sure it'll work – but let's hope it does!'

The Meshkis responded with loud and generous clapping.

'Thank you,' continued Cyrus. 'Now if you'd all stand back a bit so we can see what we're doing, my friend Miouda will switch the machine on.'

The only sound was the drip of water from the ceiling. With Cyrus at her side, Miouda knelt before the laptop, lifted the lid and raised her finger over the start button.

'Oh Cyrus,' she said quietly, 'please let it work! After all everyone has done, after all we have been through…'

Cyrus rested a hand on her shoulder. In his mind, images of

those who had given their lives for the cause flashed across the blank screen: Roxanne, Zavar, Taja, Navid, Bahm, Jannat, and all those slaughtered Albans. Instinctively, he lifted his hands and clasped the palms together in a gesture the Long Dead would have called prayer.

Miouda brought her finger down... A faint click, then nothing. Cyrus' heart sank. No, surely not? Please...

Wait! There was a low whirring and a pinprick of light appeared in the centre of the screen. The crowd held their breath. Even the drip from the ceiling seemed to stop.

The dot spread until the whole screen was an even, pale blue. Miouda gasped and reached up to Cyrus. Beside them, Olo gripped Sammy's arm in excitement.

As they watched, four words in red lettering appeared. BOOTING UP. PLEASE WAIT.

'What's that mean?' asked Sammy, breaking an almost intolerable silence. 'What's boots got to do with it?'

''Shh!' said Cyrus. 'I expect it's thinking.'

'Think—'

Before Sammy had finished, a new message appeared. WELCOME! At the same time, a strange metallic voice began to speak.

'Welcome, whoever you are. You have in your possession one of the six computers of the Soterion. Its memory contains all the—'

The voice cut, the screen went blank, and the laptop turned off. The crowd emitted a loud moan.

Cyrus jumped to his feet. 'Hold on! It's probably the plug. Wait a moment, please.'

But it wasn't the plug.

Olo went to check the Wheel House and Sammy volunteered to go with her. On the way, he explained about the Soterion and the Mission, and why finding a reliable source of electricity was so important.

'You's meanin' back in them Long times—' she began after he had finished.

'Long Dead, Olo.'

'Ok. Back in them Long Dead times, the Safids wasn't the only ones with electricity?

'Course not! You've been up in the city. In the time of the Long Dead, all those buildings had electricity.'

She thought for a moment. 'But the Safids is sayin'—'

'Sure!' interrupted Sammy. 'Listen…'

As they made their way down the Wheel House steps, he told her what he thought of her bleached masters. Before she could reply, they arrived at the platform overlooking the pool and the conversation came to an abrupt halt. The wheel was still turning, but the noise from the adjacent machinery had stopped. Worse, there was a smell of burning, and wisps of grey smoke hung over the rusted carcass of the generator.

Sammy groaned. 'It doesn't look good, does it?' he muttered.

'Never seein' it like this before,' said Olo. 'Bad for your Mission, yes?'

'Could be very bad, yes.'

'Come on, Sammy! You's tough boy. Like you was sayin', the Mission's gonna make it, whatever.' She gave him a friendly hug. 'Maybe it's not broken bad, either. Let's be goin' back and tellin' the others. Someone can be fixin' it.'

Olo's optimism proved unfounded. For several hours, she helped Cyrus and Sammy dismantle the machinery to work out what had gone wrong. They finally concluded that it was beyond repair: the extra current needed for the laptop had overloaded the ancient and worn mechanism, and it had burned out.

During the inspection, Miouda sat chatting with the Meshkis about what they might have found on the laptop if the current had not failed. Every now and again, Olo came back up from the Wheel Room to report what was going on. Shortly after one of these visits, a youth ran into the station from the opposite direction.

'It's our Saviours,' he panted. 'They's bein' unhappy, mighty unhappy!'

'Saviours?' asked Miouda. 'You mean the Safids?'

'Yes! The kind Safids. I never seein' them like that.'

Miouda was intrigued. She invited Rama, a leading Meshkis, to accompany her down the tunnel to see what was going on. As they approached, they became aware of an eerie wailing – something between a hiss and a howl. It grew to a crescendo as they emerged on to the platform.

Miouda held her torch high and stared in astonishment. Down in the pit, the Safids lay spread-eagled, face-up on their mattresses, howling like tiny children. The Leader rose when she saw Miouda and stood quivering amid the sea of flabby flesh.

'What have you done?' she shrieked. 'Give uss back our light. Now!'

'I am... we are... er, sorry,' began Rama.

'Yes, we are sorry your light has gone out,' continued Miouda. 'Actually, the machine was on its last legs and could have given out at any time. The extra current needed for our computer was probably more than it could take. We'll know for certain soon. Cyrus and Sammy are checking as we speak.'

'Mend it!' screamed the Leader.

Miouda stared at her. 'If we can, we will. But I think it's pretty unlikely.'

The Leader's jaw sagged open. 'What... What will become of uss?'

Rama turned to Miouda. 'Perhaps we should try to help them?'

'You don't have to, Rama. Without their electric lights the Safids are nothing. As we agreed back in your station, for generations they have kept you in slavery, deceiving you with lies about their superiority.'

'I understand what you's sayin', Miouda. But it's hard to accept they's been lyin' all this time.'

'Of course. But it's true.' She pointed to the pit. 'Those people down there do nothing but eat and, well, run their feeble hands over their fat bodies. You, the Meshkis, do all the work.'

'But they was takin' us in when we was in the danger. They's allowin' us to use their platform.'

Miouda nodded. 'But they couldn't have stopped you, could they? You have the power. They have only selfishness.'

Tears poured from Flosco's saucer eyes as he rose unsteadily beside the Leader. 'Not true, Rama!' he howled over the wailing around him. 'Don't listen to that wicked brown woman!'

'Ha!' laughed Miouda, spinning around to face the pit.

'Brown? Is that the worst thing you can call me?'

Normally even-tempered, she felt an unexpected fury rising within her. 'Safids, you have twisted your colour into a badge of superiority. Listen, Flosco, it's you who are the liar! You're not better than the Meshkis or anyone else. Your paleness just means you live in darkness, in ignorance, in—'

'Bigotry,' continued a voice from further along the platform. It was Cyrus. Having finished in the Wheel House, he and Sammy, accompanied by half-a-dozen Meshkis, had come to see what Miouda was up to. They had spears with them, gifts from their new friends.

'Miouda's right,' Cyrus went on. 'And here's another unpleasant truth for you, Flosco. The machinery that created your electricity is completely broken. Finished. Your precious lamps will never shine again.'

The wailing from the pit rose to a long, dismal howl and the white bodies rolled around as if in physical agony. Flosco and the Leader collapsed to their mattress like figures of soggy clay.

'It's bein' confusin',' sighed Rama, frowning and shaking his head. 'Everythin' we have been told... I don't know... What do we do?'

Before anyone in the Mission could reply, a youthful Meshkis stepped forward. 'I been talkin' and thinkin', Rama,' she said, 'and I tell you what you do. You show these Safids the way up to the sun, and the Meshkis get on with their own lives. No more bein' servants!'

'Olo, you's only young,' frowned Rama. 'How you understand?'

She moved closer to him, her brown eyes blazing.

154

'Sometimes the young is seein' clearer than the old, Rama. Look, we're free! No more slavin' for the Safids!'

'But…'

'There is no "but", Rama!'

'Freedom!' cried the Meshkis standing behind her.

'Sorry, Rama. I know it's none of our business, but I think Olo's right,' said Cyrus. 'The Safids depend on you now. You are their masters!'

'Never!' chorused the Leader and Flosco. Lying on the mattress, entwined in each other's sagging arms, they were still listening.

A tall Meshkis woman came up and stood beside Rama and Olo. 'I am agreein' with you, Rama. It's hard. The Safids took us in when we was down—'

'And made us slaves,' interrupted Olo.

'Yes, but does we just leave them?'

'Sstay! Help uss!' cried the Leader. Her remark was picked up on the surrounding mattresses and soon the whole hall was shivering with hisses for help.

'Listen!' cried Rama over the din. 'We need to be goin' back to our station and thinkin' it over.' The other Meshkis willingly accepted his suggestion.

'And you, our new friends,' continued Rama, turning to the Mission, 'would you be likin' to stay with us longer? Hear our discussin'?'

'Yes! We'd be likin' that a lot,' added Olo eagerly.

Cyrus smiled. 'I'm sorry, Olo, but no.' He turned to Rama. 'We'd love to stay, but time – my time – is running out.'

'It's running out for all of us,' Miouda added with a wry

smile. 'Now we know the laptop works and holds the Soterion information and probably the Salvation Project data, too,' she continued, speaking directly to Rama, 'we really need to find a source of electricity as quickly as possible.'

'I'm sure you will,' said Rama. 'I've seen loads of them panel things you was talkin' about. But be takin' great care up there, won't you? There's wolves at night.'

'Don't worry!' chuckled Cyrus. 'We know all about the wolves, eh Sammy?'

The young man went down on his haunches and patted Corby's huge head. 'Wolves, tigers, snakes, Zeds... There's nothing scares my Corby and me! That right, old boy?'

The dog looked up at him with wistful eyes and licked his hand. 'See? He knows what I'm saying. There ain't nothing we can't do together.'

Miouda noticed that as he was speaking, Sammy raised his eyes and looked towards one of the Meshkis. Although Miouda could not be sure, she thought she saw his lips mouth 'please'.

The final farewells were soon over. After checking his friends were ready, Cyrus took Miouda's torch and led the way along the platform.

He hadn't gone far when Sammy ran up to him. 'Er, Cyrus?'

'Yes, Sammy? Have we forgotten something?'

'Well, maybe. Sort of.'

Cyrus stopped. 'What do you mean? Corby's with us, isn't he?'

'I don't think he's talking about Corby, Cy,' said Miouda. She nodded at Sammy and grinned.

Cyrus turned and saw a figure standing a few paces behind

them. 'Ah! I wondered… But does she know what she's letting herself in for, Sammy?'

'She knows what it's all about – and Corby likes her.'

Cyrus walked back to Olo and put his hands on her shoulders. Looking her straight in the eye, he asked, 'Is this true, Olo? Do you really understand what might happen to you? There are worse things than wolves, you know.'

She nodded. 'Yes, I know, Cyrus. While we was workin' in the Wheel House, Sammy's been explainin' it all. I wanna be part of it, part of the Mission. Please?'

'And your Meshkis friends and their chiefs – they all agree?'

'I was speakin' to them back in the station, about how your Mission is bein' the most important thing in the world. I was not decided back then, mind you, just thinkin'. Now I's certain and they says I'm free to be doin' as I wishes.'

Cyrus looked at Miouda.

'Be nice to have another woman with us,' she said, putting out her hands. 'Welcome to the Mission, Olo!'

With the Safids' howls of self-pity fading in their ears, the four friends began the long climb up to the uncertain streets of the city.

There were moments when Kamal wished he were not a Malik, and this was one of them. He was coming to see that he had made a serious mistake by concentrating his forces on Tarangala's section of the Kogon. She had killed herself before he could gather information about the whereabouts of Giv and the Head. He had hunted the rest of the Kogon with dogs, but the scent always disappeared when they came to water. Now

157

there was no hope of finding them.

Kamal sat on the trunk of a fallen tree and glared about him. What would Timur have done in this situation? The only answer he could come up with was that Timur would never have got into such a situation in the first place. That was no help at all.

Another idea floated into Kamal's brain. The information he wanted could be extracted from prisoners... He sighed. No, this line of thought was no good either. His only useful prisoner, Tarangala, was dead, and the breeding slaves he had captured knew nothing.

What could he do?

The frustrated Malik picked resentfully at a pimple on his forehead. He had not made much progress before he became aware of someone standing before him. It was Thog of the Gurkov, one of his more eloquent Captains.

'Yes? Speak!'

'Men not happy, Malik,' Thog muttered, scratching his filthy beard.

''Happy? You think Malik Kamal happy, Thog?'

Thog examined him carefully. No. The downturned mouth, the twitching fingers of his intact left hand, and the way he kept shifting his position were all signs that his master was not happy. 'Malik sad,' he concluded.

It was not the right thing to say. 'Sad?' growled Kamal. 'Sad is flabtoad word, idiot. Malik Kamal angry.'

Thog took a step back. 'Ah!'

Kamal remembered why the man had come to see him. 'Well, Thog?'

The Captain scratched his beard more savagely. Was the Malik enquiring about his health? Best say nothing.

Kamal leapt to his feet and thumped Thog hard on the chest with the scabby stump at the end of his right arm. 'Idiot! Idiot! Idiot!' he screamed. 'Malik ask why men not happy – you say nothing! Idiot!'

He calmed down as another idea came to him. 'Thog not traitor, eh?' he sneered, prowling around the Captain like a cat. 'Thog not tell men to be unhappy? Stir up trouble?'

'No, Malik! Captain Thog very goodest man.'

Having faced mutinous warriors once before, Kamal was alert to the danger. 'So – why – men – not – happy?' he repeated, leaving a gap between each word in order to emphasise the gravity of the question.

'Men want flabtoads who taken Timur,' explained Thog. 'Gurkov want flabtoads and Over-Malik.'

So it was the Gurkov who were discontented, not the Grozny, Kamal realised. That was a relief. Still circling the Captain, he tried to think.

Maybe, if the Gurkov were becoming a nuisance, he should get rid of them? The easiest way would be to massacre them when they were asleep… But that would be too risky. If one of them raised the alarm, a fight between the tribes would probably result in their both being wiped out.

Kamal made another three circuits of Thog and told him to repeat the reason for Gurkov dissatisfaction.

The Captain duly obliged. 'Men want flabtoads who taken Timur.'

Kamal stopped. That was it! If the Gurkov were so keen to

find the flabtoads and the Timur totem, let them try. But on their own! They'd not succeed, but at least they'd be out of the way and Kamal would be left with only the Grozny to manage.

So, how could he get the Gurkov to leave? Mmm…

Kamal returned to the tree and sat down. He felt better giving orders when seated; it was more dignified, more Malik-like.

'Captain Thog,' he began, doing his best to sound flattering, 'you are clever man.'

Thog looked startled. Compliments were the last thing he had been expecting. 'Thank you, Malik,' he muttered. Where could this be leading?

Kamal leaned back and lifted his arms. 'Zed hunters catch deer with trap, yes?' Thog nodded cautiously. He was starting to wonder whether the Malik had gone a bit crazy, like that weird man Giv.

'Some men go this way,' Kamal continued, extending his left hand, 'and some men go other way.' He stretched out his stump. 'Deer in middle – no escape!'

'Ah!' grunted Thog. 'Deer dead!'

'Very good, Captain,' said Kamal, lowering his arms. 'That what we do now – make trap.'

Thog grinned. 'And catch deer for eating!'

'No, idiot!' shouted Kamal, his flattery evaporating even quicker than it had arisen. 'Not deer! Grozny and Gurkov trap Kogon flabtoads.'

'Oh! Er, Kogtoads…' mumbled the Captain, obviously a bit lost.

Kamal explained. 'Grozny go one side, Gurkov go other

side – flabtoads in middle. No escape! Zeds have breeding slaves and Over-Malik Timur! Clever plan, eh?'

Yes, the Captain got it now. It was a very clever plan. He set aside a vague reservation lurking at the back of his mind and waited to be told what to do. Starting out in the direction of the rising sun, over several days he was to lead his Gurkov warriors in a long, sweeping circle. At the same time, Kamal would take the Grozny and the breeding slaves on a circle in the opposite direction. When the two tribes met, the Kogon would be trapped between them.

'Ho-ho!' laughed Thog as he went off to prepare his men. 'Fine flabtoad plan!' He knew there was one further question he ought to ask before setting out, but he couldn't quite put his finger on it.

He finally realised two days later, as he was leading the Gurkov across a shallow river. How could they trap the Kogon if they didn't know where they were? He cursed himself for not asking Kamal. And now it was too late. The Grozny were far away – and they had all the breeding slaves.

Kamal was so far away, in fact, that the two tribes never met again. Just as he had intended.

14
The Meeting

Truth, they say, is stranger than fiction. If Xsani's tracking of Cyrus along the valley and over the mountains had happened in a book or film, no one would have believed it. And yet it really did happen.

The Malika got off to a fortunate start. Quite by accident, she, her kumfort Jinsha, and the increasingly eccentric Giv (still carrying the Head of Timur on his spear) found the alpine village where the Mission had sheltered before Kemran drove them away. It was not too difficult to guess that from there they had gone into the hills then dropped down into the long valley. Here the Zeds followed the trail of encampments to the blocked tunnel at the foot of the mountains.

Jinsha looked at the rocky escarpment rising before them like an enormous wall. 'Up there?' she frowned.

'If they went that way, tho mutht we,' lisped Xsani. 'Do you think that'th where they went, Giv?'

The eccentric Grozny was proving a lot more helpful than

she had anticipated. His confidence had grown now Pram was out of the way, and his early nomadic life had made him an expert at catching rabbits and cooking them on fires lit with sparks. He stuck the blunt end of his spear in the ground and turned to face the black, shrivelled head of his former master. 'O Mighty Timur,' he intoned softly, 'where go Man in Yellow Hat?'

Though neither Xsani nor Jinsha heard any response, Giv left them to guard his totem and went bounding off in the direction of the ruined mountain road. 'Timur tell me go see,' he called over his shoulder.

Xsani watched him clamber upwards between the rocks and trees. 'Ith he mad, my thweet Jintha?'

The younger woman smiled and shrugged her shoulders. 'Sometimes, my Malika, yes.'

'And dangerouth?'

'At night he frightens me. When Jinsha and Malika lie down and Giv is apart, he makes bad sounds. I'm afraid he attack us.'

'No, I don't think he will attack uth,' said Xsani. 'But he ith tho thtrange! Not like any other Thed dumbman. And that thtupid head! It hath no uthe anymore but he thtill bringth it with him, he thtill talkth to it.'

'He said he worships it – and you.'

The Malika smiled and ran her fingers thoughtfully over the Z marks branded on her forehead and cheeks. 'Yeth. Worthip. Mythteriouth word, Jintha. He thaid I wath like Timur, a god.'

'God?'

'I don't know what that meanth, either. The word came to Giv from Timur – godth are thingth thtronger than Thedth and

Conthtantth.'

'Like tigers?'

'Maybe like tigerth. I think Thyruth, the Man in the Yellow Hat, underthtandth. That'th why we mutht meet him. Thakamir thaid he knowth everything.'

Two hours later, Giv came panting back with the news that he had found the ruins of a Constant camp some distance up the road. Xsani thanked him and led her small posse of pilgrims up the mountain.

The weather had changed since the Mission had passed that way. The tumbling streams had dwindled to mere trickles and the meadow at the summit was strewn with daisies, lilies, sugarbowls, and a hundred other species of wild flower. Intoxicated by the scent, Jinsha danced a few steps and threw herself down laughing into the long grass.

'Jintha, what are you doing?' asked Xsani, smiling quizzically at her. Her instinct had already given her the answer.

'I don't know, Malika,' giggled her kumfort. She threw wide her arms and stared up at the sun. 'The smells, the colour, the warmth – they spoke to me. "Come and join us!" they said.'

'And I will join them ath well,' said Xsani, lifting her robe over her shoulders. 'But we will join them properly. The flowerth, the thky, the thun – they don't wear clotheth, tho neither will we.'

No more words were needed. Together they lay naked in the long grass with arms outstretched, the tips of their fingers barely touching. They breathed in easy peace and through half-closed eyes watched the clouds slide gently across the pale-blue dome overhead.

Nearby, Giv stared in uncomprehending horror. It was not the unusual behaviour that shocked him, nor the women's nakedness. It was the change that had come over their faces. For some reason – he later decided he had been blinded by the glare of the mountain sun – from cheek and forehead the disfiguring scars of a Zed had completely disappeared.

Xsani and Jinsha spoke frequently about the 'Soterions', the name they gave the people they were following. From the group's detritus, they worked out that it consisted of three Constants – and a dog. But figuring out the purpose of their irregular route was much harder. They avoided the ruins of large conurbations but not smaller settlements. And why had they stayed in an alpine village for several days?

Xsani wondered whether the answer lay at the start of their journey. She knew the Soterions had gone to the vault and, presumably, collected something from it before setting off. Had they taken a book? Possibly. But why did they need to come all this way with a book?

Xsani concluded they would never know what was going on until they finally caught up with their quarry and talked with them face to face.

'If we find them, Malika,' said Jinsha quietly.

'Jintha!' snapped Xsani in a rare show of irritation. 'Don't thay that!'

'I am sorry, Malika,' she blushed. 'We will find them, of course.' She paused. 'But when we meet the Soterions, will they speak with us? Constants kill Zeds – always.'

'Yeth, I know. And Thedth alwayth kill Conthtantth –

166

exthept oneth.'

'Malika means the time she spared Cyrus, the Man in the Yellow Hat?'

'Prethithely. Thyruth oweth me a life. Tho when we meet, I think it would be a good idea to remind him of that.'

The decision whether or not to enter the city was as difficult for Xsani as it had been for the Mission. The Kogon had avoided the remains of towns, preferring the safety of woods and remote vales. Neither Xsani nor Jinsha had ever seen the ruins of a Long Dead city before. Looking down from the wooded hill where Cyrus and Miouda had stood not long before, they stared anxiously at the wide panorama of crumbling buildings and overgrown streets.

'Why did the Thoterionth thtay a night here if they did not go into the thity?' mused Xsani, referring to the ashes and debris nearby. 'But we need to be thertain they went down there before we follow.'

Once again, Giv solved the problem. Leaving Xsani and Jinsha on the hill, he ran through the scrub towards the distant ruins. He was gone some time, and when he returned he was grinning broadly.

'Giv find dog shit!' he panted. 'Same as before. Constant dog shit!'

'Then we go where they went,' said Xsani grimly. 'Into the thity. Quietly and very, very carefully.'

After explaining that it could go back on the spear when they stopped, she persuaded Giv to tie Timur's head to his belt by the hair. This freed his spear as a weapon. The move was only partially successful because the skull bumped heavily against his knee as he walked, dislodging several of its teeth. Knife drawn, Xsani came next. Jinsha brought up the rear, spear at the ready.

With senses alert to the slightest sound or movement, they stuck to shadowy side streets rather than broad avenues. Giv crossed open spaces first, listening and looking around before signalling the women to follow. They were all acutely aware of the danger of ambush by man or beast.

By the middle of the day, they had advanced no more than a few thousand paces nearer the city centre. They stopped amid the rusted hulks of cars in a ruined garage and ate some of the food they had brought with them. The two women sat together and Giv squatted down opposite them, cradling the battered Head between his knees.

The stillness was ominous, Xsani warned. Jinsha shivered and moved closer to her.

Giv, who had been running his fingers around the gaps where Timur's teeth had been, raised his head and announced in a weird, penetrating voice, 'Over-Malik say death hide in this city! Beware Constants! Beware Zeds! Death approaches!'

Xsani stared at him. 'Thometimeth, Giv,' she said slowly, 'you are very utheful and helpful. At other timeth, I would like to think my knife into you. Thith ith one of those timeth. Shut up!'

Giv was devastated. 'Oh no, Malika! Please Malika! Giv worship goddess Malika, even when Malika not have Zed mark—'

'What did you thay?'

'On mountain, when Malika and friend lie in grass, Z marks vanish from flab... er, women's faces.'

Xsani shook her head. 'Oh Giv, you do talk thuch nonthenthe. My Z markth are thtill here' – she pointed to her face – 'and death ith not approaching.'

Giv lowered his eyes. 'Timur tell Giv that death approaching,' he said sheepishly.

Xsani ignored him and turned to talk to Jinsha. They resolved to press on towards the centre, and if they hadn't found a clue to the whereabouts of the Soterions by nightfall, they'd find a safe place to sleep and resume their search in the morning.

Accordingly, when the streets were deep in shadow, Xsani led the way to a large brick building in the middle of a small copse. The trees had sprouted after the Great Death, forcing their way upwards between flat, moss-covered stones. It was, Xsani said, as safe as anywhere in that desolate city.

The heavy wooden door, reinforced with iron, had not been moved for generations, and they had great difficulty wrenching it open. Once inside, they shut it behind them and looked around.

Xsani gasped. 'It'th... it'th like the other one,' she stammered. 'Amathing!'

The building had been ransacked and set on fire by vandal Zeds. Fortunately, a rainstorm had extinguished the flames before they devoured the entire building. At both ends, the roof was still intact but the space between was strewn with weeds, broken statues and the charred remains of bench seats with high backs.

The scene evoked contrasting emotions in the three Zeds. Giv, who had never seen anything like it before, was awe-struck by its fractured glory. The women were confused. The resemblance to Xsani's headquarters in Filna was uncanny: the same sword images, the same Constants, and on the walls the same weather-ruined paintings.

Xsani turned to the wall above the door and gasped. Gazing down at her from a faded fresco was the Man in the Yellow Hat. 'Jintha,' she whispered, 'he'th here.'

As she spoke, the door below the picture swung back and the figure of a man stood framed in the opening.

It was Cyrus.

15
Kamal the Great

'Teach Kamal!' the Malik of the Grozny barked at the heavily pregnant Constant prisoner sitting on the ground before him. 'Kamal want be like Timur – Great!'

He was sitting, arms folded, in a battered armchair he called his 'tone'.

The woman hesitated, trying to work out the best approach. Having been held as a breeding slave for the last three years, she remembered Timur. Oh yes! She remembered him alright. The most terrifying, evil human being – if indeed he was human – she had ever met.

'You want to be like Timur, Malik?' she asked cautiously.

Her years in captivity had taught her the art of survival. However vile or stupid a remark made by a Zed, never contradict or question it. Flattery, strength and patience kept you alive.

The fact that the woman had fallen pregnant early on in her captivity had helped her, too. Although the Zeds had no respect whatsoever for flabtoads, one of the few rules universally obeyed was that breeding slaves with child were to be guarded and cared for. They were, as Timur had once put it, 'golden Zed-makers'.

'Yes. Kamal want be like Timur.'

The woman gazed at him with weary eyes. She had been here before, trying to teach Zed commanders how to improve their semi-grammatical grunting.

'Very well, O mighty Malik,' she said, forcing herself to smile. 'Timur was a fine man and I will help you become like him.'

Kamal's mean features split into a thin grin of self-satisfaction. 'Teach!'

'Well, Malik, first you do not call yourself "Kamal"'.

'That my name, idiot flabtoad! Kam-al!'

The woman closed her eyes momentarily. This was going to be tricky. She took a deep breath and began again.

'My name, mighty Malik, is Seyda.' Kamal nodded. 'When Seyda talks about herself, she does not say "Seyda" but "I". Understand?'

'You "I", me "Kamal",' replied the Malik proudly.

'Sort of. Now you say "I", please.'

'Aye.'

'Good, O Malik. That will do. Now say, "I am the Malik of the Grozny Zeds".'

Kamal frowned. 'Aye am Malik of Grozny Zeds.'

'Almost. But put in the word "the": the Malik of the Grozny Zeds.'

Kamal puffed out his bony chest. 'Kamal thee Malik of thee

Grozny Zeds!'

'So close, Malik. Now all together: "I am the Malik of the Grozny Zeds".'

'Aye am thee Malik of thee Grozny Zeds!'

Seyda smiled with relief. 'Excellent, O Malik! Soon you will be like Timur.'

She knew it was a lie, of course. Successful tribal chiefs were educated by captured Constants from at least the age of eight – Kamal was way beyond significant help. This was shown all too clearly by what he did next.

Leaning back in his chair, Kamal screamed, 'Erzo!'

A Zed of some eleven winters ran up and knelt before him. 'Malik call?' he mumbled.

'Yes, Erzo. What is thee name of thee Malik, eh?'

'Er, Malik Kamal?'

'No, idiot! That old name. Now thee Malik edinkated, thee name is "Aye" – Malik Big Aye!'

At his feet, Seyda groaned inwardly. She knew teaching Kamal was going to be hard – but not this hard.

The Malik's sudden thirst for what he termed "edinkation" was born of frustration. Having combed the countryside for a whole moon, he had uncovered not a single clue as to the whereabouts of either Giv or the missing Kogon. He decided that the only way to find Timur was to think as the Over-Malik thought. To do that, he needed training – hence his sessions with the wretched Seyda.

Tuition did not bring Kamal – or "Big Aye" as he was now officially known – the benefits he had hoped for. He spoke marginally more coherently, could now count up to fifty, knew the names of some trees and plants, and could even sing the first verse of the nursery song Lavender's Blue – but he could not find Timur.

Another moon passed, then another and another. Gradually, the Grozny slipped back into their pattern of life before Timur had encountered Roxanne. They hunted and scavenged, and from time to time raided vulnerable Constant settlements. New members of the tribe were born, others died, killed in fighting or passing away more peacefully at the end of their Death Month.

Kamal himself felt the end of his nineteen-year span drawing to a close. In rare moments of reflection, he feared he would never see Giv or his beloved Over-Malik again. And then, one wet afternoon when all hope seemed lost, a cry went up from the edge of the Grozny encampment.

'Malik Big Aye! Malik Big Aye! Come! Zeds see strange man!

'Zeds!' cried Cyrus to Sammy, Miouda and Olo as they followed him into the ruined church. He lowered the sack containing the laptop and thrust his new Meshkis spear out in front of him. Somewhere to his left Corby gave a low growl.

The Mission instinctively spread out to encircle their enemy. Cyrus, who had been in similar situations a dozen times, knew exactly what to do. Check they weren't too heavily outnumbered and that it wasn't an ambush, then close in.

Zeds were strong and ferocious fighters, but unskilled. In hand-to-hand combat, a Constant's superior weapons and training nearly always gave them the upper hand. As most fights took place outside the safety of a settlement, usually when Constants were looking for supplies, they were taught to show no mercy. The rule was simple: kill or be killed. If even one Zed got away, they were likely to return with a far larger force.

All this flashed through Cyrus' mind as, stepping carefully around the debris at his feet, he edged to his left. Sammy, employing the military training he had received in Alba, advanced on the opposite flank with Corby at his heel. The hairs on the dog's neck bristled like teasels. Olo and Miouda held the centre. If the Zeds made a dash towards any one of them, the rest would move in and surround the assailant.

Cyrus had made an instant appraisal of the enemy: three figures, no gut-rippers or bows and arrows. That gave the Mission the advantage in both numbers and arms. As long as they didn't do anything stupid, they'd get this over and done with quickly. So intent was he on not tripping over the tangle of weeds and bits of broken stone that he didn't examine his foe too carefully.

'Alright Sammy?' he called. 'No sign of others?'

'Nope, Cyrus. Just the three.'

'Olo, you done this sort of thing before?'

'Been out on food patrol,' replied the new recruit. 'Plenty trainin'.'

'Good. Stick to my orders and you'll be alright.' Cyrus glanced at his copemate. 'Ok, Miouda?'

Her reply, in a voice quivering with disbelief, took him completely by surprise. 'Cyrus, look! Have you seen who it is?'

Cyrus stared in astonishment. Impossible! The tall, sallow-faced man with maniacal eyes was the leader of the procession they had passed on their way out of Alba! He had Timur's shrivelled head on the end of his spear, too.

As if to confirm his identity, the fellow let out a sinister, high-pitched scream. 'Ayeee! Vile Constant adderbile!' he shrieked. 'How dare you threaten the mighty Over-Malik, Timur the Terrible? Tremble, wolfspittle! Fall to your knees, elktools, before I drain the piss-yellow blood from your veins and grind your bones to powder!'

Cyrus ignored the noise and used the opportunity to study the man's companions. Both were female. The well-built, dark-skinned woman with flowing black hair he had never seen before. From the way she held her spear, he had already marked her down as probably the most dangerous of the three.

But the second woman, a slight figure with a pretty, oval face... Yes, he certainly recognised her. And he wished he didn't. It was the Kogon commander who had let him escape during the sack of Alba. Her intelligent, unblinking gaze told him that the recognition was mutual.

In that instant, Cyrus understood. It was this woman, not some lumbering Zed chieftain, who had been the brains behind the attack on Alba. She had exploited the magic of the Head of Timur, she had conspired with the traitor Sakamir, and now she had tracked him down because of his knowledge of the Soterion. Like Timur, she knew its power and wanted it for herself.

For that, Cyrus told himself, she had to die.

'What's the order, Cyrus?' called Sammy when the Head-carrier had finished his rant and stood watching, pale and

176

trembling, to see what its effect would be. 'Go in and finish them off?'

'No! Lithen to me!' And after a slight pause, 'With all my heart, I beg you.'

Cyrus cursed inwardly. Whatever the tattoos, this was no Zed. How could he kill someone who spoke like that?

'We have come here in peathe,' she lisped in a quiet, husky voice, not once taking her eyes off him. 'Yeth, we are Thedth...'

Sammy took a step towards her. 'Hang on, Sammy,' muttered Cyrus. 'I want to hear what she's got to say first.'

'Thank you, Thyruth. Perhapth I should thay that we were Thedth. I was born a Thed, I wath raithed a Thed, and for motht of my life I lived ath a Thed. A female Thed. Then...'

She paused. Looking at Jinsha, her mouth twitched in the hint of a smile. 'Then thomething happened to me. I could not underthtand how a Thed could have the thort of feelingth I have for...' Again, she gazed at Jinsha. 'For thith thweet young woman.'

If any remark was going to touch the hearts of the Constants, that was it. Miouda and Cyrus, like Sammy and Olo, understood exactly what she was saying. It was extraordinary, nevertheless. All their experience had taught them that Zeds did not feel, let alone talk in this manner.

Warnings flashed through Cyrus' mind. Wasn't this a sham, a clever device to save her life? Hadn't Timur, another fiendishly clever Zed, lied his way into Alba and succeeded in persuading the entire community that he was a Constant?

The mantra of Cyrus' childhood hammered away in his brain: never, ever trust a Zed. He tightened the grip on his spear.

'Ok,' he said, keeping his eyes on the woman. 'We'll let you live – but we'll kill your companions. Now!'

He raised his spear and took a step forward. Opposite him, Sammy did the same.

Miouda saw what Cyrus was up to. Worried lest the other two Constants did not, she called out firmly, 'Wait for Cyrus' command, Sam. That younger one's dangerous.' Xsani moved closer to Jinsha and stretched out a hand to her. With the other she drew her knife. 'If Jintha dieth, tho do I. I will fight to protect her. You will have to kill uth both.'

Behind them, Giv remained as motionless as the shattered stone images on the wall behind him. Only the swirl of terror and incomprehension in his eyes hinted at the turmoil within.

Cyrus looked at Miouda. 'Convinced?'

'Is she who I think she is?'

The reply came from Xsani.

'Yeth. You know who I am. And I know who you are. All three of you.' She regarded each of the Constants in turn. 'Thyruth, Miouda, Thammy – but the other one, the good-looking dark girl, I don't know her.'

Cyrus frowned. This woman was a witch. He knew what he had to do – and yet he couldn't do it. In the past he would not have thought twice about taking the life of a Zed, but now... He knew only too well what was holding him back.

So did Xsani.

'Yeth. Thith man here – Giv – brought me the Head of Timur and I uthed it to bring dumbman Thedth under my control. I conthpired with Thakamir to theithe the Thoterion. I am the perthon who united the Thedth to attack Alba—'

'You are responsible for the massacre of my people!' cried Miouda, close to tears.

'If I tell you I am thorry for what happened, you will not believe me. Bethideth, it would have been impothible without Thakamir. Interethting, ithn't it, that she became a Thed – and I now theek to become a Conthtant.'

'Never!' shouted Sammy. 'Zed you are – and Zed you'll stay! Can't we kill her, Cyrus? She's evil!' His hand twitched on the shaft of his spear. To his right, Olo shifted her weight nervously from foot to foot.

A hundred thoughts swirled through Cyrus' mind. Of course he should kill her! Yet the whole purpose of the Mission was to return to the time when humanity was not divided between Constants and Zeds.

Wasn't this an opportunity to take the first step in that direction? After all, the Safids were hardly shining examples of Constant virtue, and in Yash and Sakamir he had seen Constants as cruel and ruthless as any Zed.

If Constants could become Zeds, perhaps this lisping, strangely attractive woman could become a Constant? And there was also the matter that neither of them had yet mentioned...

'I've one last question, Sammy,' Cyrus called to him.

'Come on, Cyrus! I don't get it. I can't believe we've been standing here chatting to a load of murdering Zeds. What's got into you?'

'I don't know, Sammy. It's just that things don't add up. There's something I need to know.'

Xsani gave him a smile of unmistakeable sincerity. 'I know

your quethtion before you athk it, Thyruth,' she said. 'Why did I order my fighterth to thpare you?'

Cyrus nodded.

'I am not sure mythelf. Thakamir dethcribed you to me tho I thought it might be you – I wanted you alive, you thee, to teach me to read, to help me underthtand the Thoterion.'

She raised her eyes to the faded painting on the back wall of the church. 'But it wath more than that. For a long time, I have been fathinated by that perthon, the Man in the Yellow Hat from the time of the Long Dead.' She pointed to the painting. 'Who wath he? What thtrange powerth did the Long Dead think he had?

'When you thtood on the hill bethide the fire, the moon was over your head. You were the Man in the yellow Hat – and I could not kill you.'

She paused for a moment before continuing. 'Now you know everything, Thyruth. I wish I had not been born a Thed. I want to change. I am athking you – all of you – to help me. My lovely Jintha and I – and the fool Giv – are at your merthy. Tho, if you want to kill uth, do it now.'

With a loud clatter, she dropped her knife on to the stones at her feet.

No one moved. Outside, the distant howl of a wolf reminded them that night was falling fast. All eyes were on Cyrus.

Slowly, very slowly, he lowered his spear. 'I can't do it,' he said, turning towards Miouda.

She took a deep breath and exhaled before saying, 'I'm torn – but nor can I.'

Olo looked to Sammy for guidance. 'Well,' he said with a

shrug, 'if Cyrus and Miouda think it's wrong, so do I. Whoever you are, Zed woman, you're very, very lucky. You've been saved.'

16
The Spire

In years to come, Sammy and Olo would often talk about the moment Cyrus decided not to kill the Zeds who had been trailing him. It proved a turning point in the whole Mission; more than that, it marked a change in how they regarded all human beings.

Neither Sammy nor Olo ever really grasped what had gone on. At the time, Sammy imagined Cyrus' refusal to kill Xsani was a chivalrous gesture – she had spared his life, so he would spare hers. It struck him as unusual that Cyrus had allowed sentiment to stand in the way of duty.

Olo, who knew very little about the Mission, had her own take on what had happened. She said Cyrus was essentially a good man, as his behaviour in the underground had shown. Despite his upbringing, he was reluctant to kill anyone in cold blood, Zed or not.

There was something in these opinions, but Miouda knew the truth was more complicated. She understood that when

Cyrus looked on the Z-branded faces of Xsani and Jinsha, he saw another face behind theirs. That of Roxanne. Her arrival in Della Tallis, scarred in body and mind after being held prisoner by Timur, had inspired him to join the Soterion Mission.

When the Tallins had doubted Roxanne and called her a Zed spy, Cyrus had trusted her and given her his support. In the end, he had been proved right. Listening to Xsani pleading for the lives of herself and her companions, his thoughts had returned to that first meeting with Roxanne. His instinct, which Miouda knew she could trust, told him that Xsani, like Roxanne, saw her tattooing as a mark of shame.

Miouda had reasons of her own for believing Xsani's story. The fact that the Kogon led secretive lives, avoiding contact with Constants and male Zeds, suggested to her that they were essentially different from the aggressive Grozny and Gurkov. No member of those tribes could have talked the way Xsani did about Jinsha. Miouda couldn't imagine how a tribe of female Zeds had come into being, but she thought it was probably out of self-preservation rather than bloodthirsty destructiveness.

Nevertheless, whatever Cyrus' motives for letting the Zeds live, the gesture created fresh problems. What were they to do with them?

The initial idea was to let them go on condition they left the area and troubled the Mission no more. But that was too risky. Xsani and her companions had to prove their trustworthiness.

Sammy put it more bluntly. 'I don't fancy going to sleep knowing there's Zeds prowling around outside,' he muttered. 'Whatever that little one says, we've only got her word that she's not going to sneak back in here and cut our throats.'

'Surely we'd be sendin' them out with no weapons?' asked Olo.

Miouda disagreed. 'That'd be the same as killing them, except wolves would do it more messily. Listen!'

As on every night in that accursed city, a chorus of menacing howls greeted the arrival of darkness. Olo shuddered. 'No need to be tellin' me what that is, Miouda.'

A sudden commotion drew their attention back to the Zeds. It was Giv. He had listened to the conversation between Cyrus and Xsani in horrified silence. His eyes darted wildly from one to the other as he tried to make sense of what he was hearing. How could the Malika, the disciple of the great Over-Malik whose head he bore, converse with Constants?

Only Timur would be able to explain. Giv had removed the dead tyrant's head from the point of his spear and set it on top of a broken pillar. There, leaning obscenely to one side, it fixed him with its chilling, empty stare. Giv went down on his knees before it.

'O Great Timur!' he chanted, swaying backwards and forwards like a tree in a gale, 'in your mighty wisdom tell Giv what is happening.'

He sat on his heels and opened his mouth. Words came out, but the voice was Timur's, not his. 'Toadbrain! Can you not see how the Malika smiles but keeps a dagger behind her back?'

No sooner had she heard this than Xsani hurried over to him, picked up the Head by its filthy hair and flung it into a far corner of the church. 'No more!' she snapped. 'Thtop your nonthenthe, Giv. It'th jutht the head of a dead man!'

'Just the head of a dead man?' he echoed. 'No, Malika! No!'

185

He began crawling on all fours in the direction of his precious relic.

'I thaid no, Giv. Leave it!' Xsani laid a hand on the back of Giv's neck, and said in a gentler, calmer tone, 'That'th better, Giv! We're thtarting a new life, aren't we?'

The touch of Xsani's hand went through Giv like an electric shock. He forgot the Head of Timur and gazed up at her in utter devotion. The Malika, his Malika, had shown that she truly cared for him. Fourteen long years of loneliness lifted from his sad, frail shoulders.

'You heard the loony one,' said Sammy, gathering up Xsani's dagger and Jinsha's spear, which she had placed on the ground in a gesture of peace. 'Smile, and keep a dagger behind your back, that's what he said. She pretended she didn't approve of him saying that,' he went on, indicating Xsani with a nod, 'but we can't be too careful, can we?'

He walked gingerly past Giv and collected his discarded spear. 'Yuk!' He grimaced at the mess of dried blood and brain on the tip. 'Wouldn't want to be stabbed by this thing.'

Cyrus and Miouda left the other three to guard the Zeds and stood to one side to discuss what to do. They would barricade the door to prevent a wolf attack and, in case they changed their minds about being friendly, they would tie their prisoners up.

'The fair-haired one is interesting, isn't she?' said Cyrus. 'She appears harmless enough at the moment, but letting her live isn't the same as trusting her.'

'I agree, Cy,' said Miouda. She nodded towards the prisoners. 'And the dark one seems pretty feisty. Not sure she

liked everything the lisping one said. As for the mad bloke
with the head, he's capable of anything.'

'Maybe. He looks too nutty to be dangerous – but you never
know with a Zed.'

'No. They just don't think like us.'

To Cyrus' relief, the night passed without incident. Miouda
woke him once when wolves came snuffling around the
door, and a little later he was disturbed by Giv carrying on
a conversation with Timur in his sleep. Otherwise, he slept
better than he had for a long time and at dawn he felt refreshed
and eager to get going.

As his friends were still not awake, he lay for a while
thinking about the prisoners trussed up opposite him. He was
sure the woman with the lisp, whose name he had learned was
Xsani, had been telling the truth. So what followed from that?

Constants… Zeds; Zeds… Constants. He was starting to
think there wasn't any basic difference between them. It made
sense. His research in the Soterion made no mention of two
very different types of human being at the time of the Long
Dead. So how had the division come about?

Cyrus glanced at Xsani. What had made her a Zed? he
wondered. If it didn't come from inside her, it must have been
her upbringing. If that was the case, then didn't it apply to all
Zeds? But there had to be exceptions. That monster Timur,
for example, who had so enjoyed his cruelty. Yes, he was sure
Timur had been born evil.

He felt Miouda stirring beside him. She yawned and
stretched out an arm.

'Morning Cy,' she said drowsily. 'What are you doing?'

'Thinking.'

She propped herself up on an elbow. 'About what to do with your Zed friends?'

'What you my mean by my Zed friends?' he smiled.

'Only teasing. What are we going to do with them?'

'No idea. Let's go and get something to eat first. I'm starving!'

Leaving the others asleep, they moved the wood barricading the door and went out into the trees that had taken over the churchyard. Along one side they found a thicket of plantains that had seeded themselves from a nearby garden. After plucking several bunches, they returned to the church to find everyone awake.

Sammy was walking up and down in front of the prisoners, glaring at them. Although deeply suspicious, he had at least allowed them to be untied one at a time and escorted to a far corner of the ruin so they could relieve themselves.

'What're we going to do with this lot, Cyrus?' he asked as they were sharing out the plantains. 'Apart from giving them breakfast?'

'Bit of a problem, Sammy. Leaving them here'd be the same as killing them, which we decided against. But if they come with us, they'll just be a pain.'

'And a danger,' added Miouda. Thinking of her need to get to a friendly Constant settlement as soon as possible, she added, 'If Constants saw us with them, we'd be dead before we had time to explain.'

Cyrus agreed. He remembered the trouble he'd had persuading Taja, his commander in Della Tallis, not to kill

Roxanne when she arrived with a Z scar on her forehead.

'Would you lithen to me?' interrupted Xsani quietly.

The Constants stared in surprise. They had been so wrapped up in their discussion that they had ignored the possibility of the prisoners contributing. The only one of them to have spoken that morning was Giv, who had muttered incoherently about Timur. Jinsha had uttered hardly a word since their capture the previous evening.

'We have thuffered very greatly to find you, Thyruth,' Xsani continued. 'We have left our people and can never go back. Ath the woman called Miouda thaid, normal Conthtantth would kill uth ath thoon ath they thaw uth. If we thtay in the thity, we will be food for wolveth. We want to come with you, wherever you are going.'

'Even if we don't know where we're going?' asked Cyrus wryly.

'Maybe they could join up with your lot, Olo?' said Sammy, turning to his new friend.

'Neat idea,' said Miouda.

Olo was unsure. 'I don't know what they're doin' now. They were talkin' of takin' the Safids up to the city and lettin' them look after themselves. They was then goin' to get a new place to live, somewhere far off. Who's knowin'?'

'The Safids won't get far outside the underground,' said Cyrus, 'and I'm sure they wouldn't take our prisoners. Not after we put out their precious lights.'

'Even if we could be findin' my Meshkis, I am not thinkin' they'd be wantin' people with a Z on them,' said Olo. 'They is havin' too bad memories of times when there was Zeds in the

189

city.'

'I don't like where this is heading,' muttered Cyrus.

'Pleathe!' lisped Xsani, wrenching out the word with an almost physical pain. She had not said 'pleathe' since she was a girl and had almost forgotten its meaning.

Regarding her closely, Cyrus realised she was struggling to express herself. All her adult life she had commanded, never pleaded.

'We can help you,' Xsani went on, uttering each word like a stone that had to be pulled from the earth. 'If you are attacked by dumbman Thedth—'

'"Dumbman"? What kind of Zed is that?' asked Sammy. 'They all seem pretty dumb to me.'

A flash of anger crossed Xsani's face, then vanished. She was no longer Malika, she reminded herself. Others could now talk to her as they wished.

'Man Thedth, Thammy. Dumbman Thedth are man Thedth. Very thtupid people.'

'Not all of them,' said Cyrus. 'But I know what you mean. As you were saying…'

Xsani frowned. 'I don't underthtand "ath you were thaying".'

'Ah. It means continue with what you were saying. Please.'

That word again, thought Xsani. And used so naturally. 'Thank you, Thyruth,' she lisped, enjoying the sound of the phrase. 'If you are attacked by man Thedth, we are warriorth. We can help you.'

'Or help them kill us,' suggested Miouda.

Xsani looked her straight in the eye. 'Lady Miouda,' she

began, hoping the words were appropriate. 'My people would never, ever help a dumbman Thed.'

Cyrus snorted. 'So what did you do in Alba?'

'I hate what happened in Alba. The Grothny and the Gurkov were there to kill. The Kogon – my people – were there to get the Thoterion.'

'And yet you destroyed it!'

'Not me. No, not me. It was Thakamir. She thet the bookth on fire – I think to thtop me getting them.'

Here, said Cyrus to himself, was a whole new angle on the destruction of the Soterion – and on Sakamir. Feeling himself being drawn into a conversation he didn't want to have just then, he brought the subject back to the matter in hand.

'Even if we did take you and your silent friend,' he said, nodding towards Jinsha, 'the creature who carries around that disgusting head wouldn't be of any use to us. He's not even armed.'

Xsani looked at Giv, standing a little way off with his mouth hanging open like a cave. He had been following the discussion between her and the Constants as best he could, his head swinging back and forth like a donkey's as he focussed on one speaker at a time.

'Giv hath hith utheth,' said Xsani.

'Such as? He could fly like a bird more easily than get us out of here.'

Though Xsani had never heard the phrase before, the image of Giv flying reminded her of the last time they had been lost... Her gaze passed from Cyrus to Giv and on to the dilapidated church spire.

'Can you climb, Giv?' she asked.

Giv stopped swaying and gazed at her. 'Climb?' he echoed.

Xsani pointed at the tottering steeple. 'If you climb to the top of that, Giv, you will be able to thee a way out of the thity.'

'Malika want me up there?'

'Yeth Giv.'

'And Over-Malik Timur?'

'Yeth,' answered Xsani, with a knowing glance in the direction of Cyrus and Miouda.

Giv's expression grew pained. 'But Great Malika and Over-Malik not speak with one voice now,' he wailed, his newly learned grammar abandoning him in his distress. 'Giv not know, Giv not know…'

Twitching his fingers and close to tears, he turned to where Xsani had flung Timur's head the previous evening. 'Timur! he wailed. 'O Mighty Timur!'

'I think,' suggested Xsani, 'if you could get the head…'

Cyrus read her mind. Wondering how on earth he had got himself into a position where he was obeying the wishes of a Zed, he made his way between the rubble and weeds to Timur's battered and barely recognisable skull. He brought it back, stuck the haft of Giv's spear in the ground, and spiked the skull on the other end.

The effect on Giv was extraordinary. He grinned inanely and, muttering a few incantations to the fly-bitten totem, said he would go as high as the clouds if his Malika and his Timur commanded it.

The Constants were fascinated to see what would happen. They untied Giv and got Xsani to explain clearly what he had to do: climb to the top of the crumbling steeple and see if there was a direct route out of the city. As she was speaking, Cyrus realised Xsani's suggestion was cleverer than he had at first realised. If Giv fell to his death, as was likely, a problem would be solved; if he did as he was asked, and came down safely, he would have more than proved his worth.

Giv did not fall. After he had been released, he rubbed his aching limbs and surveyed the ruined stonework rising before him. Spotting a doorway about fifty feet up from the floor, he scrambled towards it like a Long Dead mountaineer. Once there, he disappeared inside the weathered stonework.

The watching crowd gasped in astonishment when, a short time later, he reappeared at the point where the body of the church gave way to the wooden skeleton of the spire. The tiles that originally covered it had blown off long ago, leaving a tapering framework rising to a point several hundred feet above the ground.

Grasping and swinging like a giant monkey, Giv made his way carefully up the decaying scaffold. Several of the cross-beams gave way when he put his weight on them, and their long, clattering fall was a grim reminder of the danger he was in. One slip and he too would crash to the stone floor far below.

Half way up, a rotten slat he was holding on to broke, leaving him hanging in mid-air by one hand. When he managed to swing round and grab a solid beam with his spare hand, a wave of relief ran over those below. Olo let out a little cheer, then clapped her hand over her mouth and blushed with naïve embarrassment.

Cyrus have her a friendly smile. Zed or not, Giv's skill and courage were amazing.

He made it. Holding on to the pinnacle with both arms, as a baby ape clings to its mother, he looked about him like a sailor in the crow's nest of a Long Dead ship. He then shouted something the spectators didn't catch, pointed to the east and began his long, perilous descent. He reached the ground without further mishap and there, to everyone's surprise, he knelt before the Head of Timur and told it that in the direction of the sunrise a long avenue running beside a broad river led directly out of the city.

Giv repeated this information to Xsani. But when Cyrus addressed him directly, asking the best way to reach the avenue from the church, he said not a word. He simply stared open-mouthed at him – or rather through him – as if he did not exist.

Poor Giv! His jumbled, overloaded brain was unable to reconcile his upbringing with the present reality. Timur, his god, hated Cyrus; Malika Xsani, his goddess, was mysteriously attracted to the man.

The two rocks on which Giv's world was founded were in opposition. As they closed in, gradually but inexorably crushing him, he sought desperately for a way out.

The only escape was into humiliating insanity.

17
Once There Was a Tallin Girl

Giv's directions were spot on. Walking at a brisk pace, by the end of the morning the Mission and their captives were well away from the city centre and passing an area of what had once been leafy suburbs. The leaves had taken over long ago, turning the district into a series of small woods interspersed with the broken ruins of villas, shops and ivy-entangled office blocks.

Cyrus would not allow the Zeds to walk together. Xsani, to whom Giv had explained the route, went first. Cyrus kept a pace or two behind her, with Jinsha a few steps back, watched by Miouda and Olo. Sammy and Corby kept an eye on Giv as he loped along at the rear of the column with the Head of Timur once more swinging from his belt.

What a strange procession they were! Constant and Zed, male and female, man and beast. For some time, no one said a word, each wrapped in their own thoughts. Remembered pains and pleasures, present anxieties and future hopes jostled too close for words.

The Mission knew they were taking a tremendous risk by trusting their former enemy, and a popular Tallin cradle song echoed at the back of Cyrus' mind:

Once there was a Tallin girl
And Zeena was her name;
To see what she trusted in,
It really was a shame!
It really was a shame O!
It really was a shame!

Zeena trusted in a man
Whose face was scarréd Zed;
And when they came a-looking
They found that she was dead!
They found that she was dead O!
They found that she was dead!

The rhyme was one of his earliest memories of life in Della Tallis. Like most children born since the Great Death, he had no recollection of his parents. When he was old enough to understand, he was told his father had been killed by Zeds two moons before his birth, and that his mother had entered her Death Month shortly after her son's second birthday.

Events like this were perfectly normal in the post-Great-Death world, and the information had neither shocked nor upset him. Nevertheless, he sometimes wished he knew more about his parents, and could have had their faces and voices in the gallery of his memory.

And one day, because of the Mission, such things would

be possible, wouldn't they? Not for him, of course, but maybe for Miouda's unborn baby. That's why, against the express command of Emir Leiss, he had gone out into the wilderness with Roxanne and his friends. That's why, despite all the pain and suffering, he needed to press on with the Mission and find a way of opening the laptop and learning about the Salvation Project.

Cyrus tried to envisage the world after the Project's completion. The division between Constant and Zed would disappear, and people would live for sixty, seventy, eighty or even more years – almost a century! And what would their lives be like? He imagined the rusted hulks of cars, the crumbling buildings, the fallen wires, and the cracked roads of the suburbs all restored to their original condition. Surrounded by such comfort and luxury, he mused, surely everyone must have had permanent smiles on their faces?

Yet the Soterion books had told him it was not so. Like the Zeds and Constants of his own time, the Long Dead had been warriors. By the end of their time, they had produced armaments powerful enough to destroy the Earth. In a letter left in the Soterion vault, Dr Rebekkah Askar had explained how, in one of their last acts before they died out, the Long Dead had got rid of their weapons.

Cyrus couldn't see why it had needed the Great Death to persuade them to do this.

Rebekkah's words had made such a profound impression on him that he knew them by heart. Fortunately or not, she had written, we were saved from full-scale warfare because governments ordered the destruction of all domestic and military weaponry immediately they saw what was going on.

'Fortunately or not' – what did that mean? Had she really believed it might have been better to destroy the planet than leave it in the hands of those aged eighteen and under?

Cyrus had been surprised by the Long Dead's odd attitude towards young people. For much of their history, when they expected to live no more than thirty or forty years, people shared the same views as the Constants: by their early teenage years, human beings were capable of working and behaving as adults.

However, as the Long Dead's expectation of life increased, they had extended the years of childhood. Cyrus had occasionally found examples of seventeen-year-old men and women referred to as "children"! This struck him as extraordinary and he thought about it a lot.

In the end, he reached two conclusions. First, human beings tended to behave as they were expected to behave or as circumstances required. Because after the Great Death no one lived more than nineteen years, they became adult sooner than when they had lived four times as long.

His second conclusion was that the human species appeared to be changing. He had learned that the process was called "evolution". Now their lives were shorter, people were maturing earlier. It made sense. He had read how the behaviour of some Long Dead teenagers had been like that of nine- or ten-year-old Constants.

'So, Rebekkah, you underestimated us,' said Cyrus to himself.

'What did you thay, Thyruth?'

It was Xsani. Cyrus had been so caught up in his meditations that he had forgotten about her.

'I was talking to myself,' he replied, feeling slightly embarrassed.

She walked on for a while without replying, then asked, 'Who underethtimated uth?'

'Once there was a Tallin girl,' sang Cyrus quietly, 'And Zeena was her name; To see what she trusted in, It really was a shame!'

'I think that ith what ith called a riddle, Thyruth. What do I have to do to perthuade you to trutht me?'

'We will judge you by your actions, not by your words.'

'Aren't I leading you out of the thity of wolveth? Leading you to thafety?'

'Your safety as well as ours, Xsani. Knowing what you have done and how Zeds behave, do you think it'll ever be easy to trust you?'

Checking that the immediate way ahead was clear of obstruction, Xsani looked over her shoulder. A half-smile flickered across her lips. 'I can exthpect nothing from you, Thyruth. But you will thee from my actionth I am not the woman I wath.'

Danger! thought Cyrus. Remember Zeena! 'I'll believe it when I see it,' he muttered. 'And getting us out of this place will be a start.'

Conversation had also sprung up among the second group. It began with Miouda telling Olo about her life in Alba, and how it had changed so dramatically when Timur lied his way into their midst. That was before Cyrus and Roxanne had unlocked the Soterion.

Olo listened open-mouthed as Miouda described the Soterion books and the amazing things they contained. But knowledge is power, warned Miouda. Wicked people like Timur, Yash and Sakamir had been prepared to do anything to get it. That's why she and Cyrus were so wary of Xsani.

'She's told us how she made an alliance with male Zeds and attacked Alba to get at the Soterion, hasn't she?' said Miouda. 'Who knows what she's up to now? Why did she follow us all the way here? She doesn't know about the laptop, but she does know we're on to something very special.'

The face Miouda turned to Olo was deadly serious. 'We have to be so careful. The Soterion is – was – wonderful, but it has brought as much pain as pleasure. It killed Cyrus' friends Roxanne, Taja and Navid – not to mention Timur, Yash, Sakamir and all my people in Alba. Its attraction is truly terrible. It hooks on to people, good and bad; it gets inside their brains and won't let go…'

Olo nodded in the direction of Xsani. 'Her too,' she said. 'I mean getting hooked up in this power thing.'

'Yes, because of her and Yash and Sakamir, we are now refugees. It's a word I learned from Cyrus. He got it from Roxanne,'

'What's it meanin'?'

'A refugee,' explained Miouda, trying to sound like an entry in the Soterion dictionary, 'is a person who for some reason has left their home and cannot return.'

'So I bein' a refugee too,' mused Olo. 'I bin leavin' my people. And I can't be goin' back…' She hesitated and looked at Miouda.

'Yes?'

'I can't be goin' back 'cos I won't be leavin' my Sammy,' she said in a hurry, turning to him as she spoke.

'Good a reason as any,' said Miouda, smiling. 'Bit like me and Cy.'

'And me,' said a barely audible voice.

Miouda and Olo exchanged glances. 'It's Jinsha, isn't it?' Miouda asked.

'What is?'

'Your name.'

'Yes.

'So why did you say "and me", Jinsha? What did you mean?'

The black-haired Zed was even more perplexed than she had been when Xsani announced she was leaving to search for the Man in the Yellow Hat. On their journey, the former Malika had explained how she was torn between the Zed values of her tribe and what she believed were the values of the previous civilization. These had been explained to her by Sakamir, who had picked them up from her classes with Cyrus.

Sakamir had thought like a Zed. She craved the Long Dead's technological muscle but rejected their morality. Xsani had begun to think differently. She sensed a mysterious link between the images she had seen of the Man in the Yellow Hat and the values Sakamir had rejected. Gradually, she had found herself doubting her hostile attitude towards Constants. If the Soterion was such a rich prize, the civilization that had set it up must be equally precious. And the Constant way of life was an attempt to preserve that civilization's values.

The Zeds, especially the males, had nothing but contempt for such thinking. Timur expressed their position most clearly. One had only to look around, he said, to see that the world before the Great Death had failed. He did not understand the medical reasons for its collapse, and he would have had no interest even if they had been explained to him.

He said it was obvious why the Long Dead had died out. They were feeble and soft. Like the Constants, they hadn't seen that the only things that really mattered were power and pleasure. Everything else was laughable weakness.

Having discussed all these things with Xsani, Jinsha understood them in theory. But faced with reality, she was confused. She still had to stop herself flinching when she saw a man unchained. Although the Kogon kept a handful of male captives for reproductive purposes, a dumbman Zed meant just two things to them: stupidity and rape. Such men were to be avoided at all costs. As the unfortunate Tarangala had shown, death – even suicide – was preferable to capture.

Non-Zed males were little better. Jinsha's only contact with them had been the ambushing of Constant patrols to capture women as teachers for the Kogon elite. Heavily outnumbered, these men fought well – much better than their Zed counterparts – but in the end they were always killed.

And here Jinsha was, with one man in front of her and two behind. True, only Giv – now hardly a man at all – had a Z brand. But the other two, the ones they called Cyrus and Sammy, were at liberty and therefore potentially dangerous.

When they left the church, Jinsha had worried that the

Constants planned to let the Zeds lead them out of the city before killing Giv and making herself and Xsani their breeding slaves. To her astonishment, she now saw that their captors didn't have, or even want, slaves for breeding. The relationship between male and female Constants was similar to hers with Xsani: warm and friendly. It didn't make sense. Everything she had believed about men and women, Constant and Zed, had been turned on its head.

That is why, when Olo said she couldn't leave her Sammy, it struck a chord in Jinsha's heart. In response to Miouda asking why she had said 'and me', Jinsha confessed she was here, far from her tribe and the way of life she knew, because she could not leave her Xsani.

'I understand,' smiled Miouda.

Jinsha was so shocked by this response that she stopped, her face a mask of incredulity.

Olo gripped her spear more tightly.

'What did you say, Miouda?'

'I said that I understand. I know how powerful the feelings are between two people. Like Cyrus and myself – like you and Xsani. They are sometimes stronger than death, aren't they?'

Jinsha had no words with which to reply. Wiping away tears with the back of her hand, she turned and set off in the footsteps of her leader and lover. Stronger than death? How could this Constant know? It was impossible for the bonds between a man and a woman to be as close as those between herself and Xsani!

To her surprise, she looked up to find Miouda and Olo had lowered their spears and were walking beside her.

'Olo and I have been talking,' said Miouda. 'We have decided to trust you. There's so much to discuss, isn't there?'

Jinsha nodded.

'Right. Let me begin by putting a question to you: what's it like growing up as a Zed? I mean, did you ever think, just once, that there might be ways of doing things without killing and violence…?'

Further back, noticing Miouda chatting earnestly with Jinsha and Olo, Sammy thought he'd see what Giv had to say for himself.

'You like being a Zed, eh?' he asked, staring at the grizzly head swinging down by Giv's knees and wondering why on earth the young man was so attached to it.

There was no reply. Giv was not being deliberately rude or obstructive; he simply did not know Sammy was addressing him, or what the question meant.

Sammy tried again. 'Giv, do you like being a Zed? You know, having that tattoo thing and running around trying to kill everyone?'

Giv had been raised in the Grozny tribe under the command of Timur the Terrible. Continual physical and mental abuse had so battered and crushed the sensitive side of his nature that he ceased to recognise it. For thirteen years, his life had been ruled by pain and occasional animal pleasures.

Yet within his tortured soul, a tiny flower of sensitivity somehow survived the poison and drought of his upbringing. It showed itself in his total adoration of his Malik, not because Giv found the man adorable but because he longed for approval and affection. When Timur gave him even the slightest nod of

204

appreciation, his whole existence had brightened.

This explained why Giv had cut the head from Timur's corpse and carried it with him – it was a bizarre attempt to keep the man's spirit alive. When Xsani saw the possibilities of the head and had it preserved, Giv's worship of Timur naturally expanded to embrace her. In all this, as Xsani herself perceived, there was more than a hint of insanity.

There was another force at work, however. Praise from someone as ruthless as the Malika was praise indeed. Yet a voice inside Giv's skull whispered that there was more to Xsani than intelligence and cruelty. Though she showed it differently from him, he sensed that she too longed for human warmth. He revered her because, like Cyrus and Miouda, he sensed her inner vulnerability.

So when Sammy asked Giv what it was like being a Zed, what could he reply? To him, being a Zed meant pleasing Timur and Xsani. And now one of them was banging feebly against his thigh and the other was conversing with Constants. Her kumfort Jinsha was doing the same, too.

'Giv good Zed,' he muttered, reverting to the broken speech of his tribe. 'Timur say Giv fine Zed.'

Sammy was about to reply when Giv untied the head from his belt and held it out in front of him. 'Mighty Timur,' he intoned, 'what is Zed?'

To Sammy's astonishment, he replied to his own question in the harsh tones of Timur. 'Shrewdug wormbrain!' he screamed. 'Such a slugthought question! You know what Zeds are! Zeds are the future, Zeds are the mighty—'

Focussing on the head rather than where he was going, Giv

tripped on a kerbstone and fell to the ground. The filthy skull spilled from his grasp and rolled into the weeds.

Instead of getting up, Giv lay there moaning. 'Have mercy on Giv, Mighty Timur!' he cried. 'Have mercy on miserable Giv!'

Sammy put out a hand to help him up. 'Come on, nutcase! You can't lie there all day!'

Giv struggled reluctantly to his feet. As he went to retrieve the Head, Sammy called out to the rest of the Mission, 'Hang on a bit! Got a problem with the steeple-climber!'

At the front of the column, Xsani looked back. 'I am not sure Giv ith going to be much more help to uth,' she said. 'He ith too mad now, ithn't he?'

'Yes, you may be right,' said Cyrus. 'But what are going to do with him?'

Giv himself solved the problem. Two days later, the mission camped in a grove outside a large villa and, as on previous nights, they tied up their prisoners. But when Sammy went to check on them the next morning, Giv had disappeared. The Head of Timur was also missing.

The eccentric Grozny, devoted disciple of Timur the Terrible, had somehow managed to slip his bonds and creep away noiselessly into the night. He had not tried to free Xsani or Jinsha, both of whom said they had no foreknowledge of his escape. Questioned further, they admitted they had no idea why or where he had gone.

For a week or so, the Constants kept watch by night in case he tried to rescue his two former allies. When nothing happened, they concluded that poor, mad Giv had run off with his precious Head to die alone in the wilderness.

18
Itzac

On leaving the city, the road ran for many miles through rich tropical farmland. In the time of the Long Dead it had been divided into large estates, each with a cluster of cottages, barns and villas at its heart. The fields were now wildly overgrown and the buildings either burned-out shells or skeletons strangled by encroaching vegetation. Yet again, to their intense disappointment, the Mission failed to locate a single serviceable solar panel.

At the end of the third day, their spirits rose when they encountered a different type of settlement. Stoutly defended by a high concrete wall, the only access was through a broad archway closed by a pair of barred steel gates. Above them the word Itzac was carved into the stonework.

The wall and doors were in surprisingly good condition, suggesting they had been carefully maintained until quite recently. Although the main house was hidden, the top of a tall brick tower was visible near the centre of the compound.

On its sloping roof was a large solar panel. Apart from bird droppings, it appeared to be in good shape.

Cyrus and Miouda checked that Giv was not lurking in the vicinity, and toured the wall to see if there was a second way in. Not finding one, they discussed their next move. The villa and its compound were strangely quiet, which told them there were no male Zeds inside. When Xsani assured them that female Zeds wouldn't settle in such an exposed spot either, the only remaining possibility was that Itzac was, or had been, some sort of Constant stronghold.

Cyrus asked Xsani and Jinsha to keep well out of sight as he walked up to the entrance. 'Hello?' he shouted, hammering loudly on the gates. 'Hello! Anyone there?'

His words echoed hollowly around the compound: 'Hell-oo… hell-oo… hell-oo…!' When repeated calls brought no response, he decided either Itzac was empty or those inside were dead, deaf or too sick to talk. Whichever it was, the Mission were going in.

Easier said than done. None of them had the skill or experience necessary to scale the smooth wall. Miouda proposed throwing up a hook attached to a rope and climbing up it. The idea was dropped when, after an hour's search, they discovered neither hook nor rope. Sammy cheekily suggested throwing a bone over the wall.

'What is that doin', Sam?' asked Olo.

'Well, I reckon Corby likes his bones so much he'd dig a tunnel, and we could use it to get in.' Recalling how he had smuggled the Mission out of the Gova settlement, he added in a more serious tone, 'What I mean is, we could dig a tunnel, couldn't we?'

'Last resort,' said Cyrus. 'Simpler to get over the top – if we can think of a way.' He looked at the wall again, running his eye from top to bottom. 'Must be at least as tall as three of us.'

'If I stood on you, and Olo stood on me, she could just reach the top,' quipped Sammy.

The remark was not as daft as it sounded. If they worked as a team, they could probably lift someone to the top. It was a big 'if', and would mean Constants and Zeds not only working together but also touching each other, something they had avoided so far. Talking was one thing, but physical contact…

'We are all on thith journey, aren't we Thyruth?' said Xsani. 'You thaid you would judge me by my actionth, not my wordth. Tho here ith an action.'

Before anyone could stop her, she took two quick steps forward, grabbed Cyrus' hand and held it fast. 'You thee? I do not poithon you, I do not thtab you, I do not make you thick. When we came out of our motherth, Thyruth, neither of uth had a Z tattoo. We were born the thame. If we remember that, we can cooperate, surely?'

This startling episode marked a significant turning point in the Mission's history. Trust, previously weighed down by a heavy cloak of suspicion, from this point onwards began to grow into an understanding that would eventually blossom into friendship.

They scaled the wall using what Cyrus later called the 'pyramid of comrades'. It was not easily achieved and to start with, as well as a good many laughs, it led to a few sharp words, scrapes and bruises.

The arrangement that finally worked saw Cyrus, Miouda and Jinsha locking arms and standing together two feet from the wall. On to their shoulders climbed Sammy and Olo, each with one hand resting on the wall and the other holding on to their partner's waist. Xsani, the lightest of the group, then clambered up to stand on Sammy and Olo's shoulders. From here she could just reach the top of the wall and haul herself up.

Perched on the parapet and gazing down at those below, she was briefly a Malika again. She was at the top, in charge and all-powerful; everyone looked up to her. The moment passed as quickly as it had arisen, and she hurried round the walkway and down the steps into the inner courtyard. She slid back the steel bar that fastened the gates and let in everyone else.

Working as a group, they cautiously explored the villa and its outbuildings. The features they had noticed from the outside were the same inside: everything was in relatively good order but there was not a living soul to be seen. Nor were there any signs of the sort of violence that would have followed a Zed break-in. Itzac appeared simply to have been abandoned.

In the centre of the courtyard stood a well of clean water, and the hand pump that lifted it to the surface still worked. A few of the beds in the dormitories had animal skins and blankets on them. They even found some dried meat hanging in a storeroom where the ants hadn't been able to get at it. Though it was no longer edible because of a covering of green mould, Cyrus reckoned it couldn't have been there for more than ten years.

'So what happened?' he asked when they had finished

checking out the place. 'Where did everyone go? And when they went, how did they close the gates behind them?'

'Maybe the place got too small, and they decided to move on to somewhere bigger?' said Miouda, thinking how her baby would mean they'd have another mouth to feed.

'And the closed gates?'

'Maybe some of them chose to stay?'

'So where are they now?'

'I don't know, Cy! Jumped off the wall? Carried away by eagles?'

'They may thtill be here but we have not found them,' said Xsani quietly. She was wary of joining in a Constant conversation uninvited.

As it turned out, she was correct. Two days later, searching one of the barns for dry firewood, Olo noticed a sweet, rather unpleasant smell coming from the corner furthest from the door. One look was enough. The remains of two bodies lay a couple of feet apart. Near the outstretched hand of one of them lay a rusty blade. A fight? A suicide pact? It was impossible to tell and, so long after the event, of no great importance. Nevertheless, once Olo had shut and barred the door, none of the Mission ever went in there again.

Of much greater significance was the discovery that, while the settlement's electrical gadgetry had long since ceased to work, the solar panel on top of the tower still functioned. After Sammy and Olo had cleaned off the bird muck, Cyrus sent the Zeds out of the tower. He reckoned it best if at this stage they did not learn what the laptop contained, or how to operate it.

When all was ready, they connected up the cable, flicked on

the switch, and waited. As before, the slight whirring sound, the pinprick of blue light spreading across the screen, the booting-up message – and then the voice! This time it did not cut out, and spoken words appeared simultaneously on the screen. Mesmerised, the Mission stood listening as they were told that the computer's data was in two parts. Part One contained electronic versions of the books in the Soterion vault – and hundreds of others. Part Two was the information provided by the international scientists working on the Salvation Project. The team had been 'almost there' said the voice – perhaps only a month away from producing a cure for the Mini-Flu.

'A month!' gasped Cyrus. 'One short month away!'

'Shh!' hissed Miouda, taking hold of his arm. 'There's more.'

'As you may not have operated a computer before,' continued the voice, 'I will instruct you how to use it.'

The use of 'I' sent Cyrus' brain whirling. This was a person talking to them – they were listening to the Long Dead! It was eerie, almost frightening, and he wanted to speak back to the machine.

A few minutes later, he found he could.

Having explained about the touchpad and the keys, how to pause and turn the machine off and start it without the welcome messages, the instructions moved on to voice recognition. The software was programmed to store three voices, it said, so would the operator please select which three these would be.

Miouda pressed "Pause" on the keyboard. 'Cyrus and…?' she asked.

'You,' answered Sammy.

'No,' said Cyrus firmly.

'Why not Miouda? She's the eldest after you, Cyrus, and she's the cleverest.'

'That's not what I meant,' said Cyrus. 'I meant not me.'

His remark was greeted with gasps of astonishment. 'But you're our leader,' said Sammy. 'Without you we wouldn't be nothing!'

Cyrus smiled. 'Anything,' he corrected. 'Think about it carefully, Sammy. I'm the leader, yes, but I'm also the oldest. There isn't much of my life left—'

'But that project thing the voice was talking about – the Salvation Project – one month's work and you'll be able to live as long as the Long Dead. For ever!'

'If only, Sammy. The people working on the Project must have had years of education. Just as we don't know how to fight properly until we've been trained, they wouldn't know how to discover a cure until they'd been trained.'

'Unless it was something really simple, like eating a certain kind of plant,' said Miouda.

'Yes, that's possible,' said Cyrus, 'but it's not very likely, is it? We've got to educate ourselves, learn about the Salvation Project, then find some Constants willing to take us in... It'll take a long time – and time's something I don't have. So I suggest the machine learns the voices of Miouda, Sammy and Olo. Ok?'

Hard though the decision was, the others knew it made sense.

The next question was how far to trust the Zeds. Jinsha, while uncommunicative, did not worry them as much as Xsani. For all her smiles, friendly talk and cooperation, they couldn't forget her murderous ambition. She was closer than ever to what she had wanted, and hadn't so much as lifted a spear. It was either fiendishly clever manoeuvring on her part or a genuine change of heart. Having watched her closely for several days, they were strongly inclined to believe the latter. But they had to be absolutely certain.

Early the next morning, Miouda woke Xsani with terrible news. Jinsha was missing. Worse still, she appeared to have run off during the night and taken the laptop with her.

Xsani was too stunned to speak. Miouda led her across the courtyard, pointing to the open gates on the way, and entered the room in the tower where the computer had been kept. The plug and lead remained, but the machine itself had gone. Cyrus, Sammy and Olo, faces grim as night, were staring at the table on which it had rested.

'And we trusted you,' said Cyrus angrily as Xsani entered.

She stared at him, hollow-eyed. 'Jintha,' she whispered, her bottom lip quivering.

'Jinsha?' shouted Cyrus. 'Is that all you can think about? Can't you see what she's done? It's gone! She's ruined everything! Everything!'

Trembling with pent-up emotion, Xsani groaned, 'Yeth, you are right, Thyruth. She hath ruined everything. Everything in my life. Do you think I care about your thtupid machine or about your thtupid Thoterion?'

'Stupid?' cried Cyrus.

'Yeth, thtupid! I have lotht the only thing that really mattered to me. Oh Jintha! Jintha! How could you do thith to me?' Tears flowed freely down her scarred, crumpled face.

'Do you mean to say,' said Cyrus angrily, 'that you care more about the loss of Jinsha than about the loss of the computer, our one hope of learning the powers of the Long Dead?'

'Of courthe!' she sobbed. 'Of courthe!'

Cyrus went over to her and, despite her protests, wrapped his arms about her. 'I am so, so sorry, Xsani,' he said. 'But we had to be sure.'

As he was speaking, Miouda slipped out to get the laptop. The result of the test they had devised for Xsani had been a double relief for her, and she smiled happily to herself. Though she was sure the former Malika cared for love and personal loyalty above all else, Cyrus' reaction was even more reassuring. She had never been completely certain that, if put to the test, he would share the values Xsani had expressed. Now she knew. However obsessed Cyrus was with the Mission, he had shown that in the end he would always be there for her.

When Xsani saw the laptop, she let out another groan. 'Tho she didn't take it! She jutht left me.'

'No, she didn't,' said Sammy, leading Jinsha into the room.

After Olo had unfastened the young Zed's gag, she moved hesitantly nearer her beloved Malika. 'They kept me prisoner,' she said quietly.

As Cyrus released Xsani, Miouda stepped forward and grasped the two Zeds by the hand. 'I beg you to forgive us,' she said, looking earnestly at each of them in turn. 'Believe me, it was the only thing we could think of to be absolutely certain.'

Xsani put her head in her hands. She took a deep breath and exhaled very slowly. 'You have theen into the deepetht thentre of my heart,' she said, wiping her face with her sleeve.

'I underthtand why you did it, but pleathe never, ever do anything like that again.'

'We won't,' said Cyrus. 'I promise. From now on there is one Mission of six people. No Constants, no Zeds. Just friends and comrades.'

And so it was.

What was this thing the Grozny guards had hauled before Kamal, the self-styled Malik Big Aye?

It had the shape of a man, but with one arm extended to a sort of swinging club. It wore no clothes, and the dry and wrinkled skin was a mass of weals, sores, cuts and abrasions. It didn't appear able to speak, either, but emitted high-pitched rasping noises from a dark hole in its face.

Kamal was about to order it to be killed and thrown out of the camp, when he examined the face more carefully. There was something vaguely familiar about it, but he couldn't remember exactly what.

'Stab and cook on spit?' asked the Grozny guard who had captured the thing.

'No!' growled Kamal, staring at the creature more intently now. Was it trying to speak? That hole where the sound was coming from… Yes, it was a mouth. So the scabby, broken projection above it must be the nose. That meant those two bleary discs near the top were the eyes.

What was it about that face? he wondered. He shifted his gaze to the legs and the two arms, one longer than the other. No, wait! The club-like thing at the end of the longer arm wasn't a club at all. It was… it was…

Kamal leaned forward to get a better look. Yes, it was a human head – the Head!

In a flash of inspiration, Kamal realised what he was staring at. It was Giv, the sometime Malik of the Grozny Zeds who had disappeared when the Kogon flabtoads sneaked out of Alba. And in his hand he held what Kamal had been seeking ever since he took command of the tribe: the living Head of the Mighty Over-Malik Timur. Incredible!

Confused thoughts darted through Kamal's wily brain. The return of the Head was a great moment, and if he killed Giv before anyone saw who he was, Malik Big Aye would become the prestigious new Guardian of the Over-Malik. But could he speak as Timur did, as Giv did? And what if someone recognised Giv's body? Were he to let Giv live, might the miserable wretch not reclaim command of the Grozny and condemn him as a usurper?

In the end, Kamal decided to save Giv's life. As flabtoad prisoners were nursing their patient back to physical health, feeding him with liquids and tending to his many injuries, Malik Big Aye Kamal raised the Head of Timur on a spear spike once more and made it clear that he was responsible for restoring their great leader and inspiration.

The claim was never challenged. What little sanity Giv possessed before he set out on his epic solo journey from Itzac had now deserted him. When talking, he either adopted the shrill tones of Timur or gabbled incoherently about crossing rivers and mountains, fighting off wolves, and wrestling with bone-crushing snakes in the jungle.

Kamal managed to salvage two important facts from the

stream of nonsensical babble. One, the cheating flabtoad bitch Xsani had betrayed them and run off with the Head. Two, Giv, who had rescued the Head and now made the journey twice, would be willing to guide the Grozny to the traitorous Malika.

So it was that, two weeks later, the entire Grozny tribe packed up its few possessions, chained together its flabtoad breeders, and set out behind the Head of Timur the Terrible on the longest journey in its history.

The goal was simple – bloody and merciless revenge.

19
Corby's Nose

The Mission began exploring the world inside the laptop, happily unaware that a murderous horde was hell-bent on exterminating them. Miouda soon got the hang of operating the software, and the first time she and Cyrus were alone they skipped the digitalised books and information and went straight to the Salvation Project section.

'Here we go,' said Cyrus eagerly as the title "Part Two: The Salvation Project" appeared on the screen. He glanced at Miouda and smiled. 'Four weeks for a cure for the Mini-Flu,' he said. 'Just four weeks!'

'Careful, Cy. Remember what you said. They were experts. We're only... Well, we know almost nothing!'

'No matter. We can learn. Anyway, let's see what it says!'

The heading was followed by a Note of Introduction:

Please find below the results of the research conducted by the International Research Project of Qatar (IRPoQ) into the behaviour of Influenza Strain IBN-398B, commonly known as Mini-Flu.

This research had identified the DNA-altering characteristics of IBN-398B and was close to producing an effective vaccine. Tragically, all those working on the project succumbed to premature death before their work was finished.

Shortly before her demise, Professor Eugenie De La Mar, the last surviving member of the IRPoQ team, collated her colleagues' findings and presented them to Dr Rebekkah Askar for inclusion in the Soterion vault.

The IRPoQ findings are presented below in two formats: (a) the original material as emailed by Professor De La Mar; (b) a simplified version for those with little scientific training.

Important: The simplified version of the IRPoQ's work will enable those able to read and write, but with a minimum of formal education, to complete the Project and produce an effective vaccine against IBN-398B. For students in this category, we recommend the following three-year programme:

Familiarise yourself with the contents of the digital encyclopedia in Part One of the computer's memory.

Follow the step-by-step courses in Chemistry and Medical Biology that follow this note.

Using the knowledge acquired in steps 1 and 2 above, complete the work of IRPoQ – and produce a vaccine for the disease that has destroyed our civilization.

Good luck!

'Understand it, Cy?' asked Miouda when they had finished reading.

'More or less,' he replied solemnly. 'Not sure about "international", "emailed" and "Chemistry", but I get the gist of it.'

'Me too. It's what the Long Dead called bittersweet, isn't it?' She gave him a long, sorrowful look before stating what they were both thinking. 'It's going to take too long for you – and for me.'

He leaned over and kissed her. 'I knew it would be for me – but you… I'm sorry. So sorry.'

'But three years won't be too long for our baby,' she said, brightening. 'Nor for Sammy, Olo and Jinsha.'

'Nor for all the hundreds and thousands who come after us as they rebuild the civilization of the Long Dead.' He tapped the side of the laptop. 'With this,' he went on, 'we're going to change the world, Miouda my love. Starting now!'

'Here?'

'Why not? At least in Itzac we've got electricity. We'll stay here until everyone can read really well and we've gone through some of the encyclopedia, then we'll find a Constant settlement and spread the word among them, like we were doing in Alba.'

'Yes, but we can't wait here too long, Cy. The baby… And you, as you said…'

'I know, I know.' He jumped up and called the others to join them. 'No time to lose, eh?'

'Cyrus,' she smiled, placing a hand on her stomach as she rose carefully to her feet.

'Yes?'

'You're incorrigible.'

He frowned. 'What's that mean?'

'Not sure. But I read it in a book talking about someone like you, and I liked the word.'

'Ok, as long as you're not calling me a loser.'

'I'm not. The opposite, in fact.'

The Mission established a daily routine. It began with one of the Constants giving reading lessons to Olo and the two Zeds while the remaining two, with Corby bounding along beside them, left the compound to forage for food.

After breakfast, when they were all sitting in front of the laptop, Miouda turned it on – and they immersed themselves in an experience beyond anything they had ever imagined. Like fallen leaves, they were swept up by the astonishing collage of sounds and moving images and carried away to the lost world of their ancestors.

Rather than try to take in the whole of the enormous encyclopedia from A to Z, they each chose an area of interest. The original plan was to finish a topic in a day, but there were so many optional videos and sound clips – and they insisted on playing every one – that they ended up spending a week on each subject.

Walking through the City of Wolves, as they called it, they had tried to imagine the buildings, the cars, the streets, the shops, and the people before the Great Death. Now, when Cyrus chose Cities as the first encyclopedia topic, they could actually see those things. Hear them, too. One of the biggest differences between their world and the world of the Long Dead was noise. The Mission were accustomed to a background of birdsong. The city soundscape of the Old World, with its constant cacophony of cars, lorries, hooters, sirens, bells, and aeroplanes, was both thrilling and unsettling.

Sammy wondered how anyone managed to think or even make themselves heard amid all that din. He said it was like two Givs screaming in Timur voices at the same time, one in each ear.

Olo and Jinsha, sitting side by side, kept begging Miouda to freeze the video clips so they could get a better look at the people. 'They're bein' enormous!' laughed Olo. 'Fat and flabby like the Safids. Yuk!'

'And quite a lot of them seems half-dead, like in their Death Month,' exclaimed the horrified Jinsha.

Xsani smiled. 'That'th what happened in thothe dayth, my dear. Death did not come quickly, ath it doeth with uth. The Long Dead grew old very, very thlowly, tho they lived for yearth and yearth and yearth.'

The two younger women nodded. 'Was that good, my Malika?' asked Jinsha. 'I mean, they don't look very happy to be living so long.'

'But we would be, wouldn't we, my dearetht Jintha? Together for ever – almotht!'

That would be lovely, Jinsha agreed. Nevertheless, she and Olo were unsettled by images of elderly people shambling slowly towards their end.

Olo chose Music as her topic. The rest of group had heard the crude band that played at Yash's coronation, and all the Constants had learned simple songs such as Cyrus' nursery rhyme. But they knew only drums and human voices. So when music of some sort accompanied almost every item on the computer, the sounds fascinated them. Olo was eager to learn more.

It took them six days to finish the encyclopedia article. Miouda and Sammy, the two controlling voices, were so often asked to repeat sections that in the end they gave up and let it run without stopping. They said those who wanted could listen again when there was time.

There never was time.

The article began by saying what music was and giving a brief history of its development. Next it presented the vast range of instruments, from the accordion (Olo's favourite) to the zither. This was followed by a complicated section on how music was written down. To the Mission, the script was like tadpoles dancing on wires.

The final part contained a selection of full-length works. There was an Aboriginal Australian playing a didgeridoo; dancing bands from Nigeria, Sri Lanka and China; a New Orleans jazz band; a series of pop videos as bewildering as they were enthralling, and an incomprehensible opera in Italian. Finally, as night closed in and the room was lit by the flickering screen and the gleams of a tropical moon, the air trembled to the ominous opening beats of Beethoven's Fifth Symphony. The Mission, who earlier that day had been up on their feet dancing, instinctively drew closer to each other. What, they wondered, was this dark, menacing music trying to tell them?

Eventually, Cyrus spoke. 'It's a warning,' he whispered. 'I have felt it inside me all along, and now I know it's true. It's telling us that Giv is coming back.'

Miouda, startled by a side of Cyrus she had not seen before, shivered and switched off the computer before the end of the first movement. No one objected. Wrapping their arms around their partners, the three couples retired into the night without saying a word.

Next morning, Cyrus made light of his remark. It was the effect of the gloomy music and the darkness, he said. Of course Giv wouldn't return. Even if he did, what could he do on his own? It would be impossible for him to find the Grozny and persuade them to accompany him to Itzac.

'Sorry,' he concluded. 'I got carried away. We're as secure here as anywhere.'

Olo, Miouda and Sammy agreed. But Xsani and Jinsha, who understood the power of Timur's preserved head better than any of them, were less sure. To be on the safe side, they asked Cyrus to organise Alba-style weapons training every morning. A precaution, they said. As the experiences of the last year had shown, no one could be sure what the future held.

Jinsha's topic was what the Long Dead called Geography, and the Mission were soon spellbound. They knew about the areas where they had lived and through which they had travelled, but none of them had seen the sea. Olo and the two former Zeds had never even heard of it. Without exception, they were astounded by images of vast expanses of water, sometimes calm and blue, sometimes surging in green-black anger.

Once they understood the shape of the continents and oceans, they spent a long time trying to work out where Itzac was. Because of the climate, they knew it must be somewhere in the band around the middle of the Earth known as the tropics. But when they added in the features they had come across – the arid uplands, the green valleys, the soaring mountains with snow on their peaks, and the dense forests, they became more and more confused.

Xsani suggested it might be Australia, Miouda India, while Sammy and Olo were sure they were in Oman. 'Let's face it,' concluded Cyrus, 'we could be almost anywhere.'

He was right. There were dozens of rivers that might be the No-Man and hundreds of cities like the City of Wolves. Road signs, in the rare cases where they had not corroded away or been covered by vegetation, had meant little to them, and they had made no effort to memorise them. The only exception was Highway 24, along which the Mission had travelled on the way to Alba, but a quick search showed almost every country had a road numbered 24.

The concept of a "country" was itself a bit of a problem. Having grown up in nomadic tribes or settlements of a few hundred people, it was hard for the Mission to imagine a world divided into blocks of land, large and small, each with its own government and customs.

'With all the clever ways they had of keeping in touch, it would have been much easier if they'd had just one country,' mused Sammy.

"Frontiers" was another in the growing list of topics they had difficulty grasping. The more they learned about the Long Dead, the more aware the Mission became of their own ignorance. If anything, the suggested three years of study needed to understand the Salvation Project and its background was an underestimate. Economics, for instance, was an undecipherable mystery. What was "money" and what was the point of it? How did "industry" operate? Why were some people described as wearing blue collars and others white? And what on earth were "salaries" and "GDP"?

In contrast, the Environment section made much more sense to them. For over a century, they had lived close to nature and had learned to respect it. They had names for most birds, animals, insects and plants, and knew which were good to eat and which were dangerous. They foretold the weather from the sky, and the seasons from the sun. As their remote hunter-gatherer ancestors had been, they were an integral part of the natural world.

The lifestyle and many of the attitudes of the Long Dead shocked them. Using a word that made every Kogon shudder, Jinsha expressed it most forcibly. 'You know,' she said, after they had watched a short film entitled Global Warming: The Environmental Crisis, 'they were raping the planet. Like dumbman Zeds, they were all take, take, take.'

Cyrus considered for a minute. 'What do you think would have happened if there had been no Great Death?' he asked, speaking more to himself than anyone in particular.

'Too many greedy people, not enough Earth,' said Xsani.

Miouda looked at her and nodded. 'It's almost as if… No, that's a silly idea,' she concluded, leaving her thought unspoken. She would remember it later, when she was with people who had reached the same conclusion.

The Grozny Zeds did not share the Mission's harmonious view of nature. Indeed, as the newly-formed Itzac community was learning about the perils of deforestation, Kamal's men were engaged in a bit of jungle clearing of their own.

Guided by Giv, who led the way from the comfort of a covered chair, they had traversed the arid region to the east of Alba, hacked their way through the Tiger Forest, crossed the No-Man by the bridge Xsani had used, and were now chopping and slashing a broad swathe through the undergrowth towards the distant hills occupied by the Murax.

Progress was slow and painful. They had lost all their horses and all but two of their dogs. Several breeding slaves, children and fully-grown warriors had also perished, some from snakebites and others from energy-sapping fevers. So eager was Malik Big Aye Kamal to reach his goal that he argued that his losses were actually a benefit.

'Weak men and flabtoads die,' he growled, pulling a bloodsucking leech from his calf and crushing it beneath his foot. 'Only strong live – Grozny now powenful, more powenful.'

Giv supported Kamal's frantic advance every step of the way. 'On, parrotheaded snakebrains!' he screeched. 'On to kill the vermin that dare insult the mighty Over-Malik! They must die! Do this in remembrance of me!'

He concluded every rant by leading the branded vandals in their infamous war cry: 'Zed blood! Zed blood! Kill! Kill! Kill!'

Up and down the sweating line it echoed, 'Zed blood! Zed blood! Kill! Kill! Kill! Zed blood! Zed blood! Kill! Kill! Kill!'

'I've chosen Biology,' said Miouda as she switched on the laptop.

Olo looked blank. 'Why you choosin' that one, Miouda?' she asked. 'What is it?'

'It's all about your body, Olo,' Miouda replied cheerfully. 'And mine – and everyone's. We can't understand the Salvation Project until we know what the Long Dead called 'Science', and Biology is part of Science. It's how bodies work, how they reproduce, what causes diseases and, I hope, how they can be cured.'

Olo glanced quizzically at Sammy. 'This "reproduce" is havin' babies, yes?'

'Yes, that's right.'

'Ah! Sammy and I ain't doin' it.'

'Good. One baby is enough until we find a Constant settlement to care for us. But I still want to know what's going on inside me. Don't you?'

Olo was not sure. 'I am understandin' a bit,' she said hesitatingly.

'So am I. But I want to know a whole lot more,' said Miouda as she set the programme running.

Within five minutes, Olo was waving her hand in the air and crying, 'Stop! Stop! I am wantin' to see that bit again.' She turned to Jinsha. 'I was never knowin' women was like that, was you Jinsh?'

Jinsha shook her head. 'Amazing!'

That was the reaction of them all, even those who had picked up a little Biology from the Soterion library. Their knowledge had previously been a curious mix of scientific fact and myth. They knew eating a balanced diet made them feel better, for instance, but they had no understanding of vitamins, proteins, carbohydrates, or the body's nutritional needs. Similarly, as all creatures did, they knew the external mechanics of reproduction by instinct but were clueless about what went on inside.

Many myths were dispelled over the next five days, and the attitude of the Mission towards their bodies – and what they put into them – underwent a change. This had an unintended and extremely important consequence.

Early one morning, while Sammy was conducting a literacy lesson, Cyrus, Miouda and Corby went off foraging for food. Their new dietary knowledge made them more particular than they had been, and searching for something new to eat, they wandered further from home than usual. While they were climbing a steep slope set about with exotic trees and creepers, Cyrus noticed Corby sniffing suspiciously at the breeze blowing in their faces.

'What is it, old boy?' he enquired, tightening the grip on his spear in case the dog sensed danger. 'Come on, show us!'

Corby, ears twitching and head held high, scampered to the top of the hill. There he stood, nose wrinkling, staring in the direction of the sunrise. The Constants screwed up their eyes against the glare and followed the direction of his look.

Below them, the lush green swathe stretched away for mile after mile. Just short of the horizon, it gave way to a smudge of yellow. Beyond that, a patch of light blue melted imperceptibly into the darker hues of the sky. Heavy clouds foretold an approaching storm.

'What's Corby got the scent of?' asked Miouda.

Cyrus' mind went back to a video they had seen. 'I think,' he said slowly, his gaze sweeping the line between Earth and sky, 'I think he can smell the sea.'

'You mean that pale blue out there?'

'Yes. It could be the sea, or ocean, or whatever it's called, couldn't it?'

'Maybe. But if it is, what's that dark shape on it?'

'Shape?'

'Yes, there.' She stretched out an arm, pointing. 'It seems to be moving.'

Cyrus put his head close to her shoulder and followed the line of her finger. 'Oh yes! You're right, it is moving. Looks too big to be a fish…'

He was interrupted by a rumble of thunder, and moments later the distant vision disappeared beneath a blanket of cloud and rain. Hurrying to get back to Itzac before the storm struck, they gave little thought to what they had seen. But that evening, when they were alone together, Miouda again asked about the dark shape gliding over the water.

'Do you think it was some sort of shadow, Cy?'

'I only got a glimpse before the storm came in. It might have been the shadow of a cloud. On the other hand…'

'You know what I'm thinking, don't you?' she said eagerly.

'Yes. It was probably a boat. And if it was, it means that somewhere, not too far away…'

'… is a settlement of Constants!'

They lay there in the darkness, hand in hand, momentarily wrapped up in their own thoughts. Eventually Miouda whispered, 'Cy?'

'Yes?'

'We need to go and find them, don't we?'

'Those boat people? Yes. We need help for you and the baby.'

Relief swept over her. Although Cyrus had talked of needing to move on at some stage, she knew how difficult it would be for him to leave Itzac and its precious power supply.

She pressed him to be more specific. 'When shall we go? Tomorrow?'

He hesitated. 'Too soon. We need to plan. We might even take the panel with us. Let's wait until we've seen Sammy and Xsani's topics, then decide. Won't be more than about ten days.'

Ten days, she said to herself. I can wait that long. Smiling to herself, she closed her eyes and allowed the gentle drumming of the rain to lull her to sleep.

In the mountains above the City of Wolves, the same rain fell as sleet, soaking the weary Grozny and making Malik Big Aye Kamal more fractious than ever. His horses and dogs had all perished; so had half-a-dozen warriors and a couple of precious breeding slaves, including his tutor, Seyda. If they didn't catch up with their quarry soon, he would have no tribe left to command.

Kamal rose at first light and splashed over to where Giv lay in his covered chair. 'Where flabtoad bitch?' he snarled.

Giv sprang upright, rolled his eyes and looked around him. 'Soon find, soon,' he blabbered.

'What Over-Malik Timur say?'

Giv climbed out of his chair and went to consult the dripping Head. 'Mighty Timur,' he intoned. 'How long, O Lord, how long to find flabtoad?'

'Pigsnout!' came the high-pitched response from the disciple's own throat. 'What frogpricked slave questions the judgement of the Over-Malik?'

'Giv begs, Mighty One! How long, O Lord?' repeated Giv in a nervous whisper.

'Hear what the Great One says, hipposhit! Before nine times the sun has slept, I will rip the traitor flabtoad open and feed her stinking guts to the vultures!'

Kamal nodded. Better news at last. If Giv interpreted Timur's words correctly, in just nine days Xsani and whoever was with her would be in his hands. Would the expression Seyda had taught him – having them 'at his mercy' – be appropriate? No, it would not! Mercy was the last thing on his mind.

He wasn't even sure what the word meant.

20
The Siege

Sammy was a straightforward, practical young man whose suspicion of all things mysterious could be traced back to his childhood. The community in which he grew up was kept safe from attack by a massive, solar-powered electric fence. Corrupt, unelected rulers, exploiting the ignorance of ordinary citizens, called the solar-generated power "Gova" and twisted it into a sort of religion. They set themselves up as pseudo priests and brainwashed their congregation into worshipping Gova with rituals and endless reciting of a ridiculous chant, "Glory to Gova! Polish the Panel!"

Sammy and some of his friends had seen through the fraud. After escaping from the Children of Gova community and joining the Mission, he remained deeply sceptical about anything that went under the name of "religion". As he was eager to learn whether the Long Dead shared his doubts, when his turn came to select an encyclopedia topic, he straight away opted for Religious Faiths.

The programme opened with chanting. 'Oh no!' groaned Sammy. 'Not that "Glory to Gova" stuff again!'

'Shh!' hissed Miouda and Cyrus. Religion was one of the aspects of Long Dead civilization they were most keen to make sense of.

Beside them, Xsani stared intently at the screen. At last, she whispered to Jinsha, they would find out about the Man in the Yellow Hat. It was not to be. Though the Mission learned many things about religion, certainty was not one of them.

They were told that the Long Dead, who called themselves Homo Sapiens Sapiens, had always been confused by what they didn't understand. Thousands of years before the Great Death, they couldn't explain things like the creation of the earth or crop failure. They responded by imagining they were the work of mighty beings called "gods". Obviously, as these gods were so powerful, men and women had to keep on the right side of them through worship.

The Mission had no problem grasping this idea as it was precisely what had happened in the Gova settlement. But what followed left them really bewildered. Sammy put it most clearly: 'It's Gova plus goodness – and I don't get it.'

As they discovered more about the world, the Long Dead decided there was one super god. It was a man, apparently, who went by various names. He was all-powerful, all-understanding, and was the beginning and end of everything. Strangely, most religions also taught that he was incredibly good and kind.

Once more, it was Sammy who put his finger on the problem. 'If this god-thing is so good, why did he make Zeds?'

'For a joke?' suggested Olo.

'Pretty nasty one,' snorted Cyrus.

It was left to Xsani to defend the kindly mega-god. 'Maybe we don't know why there are Thedth? We jutht have to acthept it because, ath my Jintha and I know, there ith Thed in all of uth.'

'But who put it there, Xsani?' insisted Sammy. 'And what for?'

She shrugged and gave him a look that implied this was a matter on which they would never agree. 'Forget thothe quethtionth, Thammy,' she said earnestly, 'and think about how thith god thayth we should live. If we all did ath he taught uth, there wouldn't be any Thedth.'

'You bein' thinkin' a lot about this, Xsani, ain't you?' said Olo.

'Yeth. Ever thinthe I thaw the picture of the Man in the Yellow Hat. He thpoke to me, and now I know what he was thaying.'

Miouda had stopped the programme in the middle of a short film on the history of the world's major religions. A painting of men sitting around a table having supper was frozen on the screen.

'There he ith,' said Xsani, pointing to the bearded figure in the centre of the image. 'He thaid that if we all treat otherth ath we want them to treat uth, the world will be perfect.'

'Fat chance!' muttered Sammy. 'So I go up to Timur and give him a big kiss and say I love him… and he cuts my head off! There we are, a perfect world – except poor old Sammy hasn't got a head!'

'That ith thilly!' retorted Xsani.

Cyrus intervened. 'Ok you two, let's leave it. The Long Dead didn't understand this religion business – and neither do we.'

'It's about the word "belief",' ventured Miouda. 'They keep using it in the programme. Not all people believe the same thing.'

'And I believe it's all a load of nonsense,' said Sammy quickly.

'Sammy, please!' cut in Cyrus. 'Religion is a difficult and dangerous topic. The Long Dead actually went to war over it – they killed those with different beliefs from their own.'

'Horrible, ithn't it?' said Xsani. 'It maketh me wonder about thothe Long Dead. They thaid and did thuch wonderful thingth… and thuch terrible thingth.' She paused. 'I thometimeth wonder…'

'… why we are trying so hard to be like them?' said Miouda, finishing the sentence for her.

Cyrus' face fell. 'That's enough,' he snapped angrily. 'We'll finish Religious Faiths and move on to Xsani's topic.'

Miouda and Xsani looked at each other. It was so unusual for Cyrus to get angry, yet they understood why. Deep within him, out of sight and almost out of mind, his blind faith in the superiority of the Long Dead was beginning to crack.

Xsani's topic made the situation worse. They had met many references to it already. It was there in The Odyssey, one of the first Soterion books Cyrus had opened; it was there in the letter of Rebekkah Askar, and it was there in most of the encyclopedia articles they had studied.

Xsani's topic was War.

They found the programme as exciting as it was depressing. If the Long Dead hated war so much, they kept asking themselves, why did they keep indulging in it? There wasn't a time in their history when one group wasn't slaughtering another, and it was worse than the conflict between Zeds and Constants because the numbers were greater and the weapons more terrible.

Three days later, when the Mission had completed a brief history of warfare and moved on to the development of weapons, Xsani raised an interesting point.

'You thee, Jintha,' she said, 'it was alwayth the men. Like Thedth nowadayth.'

'Constant women can fight as well as men,' said Miouda, eager to defend her sex's physical prowess.

'But they don't thtart the fighting, do they?' said Xsani gently.

As if to support her, at that very moment Corby began to bark.

Sammy recognised the tone at once. 'That's not asking for food,' he gasped, leaping to his feet. 'It's a warning. He's heard something – and by the sound of it, he doesn't like what he's heard!'

Not far away, in the grove where the Mission had sheltered before entering Itzac, Giv also heard Corby's barking. The sound came as a great relief. Having abandoned the Mission outside the walled compound, he had guessed they would have managed to get in and would still be there. Speaking largely in meaningless gibberish, he sought to explain to Malik

Big Aye Kamal that, as promised, he had led the Grozny to their target. The Malik managed to pick out a single reasonably coherent sentence. 'Giv recognise barking – dog is of Sammy, Constant.'

That was all Kamal needed. Peering between the trees where he and his men were hidden, he gazed at the concrete walls in front of him. In there – yes, a few paces away! – was the flabtoad traitor bitch, Xsani. Now he had her! Now would his revenge be terrible, more terrible than anything even Timur could have devised. He licked his thin lips at the prospect of what lay ahead.

How to get in? Kamal summoned Captain Peng and told him to go around the compound to see if there was a door. On being told that there was indeed an entrance, but that it was closed by a hefty steel gate, Kamal sat down and forced his brain to work logically. Peng stood awkwardly beside him, picking his nose.

Thinking along the same lines as the Mission, Kamal concluded that if one couldn't get through a wall, one had to get over it. That meant steps (which there weren't) or a rope (which there wasn't) or a ladder (which he hadn't). Frustrated, he looked at Peng.

'Grow!' he growled.

'Eh?' mumbled the Captain, removing a filthy finger from his nostril.

'Fool! Get bigger so you can climb over wall.'

Completely nonplussed by his master's idiotic command, Peng said the first thing that came into his head. 'Two Pengs bigger than one Peng,' he muttered.

Kamal thought about this. As he did so, his mouth slowly twisted into a weak smile. Of course! One Peng could not get over the wall – but a heap of Pengs…

The Mission had managed to scale the wall by making a pyramid from six people. It took almost ten times as many Zeds to perform the same task. Urged on by Kamal, they piled on to each other until four of the lighter men were able to scramble up the heap of bodies and reach the top of the wall.

Peering out of gaps in the parapet, the Mission had watched the operation with disbelief. When the mound of Zed bodies was large enough for the attackers to make their move, Cyrus lined up his forces.

'Now!' he shouted as the fingers of the leading Zed appeared over the parapet.

Moving as one, the Mission stood up, raised their spears and thrust down at the defenceless attackers. Sharp steel points pierced Zed skulls, throats and chests. Blood seeped down through the sweating bodies below.

Kamal sent four fresh attackers up the mound, now slippery with the blood of the fallen. When they too failed, he tried a batch of five, then six. These met with no more success than their predecessors, and Kamal angrily called his men off. Every assault had been repulsed so easily that Cyrus had difficulty keeping the Mission focussed. Nevertheless, he understood that these little victories brought only temporary security. They could not remain under siege in Itzac for ever. Sooner or later, they had either to drive the Zeds away or escape.

He remembered the vision of the distant ocean. Somewhere out there were people who had learned how to sail a boat. They had to be Constants – no Zed would ever master the skills of seamanship. If the Mission could sneak out of Itzac and make it to the coast…

That evening, as Xsani and Miouda patrolled the parapet in the company of Corby, Cyrus, Sammy, Olo, and Jinsha discussed the Mission's predicament.

'Not sure how we're going to leave unseen,' said Sammy. 'To stop us making a run for it, they've spread out right around the place. Guards at night, too.'

'I know,' replied Cyrus. 'But there's no hurry. We've got all the water we need and enough food to last us for a few days. I say we sit tight and see what happens.'

Jinsha, who spoke little, gave her support. 'Xsani and I know dumbman Zeds well, Cyrus,' she said. 'I think they become bored and go away.'

Unfortunately, Jinsha was wrong. Malik Big Aye Kamal did not get bored. In fact, the longer the siege of Itzac went on, the more determined he became. And after two days, he finally hit upon a way of getting inside. His inspiration came from watching a rabbit innocently hopping past his feet one evening.

At dawn the following morning, working with their bare hands and bits of wood, parties of Zeds began digging three tunnels under the walls of Itzac. Their progress was slow but steady. Within a week, Cyrus estimated, the tunnellers would be beneath the compound. The Mission might be able to block off the mouths of the tunnels for a while, but if there was an attack over the walls at the same time… In the end, they would be overwhelmed by sheer weight of numbers.

The defenders' morale flagged. Tempers frayed, and Xsani,

her face creased with anxiety, withdrew deep into herself. From the continual barrage of yells and taunts that came floating over the parapet, she gathered she was the Grozny's principal target. The prospect of what they would do to her if they caught her was too horrible to contemplate. More than once, Jinsha caught her staring at her dagger. Both of them knew, as did all Kogon, that if the worst came to the worst, suicide was the only way out.

On the fourth morning, when Cyrus and Miouda were in the computer room going over their options, Jinsha came down from the parapet and crossed the courtyard to join them.

'Hello,' said Cyrus. 'Everything ok outside?'

'Yes, Cyrus. Dumbman Zeds never move before sun gets high.'

Miouda looked carefully at the younger Kogon. Her expression, normally relaxed, was tense and her voice had an unusual edge to it. 'What about you?' Miouda asked. 'Are you alright?'

Jinsha nodded. 'I am well, but I worry about my Malika. And all of us.'

As if hesitating before making up her mind, Jinsha glanced at the two Constants. 'I know how we can escape,' she said.

Her idea was simple but extremely dangerous – especially for herself. Shortly after dawn, when the Zeds were at their least watchful, she would open the gates noisily and make a run for it. She had been famous among the Kogon for her fleetness of foot and was confident she could outrun any Zed.

In the half-light, it would be impossible to see clearly what was going on. The ill-disciplined Zeds would think the whole

Mission was trying to escape and set off after her. The remaining members of the Mission could then slip out of Itzac unnoticed. Jinsha, having shaken off her pursuers, would rejoin them at a pre-arranged meeting place.

Noble though the gesture was, Cyrus and Miouda wouldn't hear of it. But Jinsha revealed a side of her personality they had not previously seen. They had tended to regard her as Xsani's friend rather than as a powerful individual in her own right. Now, listening to the determined way she defended her proposal, they saw why Xsani had once chosen her as her successor.

Calm and even gentle on the outside, inside she had a core of steel. When she persisted in her proposal, saying she would make a run for it whether they liked it or not, they backed down and said they'd get the opinion of the whole group.

Xsani was horrified. Reverting to Malika mode, she told Jinsha to forget the suicidal plan immediately. But the young woman's mind was made up. She was no longer Xsani's to command, she pointed out. Moreover, as she would be acting out of affection for the Mission, especially for Xsani, she hoped their parting words would not be angry.

This was more than Xsani could take. Shaking with emotion and signalling Jinsha to follow her, she hurried into the courtyard. The couple returned half an hour later, hand in hand. Having talked the matter over, they said, they had agreed Jinsha's suggestion was probably the best chance they had of getting out alive.

'And she hath promithed me,' said Xsani in a voice tinged with resignation, 'that she will not get caught by the Thedth. I have alwayth truthted her – and I do now. I am sure Jintha will thave uth.'

'So am I,' echoed Cyrus, relieved that the two women had reconciled their differences.

'I'm with you, Xsani,' said Miouda. She explained that she had been studying how the Grozny were spread out around the walls. Those involved in the tunnelling were quite alert, but the men nearest the gate appeared bored out of their simple minds. Some slept, others threw stones or played childish games to keep themselves occupied. She was convinced that the moment they saw Jinsha they would charge after her like hounds after a hare.

Sammy and Olo also accepted the escape plan, with one proviso: Jinsha was to take Corby with her. He could run as fast as any man or woman, Sammy said proudly, and would be the perfect bodyguard if any Zed managed to catch up with her.

He spoke with all sincerity and in a manner that seemed matter-of-fact, as if he were lending Jinsha a spear or sword. Only Cyrus understood how great a sacrifice his friend was making. Boy and beast had struck up a strong friendship as soon as they met, and after the death of Navid, the dog's original owner, the two had been like brothers. Cyrus remembered how devastated Sammy had been when Corby went missing during the sack of Alba.

The faithful, fearless companion had done as much as any of them to help the Mission succeed. He had saved Sammy's life at the time of the tiger attack; he had led them to the River No-Man when they were lost in the forest; he had fought off wolves, and he had warned them of the arrival of the Grozny

Zeds. Cyrus wondered whether Sammy would have let him go had he not met Olo.

That night they unplugged the laptop and wrapped it carefully in the special backpack. While Olo patrolled the parapet, the others told Jinsha all they could remember about the surrounding countryside. Her best bet, Miouda advised, was to stay off the Long Dead roads and go through the former plantations to the hill she and Cyrus had found. From there she would be able to see the yellow of the beach, with the sea beyond. That's where they'd meet up.

Assuming they got out of Itzac unseen, the rest of the Mission would head in the same direction by the shortest possible route. They would wait on the beach until Jinsha joined them.

It was, they all recognised, not much of a plan. Even if the escape was a success, there was no guarantee that Jinsha could throw off her pursuers, or that she'd find the others on an expanse of beach many miles long. And even if they did meet up, what then? Assuming the mysterious 'sailing Constants'actually existed, and the boat seen by Cyrus and Miouda had not been a trick of the light, how were the Mission to contact them?

Though questions such as these were at the back of everyone's mind, no one gave them voice. They all knew they were taking a desperate gamble, and they all knew why. The alternative was far, far worse.

None of the Constants slept much that night, and shortly before dawn they gathered in silence behind the gates. Jinsha checked the food and water in her backpack and ensured her knife was loose in its scabbard. She squatted down beside Corby and patted his broad head.

'Thank you!' she whispered in his ear.

He licked her hand. 'Don't worry,' he seemed to be saying. 'We'll make it!'

The pale colours of dawn were now lightening the sky to the east. It was almost time to move. If they left it much longer, the Zed camp would start to stir and the guards would be able to see clearly that the break-out was being made by a single runner.

Cyrus looked up at Miouda on the parapet above the gates. She signalled to him that the coast was clear – there was no Zed within fifty paces of the entrance. Most were still asleep.

Jinsha positioned herself behind the doors, her face taut with concentration. Xsani emerged out of the shadows, kissed her briefly and, without a word, moved quickly away again. As she did so, the first rays of the sunrise glinted on the panel at the top of the grey tower.

'Now!' whispered Cyrus. With a loud clang, he threw back the bar across the gates. Sammy heaved the right-hand door open, and Jinsha sprinted out and into the gloom beyond.

From her vantage point on the wall, Miouda observed the reactions of the guards. Not until Jinsha had almost reached the trees did one of them notice her. Unsure what he had seen, he shook his head and pointed. Moments later, he gave a bloodcurdling yell and set off in pursuit.

He had taken only a few strides when a second guard stopped him to ask what was going on. The two of them took up the chase, howling wildly. The noise alerted others, and soon every Zed on that side of the settlement had joined the hunt. As Jinsha had hoped, minutes after her break-out the area in front of Itzac was empty.

Cyrus cautiously opened the gate wider and peered around. Not a soul. Miouda hurried down the steps from the parapet and, leaving the door ajar so the Zeds would believe Jinsha had not been alone, the remaining members of the Mission slipped out into the surrounding trees.

They soon picked up the remains of a track leading more or less due east. From their left the confused shouts of the Zed guards floated through the undergrowth. 'Here! Here! Flabtoad Malika! Escape! Follow! This way!'

It was all going far better than Cyrus and Miouda could have expected. Judging by the hunters' cursing and squabbling, they appeared to have no idea who they were chasing or where their quarry had gone.

Cyrus turned to Xsani and smiled. 'You said Jinsha would save us, didn't you? Seems you were right, Xsani.'

'Thave uth, yeth,' she replied, her face contorted with anxiety. 'But I am not sure she will thave herthelf.'

21
Trapped

The Mission travelled fast down the Long Dead highway running east from Itzac and reached the coast in a little over a day. On the way, they encountered neither Zed nor Constant. Their sole companions were flocks of rainbow parrots and armies of monkeys that chattered angrily and threw nuts at them as they passed.

Where the land met the sea, the road ended at the site of a small fishing village. Blankets of tropical vegetation canopied the shops and houses and sprouted from the roofs like grotesque chimneys. The harbour, nestled behind a crumbling sea wall, had silted up long ago, and the pounding of the waves had reduced the vessels once moored there to unrecognizable hulks.

The Mission skirted around the village to the beach. Here they paused and gazed spellbound at the sea.

Sammy exhaled loudly. 'Wow! I never imagined…'

'Nor did I,' said Miouda, reading his thoughts. 'So huge. It's quite frightening, isn't it?'

'Yeth,' agreed Xsani. 'And lithen to the thound of the waveth – on and on and on, never thtopping.' She ran a hand through her hair. 'I don't know why, but it maketh me feel rather thad.'

Not far away, they came across a faded blue fibreglass hull half buried in the sand. On the leeward side, sheltered from the worst of the spray and rain, they could make out three letters of the vessel's name.

Cyrus was intrigued. 'S… GO…' he read. 'What d'you reckon the boat was called, Miouda?'

'Could be almost anything.' She looked at the letters. 'But you know how the Long Dead thought ships were female, so what about Sea Goddess?'

'Or She Hath Gone?' lisped Xsani wryly. Since their arrival at the coast, she hadn't taken her eyes off the trees in the hope of seeing Jinsha running towards them out of the shadows.

Cyrus understood her pain and let the remark go. But he was worried. Nothing would undermine their chances of success quicker than negative thinking.

For much of the afternoon they struggled along the shore, staring intently about them and saying little. Eventually, exhausted by the heat, they stopped beneath a clump of palms that stood like monuments on the fringe of the beach. Stretching out on the warm sand, for a while they lay listening to the cries of the birds and the regular splash of the waves.

Sammy spoke first. 'Still no sign of Jinsha,' he muttered.

'No sign of anyone or anything,' said Miouda. She brushed back her hair and turned to Cyrus. 'What now, Cy?'

Cyrus, aware that everyone's eyes were on him, felt the

burden of his responsibility more keenly than ever. He had led them out of Itzac and probable death at the hands of the Grozny – but to what end? They were now alone on a distant shore, far from any source of power for the laptop, and probably far from any other Constants. Had Jinsha and Corby sacrificed themselves for nothing?

'That shape we saw out there, do you really think it was a boat?' asked Miouda, adding to his discomfort.

As he had done several times since leaving Alba, he dredged the very core of his being for strength to hold the group together. 'We did the only thing we could have done,' he said with as much confidence as he could muster.

'We do not give up,' he continued, raising his voice and looking at each member of the Mission in turn. 'We will find Jinsha and Corby. We will meet up with friendly Constants. We will pass on to them the knowledge of the Long Dead. We will finish the Salvation Project.'

He stood up. 'Here, on this hot and deserted beach, we are sowing the seeds of a new world. A brave new world.'

Olo, who had never heard Cyrus in this sort of mood, rose and stood beside him.

'You are bein' the best leader, Cyrus,' she said softly.

Sammy joined her, then Miouda. Finally, Xsani got to her feet and said dryly, 'I have followed the Man in the Yellow Hat thuth far, tho I thuppothe I had better thtay with him now.'

'Thank you, Xsani,' said Cyrus. 'I don't have a halo, and when I die that will be the end of me. But while I live, I won't let you down.'

He turned to the rest of the group. 'No more gloomy

talk, please.' He clapped his hands and smiled. 'Let's have something to eat and drink while we work out how to contact Jinsha.'

'And Corby,' reminded Sammy.

They broke open coconuts and drank their milk, and feasted off wild fruits and berries. Rested and no longer hungry, their mood lightened. Sammy and Olo even managed to laugh when a monkey swung down and stole a plantain out of Olo's hand.

While they were eating, Cyrus explained the plan he had come up with. The best chance of finding Jinsha, he suggested, was spreading out in a line to cover as much of the beach as possible. When they could only just see and hear the person on either side of them, he estimated they'd be covering about 5,000 metres of shoreline.

'Miouda and I will stand at either end,' he went on. 'When I give the signal, we all shout Jinsha's name as loud as we can. If there's no reply, we repeat it, five times if necessary. If there's still no response, we'll move up the beach and do the whole thing over again. If Jinsha's anywhere around here, she'll hear the noise and come to join us.'

'As long as it's Jinsha and not the Zeds that turns up,' said Sammy.

'It's a risk, of course,' said Cyrus. 'but not as great as the one she took for us. Anyway, the Zeds will have given up the chase ages ago. There's no way they could've pursued us down here.'

His eyes met Xsani's as he was speaking. Though she didn't say a word, the message he read there was clear. Be careful, Cyrus! Dumbman Zeds may be stupid, but underestimate them at your peril.

The Mission spread out in a long line along the beach as Cyrus had suggested. When their colleagues were no more than shapes in the heat haze, Cyrus called out at the top of his voice, 'Jinsha! H-E-R-E!'

As the others took up the cry, hundreds of birds rose screaming into the air. There was no human response. A minute later, they tried once more. 'Jinsha! HE-RE! Jinsha!' Again, no reply. The shout went up a third time, and...

On the fourth attempt, Cyrus noticed movement under the palms in front of him. Seconds later, three fully-armed Zeds came running out of the undergrowth straight at him. His instinct was to stand and fight. Previously, he had seen off more than this number single-handed, and he was confident he could do so now. But there were bound to be more of them. Besides, he had the rest of the Mission to consider.

'Zeds!' he yelled, turning and sprinting towards Olo. 'Run to Miouda! Form a group! We must fight as a group!'

Olo set off in the direction of Sammy and Cyrus sprinted after her. Glancing over his shoulder, he saw more Zeds emerging from the trees. Six... ten... fifty or more, all yelling and waving their weapons as they hared down the beach after the retreating Constants.

At the other end of the line, Miouda understood the noise to mean the others had found Jinsha. She smiled and scanned the beach to her left. Beyond Xsani she could make out three figures running in her direction and beyond them... Her heart sank.

Turning away, a movement far out to sea caught her eye. Something was bobbing up and down on the waves. A fish? A bird? No, it was too large for that. She raised her hand to shield her eyes from the sun.

It was a boat – like the one she and Cyrus had seen from the hill. She wrenched off her smock and waved it frantically above her. 'Help!' she screamed. 'We're Constants! Help!'

A finger of sand, no more than five paces wide, stretched out into the sea from where she stood. In normal circumstances it would have been a death trap, the sort of place in which to make a brave but futile last stand. But now, if help really was on its way, it could be their salvation.

Calling Xsani to join her, Miouda put her dress back on and hurried on to the spit. She waved her arms and shouted, louder this time. Yes! The boat people had noticed her and were paddling in her direction. They were still a long way off, and the Mission would need to keep the Zeds at bay until the boat people arrived. It would be a tough but not impossible task. The spit was narrow enough to be defended by three or four of them.

Miouda had another matter on her mind. Even if they survived long enough for the boat to reach them, could they really abandon Jinsha and Corby on this bleak, Zed-infested shore? She was fairly sure Cyrus wouldn't agree to do so, but what about Xsani and Sam?

By now Cyrus, Sammy and Olo had out-run their pursuers and were sprinting down the spit to join Miouda and Xsani. They too had seen the boat sailing swiftly towards them across the blue-green sea, and hope glowed on their perspiring faces.

Cyrus took command. 'One last battle!' he cried, drawing a line in the sand with his spear. 'This is where we stand, myself and Xsani at the front. Olo and Sammy, you guard the flanks in case they try to wade round behind us.'

He handed the laptop backpack to Miouda. 'Here, take this. And get ready to jump into the boat.' He scanned beyond the Zeds to the fringe of trees. 'Let's hope Jinsha and Corby make it – there's still a chance!'

Xsani looked at him quizzically but said nothing.

The first attackers, exhausted by the long chase, were dealt with easily. One almost fell on to the point of Cyrus' spear and the second, lunging forward, tripped over the body of his colleague. As Cyrus dispatched him with his knife, Xsani slew the third with a deft thrust to the chest. Cyrus was astonished by her speed and skill. He had rarely seen such a fighter, man or woman, and he was glad the Tallins had never met the Kogon in battle.

As he had anticipated, the next Zeds to arrive, seeing three of their colleagues lying dead, attempted to outflank the Mission by wading into the sea. Olo and Sammy were waiting for them. With one foot on the sand and the other in the water, they had the advantage of height and soon the three bodies on the sand were joined by three more floating face down in the bloody ocean.

At this point, instead of charging headlong into the attack as they would normally do, the Zeds massing on the beach held back. Afraid? thought Cyrus. Surely not! He soon saw the explanation. A tall, thin-lipped figure with a stump for a right hand was walking up and down in front of them, shouting and striking them with the flat of his sword.

Xsani recognised Kamal at once. His presence filled her

with despair. To get this far, he must have overtaken Jinsha. And if he had taken her alive… She shuddered and searched the ranks of the Zeds for a prisoner: they would consider it great sport to torture a captive in sight of their friends.

Standing at the rear of the group, on the very tip of the finger of sand, Miouda turned again towards the boat. She could see it clearly now and was surprised by the appearance of the crew. Bare-chested and without weapons, they didn't look at all like warriors. She waved. A figure in the bow waved back and shouted something. The distance was too great for her catch the words.

A hideous yell drew Miouda's attention to the situation on the beach. Kamal had arranged his forces in three blocks, one in line with the centre of the spit and two on the flanks. The yell of acclamation had arisen as the centre block divided to allow a figure to pass through.

It was Giv. Holding aloft the tattered Head of Timur on the tip of his spear, he advanced unsteadily until he stood no more than five paces from Cyrus and Xsani.

The gaunt, scarred figure was barely recognisable as the bright youth who, not that long ago, had been singled out by Timur as a possible Grozny Captain. All leadership qualities had long since disappeared. He had proved too sensitive, too intelligent for the world of the Grozny, and Kamal would certainly have had him killed were it not for his possession of the Head and his extraordinary ability to speak in the voice of his former master.

'Now fishscum!' he began, giving his customary screeching a marine flavour. 'Hear the words of Timur the Terrible, your great Over-Malik!'

Awed by his rhetoric, the Grozny horde fell silent. 'There stand the false flabtoads and weedstinking Constants who stole the Head of Timur. Stole my soul!'

Unbidden, the Grozny launched into their terrible war chorus: 'Zed blood! Zed blood! Kill! Kill! Kill!'

'Silence, codpieces!' howled Giv. 'Timur will give the order.

'I have a dream that these god-stealing seaslugs will die! I have a dream that the Zeds will tear their hair from their skulls, their limbs from their bodies, their eyes from their sockets! I have a dream that the flabtoad traitor will scream and beg for mercy. I have a dream—'

And that's where his dream ended. Taunted beyond endurance by Giv's words, Xsani sprang forward and thrust her spear beneath his thin ribs and into his shrivelled, sad and blackened heart.

As he fell, the Head of Timur slipped off the top of his spear and flew towards Cyrus. Instinctively, he raised his leg and kicked it high into the air. It hung there for a few seconds, a dark token of evil challenging the brilliance of the sun, then splashed into the sea and disappeared beneath the mirrored surface.

The Zeds took a moment to realise what had happened. Then, howling like wolves, they hurled themselves forward, trampling the body of Giv underfoot as they came. To Cyrus' horror, Xsani did not return to his side but remained close to where Giv had fallen.

'Xsani! Get back!' he cried.

'Why?' she called to him as a gigantic Zed swung his gut-ripper at her head. 'Thith is what love meanth, Thyruth!'

She neatly sidestepped the blow, stabbing her opponent as he was off balance. As she did so, the man twisted and she was unable to withdraw her weapon swiftly enough to protect herself against what followed. A club crashed into her skull, knocking her   sideways. Before she could recover, a rusty blade slashed her neck. Blood poured from the wound and she collapsed to her knees.

Cyrus watched in horror as, in a frenzy of killing, blow after blow rained down upon Xsani's slight frame. A terrible scream rent the air behind him. He assumed it came from Olo.

Giv's oration and Xsani's suicide saved the Mission. By the time the Zeds had finished hacking at the lifeless body of the former Malika and turned their attention to Cyrus, the boat was no more than ten feet from the end of the spit. Miouda waded into the water and grabbed the bow. One of the crew jumped out beside her and helped her hold the craft steady.

'It's here!' she cried. 'The boat – and they're friends – Constants! Cyrus! Olo! Sammy! Get back! Get back!'

It was easier said than done. Step by step, fighting all the way, the three warriors edged down the spit. They accounted for at least seven Zeds, though they themselves were all injured. A metal cudgel broke Olo's forearm and Sammy received a deep cut above his left eye. In the end, they both managed to stumble into the boat.

Cyrus, who single-handed had kept the Zeds at bay while his friends got away, was now the only member of the Mission still on the spit. The Zeds were pressing him so closely that he fought with his knife in one hand and his spear in the other, stabbing and slicing at the wall of snarling Grozny that bore inexorably down on him.

By the time he reached the water, the shaft of his spear had been smashed by a massive blow that cut his arm from shoulder to elbow. Wading into the water, he raised his knife to fend off an axe swinging down towards his head. He succeeded only in diverting the blow. The hatchet dashed the knife from his grasp, sending it spinning off into the sea, and sliced open his forehead.

Blood from the gash poured over his face, temporarily blinding him. As he raised his hand to wipe it away, he felt himself seized and pulled backwards. The next thing he knew, he was lying on the bottom of a boat staring up at the faces around him as kind hands attempted to staunch the flow of blood from his wounds.

Miouda – thank goodness! And Sammy and Olo had made it, too! And who was that? No, it couldn't be! But yes! The grief-stricken, tear-stained face belonged to Jinsha, the lovely creature who had meant more to Xsani than life itself.

Wasn't there someone else? He tried to speak, but no words came. They were not needed, for Sammy read his mind.

'Yes, I'm sorry Cyrus,' he sobbed. 'Xsani wasn't the only one. We've lost Corby, too.'

22
Lanskira

Cyrus blinked and opened his eyes. What was that noise? Thunder. There was a violent storm going on somewhere above him – and second in his head. Ow! It hurt!

A lightning flash momentarily lit up the strange room, hurting his eyes. Where was he?

He shut his eyes again as a crash of thunder shook the frail roof, temporarily drowning out the drumming of the rain.

Gingerly, he raised his left hand and felt his forehead. It was bandaged. Quite expertly, too. He moved his hand to where his right arm lay heavy on the bed beside him. Another bandage. Who had done this? Miouda? Xsani? No, not Xsani. It couldn't possibly have been Xsani...

Very slowly, like a series of images slipping across the screen of his precious laptop, he began to remember. The dreadful killing of poor Xsani – the desperate retreat to the boat – the rescue by those strange Constants, eager to help but not to fight – the news that dear old Corby had died saving Jinsha, whom the boat people had picked up further down the beach before rescuing the rest of the Mission – the painful voyage to wherever he was now – the agony, mental as well as physical – Miouda's tearful concern when she feared he might die – the care of tender, skilful hands...

Gradually, the images merged together and, as the storm died away into the darkness, he drifted into a deep sleep.

He awoke to a different world. The air was warm and laden with the scent of flowers. Bright sunlight filtered between fissures in the woven walls of the hut and the pain in his head had gone. A familiar face was smiling down at him.

'Miouda!' he croaked through parched lips. 'How are you? Where are we?'

She laid a hand on his cheek. 'Shh! Relax. We've made it – you have led us to a wonderful place full of amazing people.'

He thought for a minute. 'Heaven?'

She laughed. 'Not quite, but close.' She gave him a sip of water from a coconut shell. 'I'll tell you more when you're stronger.'

'But the laptop?'

'It's safe. And they have a solar panel that works just as well as the one in Itzac.'

He gave a long sigh of relief. 'Oh Miouda! The Mission has finally come home. Salvation!'

'I believe so, yes.'

She gave him more water and left, placing the shell at his side so he could help himself when needed. Thinking about what she had said, he smiled, closed his eyes and went back to sleep.

It was evening when he woke again. A soft breeze rustled the leaves of the palms outside, and from somewhere to his left came the sound of children playing. A dog barked and he was reminded of Corby. Poor Sammy! He hoped Olo would bring him comfort in his distress.

When Miouda returned, she brought fruit and eggs and a strange bread he had not tasted before. Five minutes later, he was sitting up in bed, wolfing down his first proper meal for days.

As he ate, Miouda told him what had happened to Jinsha. She had easily got away from most of the chasing Zeds. But two men, both older than her and strong runners, had stayed on her tail. Knowing she could not out-run them, she had decided to fight it out.

She took on the nearest of her pursuers while Corby went for the second. Fortunately, her man had dropped his weapons during the chase and she was able to finish him off easily. But the second had kept hold of his long-bladed knife and as Corby leaped for his throat, the weapon pierced the dog's soft underbelly. The wound was fatal.

The force of Corby's jump was sufficient to knock the man off his feet, allowing Jinsha to get close enough to stab him through the heart. Having covered Corby's body with leaves, she continued to the coast where she was spotted by the boat people. When she told them there were more Constants in the area, they stayed to pick them up... And the rest of the story Cyrus knew.

'And how is Jinsha now?' he asked between mouthfuls.

'Very unhappy. When we were in the boat, she tried to jump

overboard, saying she wanted to die with Xsani. But she's calmer now and I think she will be alright. It's difficult to be miserable in this place.'

'And Sammy's not too wretched?'

'Of course he feels terrible about Corby. But he knew it might happen, and Olo is a great comfort to him.'

'She's a lovely person, isn't she?'

'Yes. They make a great couple. But I'm not sure they want to stay here.'

'Not stay? I thought you said these people – by the way, what are they called?'

'The Tiani.'

'Ah. I thought these Tiani had electricity, a solar panel?'

Miouda nodded. 'Yes, they do. But I've spoken to a few people and it's not as simple as that.'

'Eh?'

'I'll leave it to them to explain. In the meantime, I'll tell you what I know.'

They were on a tropical island named Lanskira, she said, where the Tiani had lived for more than a century. They were Constants, but unlike any others she had heard of. In fact, they were unlike any people she had even read about.

'You mean there were no Long Dead like them?' Cyrus interrupted.

'No, not that we know of, anyway.'

'Strange. I can't wait to tell them about the laptop and the Salvation Project!'

She laid a hand on his arm. 'Take it easy, Cy. All that can wait. They said you wouldn't be fit enough to move for a while.'

He lay back and closed his eyes. Ok, he'd wait. He did feel tired, and his arm was hurting quite badly.

The Tiani carried no weapons, Miouda continued, and they outlawed all fighting and physical conflict. From the earliest age, children were taught that tolerance and sympathy were the greatest virtues, and that frowning was the same as swearing. Anyone who rejected the Tiani code of peacefulness was "outed" – put on a boat and taken to the mainland. As far as anyone could remember, only three people had been exiled in this way.

Aware how unpleasant life was off the island, especially in areas where there were powerful Zed tribes, Tiani fishing boats regularly patrolled the shore to rescue desperate Constants. That was how they met Jinsha.

New arrivals took the name of the place they came from. 'And guess what name some of the people here are called by?' said Miouda excitedly.

'Alba?'

'No, but that's what they call me: Miouda Alba!'

'Sounds good.'

'Yes. But the other name I've heard – I thought you might guess – is Itzac!'

Cyrus laughed. 'You mean the Constants who left Itzac came here, like us?'

'Yes. The original arrivals are all dead now, but stories about the place live on.'

'They might still be alive if we'd been here and got our laptop working.'

When she made no direct reply and went on talking about life on the island, he wondered again why she was being so evasive.

One of the strangest things about the place, she said with a chuckle, was that no one was ever embarrassed – about anything! They talked openly about their feelings and made almost no effort to cover up their bodies. Everyone walked about naked from the waist up, and around their middle men and women wore just a brightly-coloured sort of skirt called a "tootsa". The name, Miouda heard, came from the label of a particularly lovely article of Long Dead clothing. The original had worn out long ago, but the Tiani had loved its design so much that the word had passed into their language.

The Tiani fished, did a little farming and kept chickens, but the island's fertility meant most of their food grew wild in the groves and forests. Feeding off mangoes and melons, yams and eggs, sugar cane and coconuts, they all appeared extremely healthy.

It sounds a wonderful place, thought Cyrus when he was alone. But why is Miouda reluctant to talk about the Salvation Project and the Soterion information on the laptop? In his heart of hearts perhaps he knew the answer, but he was not yet prepared to admit it.

Over the next few days, as his strength returned, Cyrus received a growing number of visitors. Sammy and Olo came in several times a day. Both were recovering well from their injuries. Olo's arm had been carefully set in wooden splints and Sammy's head was wreathed in bandages similar to those used on Cyrus. He also noticed that, like his own wounds, Sammy's were dressed regularly and kept scrupulously clean. It was as if the Tiani had access to the sort of Long Dead medical knowledge he had found in the Soterion.

Olo had helped Sammy come to terms with the loss of Corby by giving him a wooden carving of his faithful friend. It was expertly done by one of the islanders after Olo had described the dog in great detail. She wondered whether she might also ask for an image of Xsani to give to Jinsha, but on Miouda's advice she decided against it. They needed to help Jinsha move on, Miouda said, and not dwell too much on the past.

When Olo chatted with Sammy about how forcefully Miouda had used the expression 'live in the past', he nodded. 'Not surprised, Olo. It'll be interesting to see what Cyrus makes of it.'

Like Miouda, Sammy and Olo were full of praise for the generosity and compassion of the Tiani.

'Yes,' said Cyrus, 'it seems they have an almost ideal life here.'

'Almost,' repeated Sammy with a knowing glance towards Olo.

Cyrus misinterpreted the signal. 'Of course. And when we've shown them what's on the laptop, it'll be even better, eh? Why does Miouda say you two don't want to stay here?'

The couple looked at each other awkwardly. 'It's bein' hard to explain, Cyrus,' said Olo. 'The Tiani, they's wantin' to speak with you themselves.'

That reluctance again, thought Cyrus. He wondered how long he'd have to wait before he was given an explanation.

Apart from the men and women who came to tend his wounds, he didn't see much of the Tiani themselves. The self-styled "medicals" caring for him were infinitely kind and attentive, and their skill astounded him. They knew about sterilization, and treated his gashes with juice from a herb they said was 'almost the same as the medicine used by the Long Dead.'

When Cyrus expressed surprise that they had such information, which in other Constant communities had rapidly died out after the Great Death, they replied simply that they were 'very lucky'.

On the third day of his convalescence, he received a visit from a tall, elegant woman with ebony skin and long dark hair. Her name was Vaarunika Itzac she said with a broad smile, and she came as an ambassador from the Paarlimeentuva, the island's governing body. She explained, pointing to the children's faces peeping in at him through the windows of his hut, that he was already a local legend, and it was the Paarlimeentuva's wish and hope that he would agree to stay on the island.

'Of course,' he replied. 'You have all been so caring and my friends all say it's lovely here. And in there,' he went on, pointing to the laptop, 'We've got something to give you in return.'

'A kind gesture, Cyrus Tallis,' she said, disregarding the computer. 'We shall discuss it when you come before us.'

Six days after his arrival, Cyrus was well enough to leave his hut and wander about the Tiani community arm in arm with Miouda. She had already adopted the tootsa and, feeling awkwardly overdressed, he readily did the same. When they met Sammy and Olo, however, he noticed they had chosen to retain their mainland dress.

Life on the island was just as it had been described to him. The place was much more relaxed, more carefree, than the Constant communities he had been in previously. The most obvious reason was the absence of any warrior culture. The island was defended by the sea and its inhabitants regarded any form of violence with abhorrence – looking at Cyrus' wounds, those who had not heard his story assumed he had been in some dreadful accident.

The island's climate and fertility also encouraged the unhurried atmosphere. It did away with the tyranny of agriculture that kept Constants elsewhere slaving away at the soil all the year round.

Above all, Tiani culture placed happiness and wellbeing at its heart. Watching the islanders going about their business, Cyrus was struck by how laid-back they all were. They were perfectly content to stand about chatting and laughing for hours on end. From time to time, others came into the village with food they had gathered and shared it out among the inhabitants. By the shore, he watched a crew launching their boat for a fishing trip. Yes, they told him, they would be passing near the mainland in case there were any more Constants in need of rescue.

Later, as they were wandering past a covered area where children were being taught to play tunes on bamboo pipes, Cyrus asked how Jinsha was coping in a community that was so different from anything she had ever experienced. Miouda responded by leading him to a hut near the centre of the village. Outside, a group of women were singing softly, and in their centre, sitting cross-legged on the ground, sat Jinsha. She was wearing a tootsa.

She got up as soon as she saw Cyrus and came to meet him. To his astonishment, she took his hands, smiled and kissed him on his cheek.

'Jinsha!' he exclaimed, smiling at her. He noticed she had colouring on her face that hid her triple Z scars. 'How are you?'

'Learning to heal broken heart,' she said quietly. 'My new friends' – she indicated the women behind her – 'are teaching me to live the Tiani way.'

She gestured towards his bandages. 'I am glad you recover. I tell them much about you and they all want you and Miouda to stay.'

'And why not?' he said, looking around. 'Everyone appears so happy – and I'm told they have power for the laptop.'

'Ah!' she sighed. 'The laptop and the Salvation Project... I think the Paarlimeentuva wait for you to tell them all about it.'

23
Salvation

The Paarlimeentuva met in a broad clearing on a hill near the centre of the island. Five jungle paths radiated out from it like rays of the sun, each leading to one of five Tiani villages. All the inhabitants of Lanskira were welcome to attend, and the space was amply furnished with logs as seats.

A governing council of five senior Tiani, known as the Atikari, sat on chairs on the eastern side of the clearing. Behind them rose a large, gold-painted building from the time of the Long Dead. Cyrus and Miouda recognised it as a temple. Empty niches and a large platform at the front suggested that it had once been decorated with statues. Some fifteen paces to its left, wreathed in creepers and moss, were the ruins of a burned-out building of more recent construction.

Meetings were held at dawn, starting when the sun rose above the temple's golden roof. If the day was cloudy, the Paarlimeentuva was cancelled. On the morning in question, as sunlight flooded the clearing, the Atikari descended the temple

273

steps and stood before their chairs. Bowing and chorusing 'We are your servants,' they smiled and sat down. Their words were greeted with cheerful clapping.

As the sound died away, Cyrus, Miouda, Sammy, Olo and Jinsha were invited to sit on a log at the front of the assembly. Cyrus and Miouda were at one end, with Jinsha in the middle and the younger two at the end nearer the edge of the clearing. At Sammy's feet sat Pablo, a little dog who had instinctively singled him out as a man who loved animals.

The Atikari, each representing one of the island's villages, were all of equal status, and took it in turns to chair the Paarlimeentuva. Today it was the turn of Nelith Blurutaan, a short, curly-headed man with bronze skin and protruding teeth. When he had welcomed everyone to what he called the 'Damas', he prepared to address the new arrivals.

Cyrus nudged Miouda. 'What's a Damas?' he whispered.

'It's the name of what's happening: a "go or stay" meeting for new arrivals.'

'Ah! Who decides? Them or us?'

'Bit of both, I think. Let's see.'

The couple edged a little closer and, clasping their hands together, got ready to hear what Nelith had to say.

Although the Tiani did not get the opportunity to rescue people from the mainland often enough, he began, it always gave them great pleasure to do so. The recent episode had been particularly joyful because, for the first time, they had brought back a Zed who had rejected the ways of violence and barbarism. Jinsha blushed deeply as vigorous clapping echoed around the clearing and a group of women broke into a brief snatch of rhythmic song.

Nelith then invited Cyrus, as leader of the group, to stand up and tell the Mission's story.

'Here goes,' he said, rising to his feet and positioning himself to face both the Atikari and the audience.

He started with the Albans' discovery of the Soterion, and went on to outline Roxanne's Mission and her struggle with Timur, the opening of the vault, the traitorous behaviour of Yash and Sakamir, the destruction of Alba, the conversion of Xsani and Jinsha, and the long journey to the beach from where the Mission had been so fortunately rescued.

His words were listened to in respectful silence, interrupted only by gasps of horror at the evil and cruel nature of some of the things he described. When he had finished, Nelith asked what had motivated the Mission's deeds of such extraordinary courage and bravery.

Cyrus stooped down and picked up the laptop from near Miouda's feet. Lifting it high enough for everyone to see, he said proudly, 'This is the machine we recovered from the Soterion. It contains the knowledge of the Long Dead and the means to rebuild their wonderful world!'

Instead of applause, his announcement evoked only a low hiss as the audience drew in air through their teeth.

'Perhaps I need to explain more fully?' he asked.

Miouda gave him an uncertain smile and shook her head.

Nelith politely requested Cyrus to resume his seat. There was no need to explain, he said. If the Mission wouldn't mind, he would now like to tell them about the Tiani.

Cyrus nodded and resumed his seat. He had been half

expecting this. The Tiani were a fine people and their way of life was delightful. But, except for their strikingly advanced medical knowledge, in some ways they were a bit primitive, weren't they? The combination of the sophisticated and simple confused him and, taking Miouda's hand again, he prepared to listen keenly to what Nelith had to say.

The Atikari described how, shortly after the Great Death, the mainland settlement of Tiani had been attacked by Zeds. A group of about 100 survivors trekked for over a year to the same coast where the Mission had been stranded. Under increasing pressure from Zeds, the refugees had escaped to Lanskira in boats from the fishing village. They brought with them the precious equipment left by the Long Dead founders of their settlement: two portable solar panels and several computers similar to the one Cyrus had produced. All of these contained copies of the Soterion information and the data of the Salvation Project.

Cyrus opened his mouth in astonishment. His suspicions were right: the Tiani had accessed Long Dead knowledge! That explained their medical expertise. So what, he wondered, had happened to their computers to prevent them completing the Salvation Project? Probably some disaster like the fire that had destroyed the books and laptops in Alba. Looking at the burned-out building beside the temple, he supposed that was where the tragedy had occurred.

He refocussed his attention on Nelith.

As the Mission had done in Itzac, he was saying, the Tiani had used their computers to study the vanished world of the Long Dead with a view to finishing the Salvation Project. He pointed at the ruin. They had even built a special laboratory in which to carry out this work.

Thought so, said Cyrus to himself.

At first, Nelith continued, it was all tremendously exciting and Tiani scientists developed a four-year plan for reversing the mutation caused by the Mini-Flu. But as they delved deeper into the world of the Long Dead, they began to have doubts. The more they learned, the less sure they became that the Old World was better than the one they were in now. Day by day, week by week, their opinion hardened.

Nelith looked directly at the five members of the Mission seated before him. 'Finally,' he said, 'they announced that the Long Dead were of the past and should remain there.'

Only the pressure of Miouda's grasp prevented Cyrus from jumping up to intervene.

'Wait!' she whispered. 'Let him finish!' Beside her, she felt Sammy tense with similar agitation.

Nelith sensed the two Constants' discomfort and spoke to them directly. 'Yes,' he said gently, 'the people of the Old World had amazing science and technology. They were geniuses of art and ingenuity. They wrote beautiful poems and music, painted pictures, explored every tiny nook of their planet, discovered electricity, cured diseases, and built machines that carried them into the skies. Just before they died out, billions of them lived for years and years in great physical comfort.

'What a species they were!'

He paused and passed his eye along the rest of the Mission.

'And yet, there is another side to this extraordinary story. Long Dead human beings were part-god, part-devil – I believe you know what those words mean?'

'Yes, we discussed them in Itzac,' said Cyrus.

'Good. As well as a passion for creating, the Long Dead had a strong passion for killing and destroying – slaughtering each other and all creatures that stood in their way, and devastating the Earth by stripping it of its riches.'

I know what you mean, thought Cyrus. He remembered how shocked he had been by a casual remark of Sammy's: 'They killed tigers for fun.'

'Billions and billions of them crammed on to a groaning planet,' said Nelith, 'all wanting more and more in the belief that it would bring contentment. Yet it was a mirage, my friends. It ignored the message sung by their poets and their prophets throughout the ages: happiness lies not in things but in the human heart.'

'Nor did joy grow with age. Time crusted over their imagination and sensitivity. In their place came bitterness, cynicism and bigotry, all disguised as wisdom. This was what the Long Dead poet meant when, thinking of his lost youth, he wrote: *The things which I have seen, I now can see no more.*

'Then came the Mini-Flu and the Great Death,' continued Nelith with a sad smile. 'We think those events may have been nature's response to what humans were doing. It was as if she were saying, "Well, if you refuse to care for the place we all share, I'll have to deal with you myself." She sent the great plague. The destroyers of the Earth were themselves destroyed.

'And that is why,' Nelith concluded, 'we rejected the Salvation Project. In their arrogance, the Long Dead left it for us because they assumed we would want to go back to their ways. We do not.

'As we live for eighteen years, we will not overwhelm the Earth as the Long Dead did. And since we value happiness above possessions, we will not exhaust her riches or poison her air.'

The Mission sat in silence throughout this extraordinary revelation. All of them except Cyrus had some idea what lay behind the Tiani civilization, but this was the first time it had been fully explained to them – and they found it almost impossible to take in.

Cyrus' head was spinning. Rejection of the Salvation Project made a mockery of the Soterion Mission and the last two years of his life. If the Tiani were right, Roxanne was wrong and he had wickedly misled his friends. The sacrifices, the pain and suffering had all been pointless.

But even as such thoughts were passing through his mind, others were jostling for attention. He had a strange sensation, as if a curtain was being opened in his brain. Like water held back by a dam, reflections he had not wanted to acknowledge had been building for many months. Now the dam was broken, they came flooding out.

What was it Xsani had said with her child-like lisp? 'They did thuch wonderful thingth… and thuch terrible thingth.' Towards the end, was she too having doubts about the wisdom of the Salvation Project? Perhaps that was partly why she chose not to go on…?

Cyrus forced himself to concentrate on the present. Did the Mission have any questions? Nelith was asking.

Cyrus stood up. 'Thank you, Nelith. I have many questions.

First, where are your computers now? And where is the laboratory in which you were finishing the Salvation Project?'

'I'll answer that, if I may,' said Vaarunika, getting to her feet. 'Poor Nelith has had too much to do already!' She pointed to the ruin. 'There is the laboratory, Cyrus.'

'A fire, like in Alba?' he asked.

She nodded. 'Yes, but with a difference. We burned it down deliberately so there would be no chance of restarting the Salvation Project.'

'Shame,' muttered Sammy.

Vaarunika turned to him. 'It was the Tiani's unanimous decision. I'm sorry you don't approve, Sammy. But you still have the information on your laptop.'

'And on yours – or were they also burned?' asked Miouda.

'No, they were not burned, but we deleted the Salvation Project data from them. We now have three laptops in the Paarlimeentuva building behind us. We use them as a source of practical information on matters such as health and boat-building.'

'And stories,' added Nelith.

'Stories?' queried Jinsha, who had been brought up in a culture where such things were all but unknown.

Nelith chuckled. 'Yes. Every evening, one of our five Tiani villages comes here to listen to a story read from a book stored on a laptop. We usually have singing and dancing afterwards.'

'Why aren't you showin' films?' queried Olo. 'We was loving' the films on our computer.'

'We tried that, Olo,' said Vaarunika, 'but the screens were too small. And people were depressed by the images. They said all the Long Dead looked as if they were in their Death Month!'

Sammy, who had been getting more and more agitated, suddenly jumped to his feet. 'Sorry,' he cried in a voice cracking with emotion, 'but I don't like it. All this waiting for the sun business in your Parli-whatever-you-call-it – it's a sort of religion, like it was in the Gova place where I grew up. It's creepy!

'And people don't change. You may be ok on your island, but everywhere else it's the same as it always was, Constant and Zed, good and bad, happy and sad. Our Mission's all about changing that – everywhere.'

Close to tears, he turned to Cyrus and Miouda for support. 'I'm right, aren't I?' he pleaded. 'We'll learn from what the Long Dead got wrong, and start again. "Brave new world" you called it, Cyrus. Remember?'

'Yes, of course I remember, Sammy. And you're right.' He hesitated. 'But perhaps it's not as straightforward as we thought it was.'

'Maybe not, but—'

'Excuse me,' interrupted Vaarunika. 'I believe this is the sort of conversation you might want to have amongst yourselves. The main purpose of this Paarlimeentuva – explaining the Tiani way of life – is over. We ask you to return to your village, think carefully about what you have heard, and decide whether or not you wish to stay here.

'If you do – and we very much hope you will – the Tiani will welcome you with open arms. If not, we will return your weapons, give you food and water, and carry you to the mainland to resume your mission.

'The Paarlimeentuva will gather in seven days to hear your decision.'

Two months have gone by. An old man is sitting in the shade on the edge of the beach. He stares with tired grey eyes at the distant mainland, no more than a hazy blur on the horizon. Beside him, a young woman with hair bleached by the sun is feeding her new-born baby.

'Strange to think we could be over there with them,' says Cyrus, reaching out a wrinkled hand to stroke the baby's head. 'I hope they're alright, I really do!'

Miouda smiles. 'If anyone can make it, Sammy will,' she says. 'And Olo's as tough as they come.'

Cyrus takes a deep breath and lies back on the sand. 'I still don't think they were right,' he says slowly, closing his eyes. 'The past is gone and no amount of chasing will bring it back. It's taken me a lifetime to realise that.'

Miouda gently moves her baby from one breast to the other. 'And you don't feel bad about the Mission any longer?'

'No. The more I think about it, the more I'm convinced that all those who gave up their lives – Zavar, Navid, Taja, Xsani, even Roxanne herself – would now agree that we were chasing shadows. There can be no return.'

Cyrus closes his eyes. 'I am very tired today.'

They remain silent for a long time, listening to the steady lap of the waves. Eventually, Miouda carefully places the baby Roxy between them and lies down.

'Vaarunika says we are changing,' she says quietly.

'Eh?'

'According to Vaarunika, human beings are adapting to their new, shorter lifespans. It's evolution, she says. We are maturing, becoming responsible at an earlier age than in the time of the Long Dead.'

'I thought so. I never did see why they considered sixteen-year-old men and women to be children back then.'

'Because they behaved like children?'

'Only because they were treated like them, given no responsibility.' He gives a breathless chuckle. 'I don't think we behaved like kids, did we?'

She makes no reply but reaches across the sleeping baby and places a hand on his shrivelled shoulder. Although she has seen countless people in their Death Month, never before has she witnessed its effect so closely. His hair, thick and brown only a few days earlier, is now spiderweb thin and as white as the foam that flecks the waves. Where her hand rests upon him, the skin is dry and rough.

Without opening his eyes, he says, 'Shall I tell you something?'

'Go on.'

'Just before Xsani ran into the Zeds, she looked round. I'll never forget her expression.'

'She saw you?'

'Maybe. But I think she saw the people in the boat, too.'

'You mean she knew Jinsha was in it?'

'Yes. She died to buy us time, time for us to get away.' He pauses. 'She gave up her life for her friends.'

'Oh Cyrus! People can be so good, can't they?'

'They can. That's why you and baby Roxy and Jinsha must stay in this new world. Here your goodness can grow as tall and beautiful as the trees.'

As she turns to him, joy and sadness mingle in her face. 'What is it Cyrus? What's the matter?'

'Can you hear that bird, Miouda?'

She listens. 'No, I can't hear anything.'

'It's very big. Wings like palm leaves. It's swooping down towards me, its feathers blotting out the sun.' He shivers. 'It's cold, Miouda.'

She tenderly moves little Roxanne aside so she can lie next to him, warming him with her body.

'Thank you.' His voice is so quiet now she has to lean close to his mouth to hear him. 'I love you, Miouda. You know that, don't you?'

'I do. And I love you, too, Cyrus. But it hurts so much.'

'What does?'

'This moment. You're not afraid, are you?'

'No. But I can hear the wings beating very close.'

'Yes, it's very near.'

He shivers again, more violently this time, and his mouth remains open. His speech is barely more than breathing. 'Miouda, we came seeking salvation. It wasn't what we expected, was it?'

'No, but we have found it, Cyrus. At the last.'

'Ah yes. And how good it is!'

Glossary

Alba Constant settlement where the Soterion was found.

Atikari Elected leaders of the Tiani.

breeding slave Male Zed term for a woman kept in captivity to produce children.

Captain Male Zed officer below the rank of Malik.

City of Wolves Long Dead city inhabited by giant wolves, and by the Safids and the Meshkis.

Constants Those trying to maintain the civilization that collapsed following the
Great Death of 2018-19.

copemate Alban name for a partner of either sex.

Damas Decisive meeting for new arrivals in Lanskira.

Death Month 28-day period during a person's 19th year when they age and die.

Della Tallis Constant settlement where Cyrus was born and raised.

dumbman Kogon term for a male.

Emir Elected leader of a Constant settlement.

Eyes Kogon lookouts and spies.

Filna Abandoned Long Dead town inhabited by the Kogon.

flabtoad Grozny term for a female.

Ghasar Meeting hall in Alba where the Soterion books and all but one of its computers were stored.

Gova	Constant term for a mysterious power [electricity] worshipped by the Children of Gova.
Great Death	Period (2018-19) when all those over 19 suddenly aged and died.
Grozny	Tribe of vicious Zeds once led by Timur.
Gurkov	Zed tribe led by Ogg.
Itzac	Abandoned Constant settlement occupied for a short while by the Mission.
Kogon	Tribe of female Zeds.
kumfort	Kogon term for a female partner.
Lanskira	Tropical island, home to the Tiani Constants.
Long Dead	Those whose civilization died out during the Great Death.
Malik	Male Zed tribal leader.
Malika	Female Zed tribal leader.
Meshkis	Community of brown-skinned Constants living in a former metro station in the City of the Wolves.
Mini-Flu	Seemingly innocuous strain of influenza that caused a disastrous mutation in the DNA controlling ageing.
Mission	Group of Constants hoping to use the Soterion to rebuild the civilization of the Long Dead.
moon	Constant term for a month.
Murax	Zed tribe of Captain Kemran.
Over-Malik	Title given to Timur after his death.
Paarlimeentuva	Assembly of the Tiani Constants.
Safids	Community of conceited, white-skinned

	Constants living is a former metro station in the City of the Wolves.
Salvation Project	
	Long Dead medical programme aimed at reversing the DNA mutation caused by the Mini-Flu.
Soterion	Vault and the books and laptops within it containing the Salvation Project and key elements of the civilization of the Long Dead.
Soterions	Zed name for the Mission.
Tallin	Constant from Della Tallis.
Tiani	Community of peace-loving Constants living on the isle of Lanskira.
tootsa	Garment worn by the Tiani.
winter	Constant and Zed term for a year.
Wheel Room	Safids' hydro-electric power chamber.
Zeds	Barbarians who reject the civilization that collapsed during the Great Death.
Zektiv	Officer of the Kogon Zeds.

About the Author

Prizewinning author Stewart Ross taught at all levels in the UK, the USA, the Middle East and Sri Lanka before becoming a full-time writer in 1989. He has published many works of fiction and non-fiction, including over 50 novels for adults and for children. He has also written plays, lyrics and poetry, and his books have been translated into some 20 languages. When not working in a large hut in the garden, Stewart visits schools, colleges and universities in the UK, France and elsewhere to talk about writing and pass on his passion for words.

Find out more on *stewartross.com*